"Who's that?" I say.

"Don't worry about it," says Joe.

"No, really," I say.

"No, really," he says. He jogs down the driveway toward the car.

Riot Grrl 16 is going to be big; we're all going to be big—I can feel it. I aim my camera and zoom in on the human sunbeam. I want to know who's so important that Joe would cut out on us.

"Eddy?" Rory says.

I zoom in. And zoom again.

I know this girl.

We have history.

As in *History*.

She's not a sunbeam.

She's a lightning bolt.

"Eddy!"

I'm too busy to notice that Dreads is operating a tall bike without the proper training and is coming straight for me.

About humiliating yet strangely hilarious groin injuries? Yeah. Mine gets 1,236 views on YouTube, which, funnily enough, happens to be the exact number of kids at my high school.

Also by

Laura Ruby

BAD APPLE

GOOD GIRLS

For Younger Readers

LILY'S GHOSTS

THE WALL AND THE WING

THE CHAOS KING

Play Me

Laura Ruby

HARPER TEEN
An Imprint of HarperCollinsPublishers

HarperTeen is an imprint of HarperCollins Publishers.

www.harperteen.com

Library of Congress Cataloging-in-Publication Data

Ruby, Laura.
Play me / Laura Ruby. — 1st ed.
p. cm.
Summary: High school senior Eddy deals with his patchwork family, getting the girl, and trying to make it big by winning a contest on MTV.
ISBN 978-0-06-124329-5
[1. Video recordings—Production and direction—Fiction. 2. Dating (Social customs)—Fiction. 3. Mothers—Fiction. 4. Interpersonal relations—Fiction. 5. Stepfamilies—Fiction.] I. Title.
PZ7.R83138Pl 2008 2008007117
[Fic]—dc22 CIP
AC

Typography by Amy Ryan
09 10 11 12 13 LP/RRDH 10 9 8 7 6 5 4 3 2 1
❖
First paperback edition, 2009

For Jess, who asked.

"Is it being prepared to do the right thing, whatever the cost? Isn't that what makes a man?"

"Sure, that and a pair of testicles."

—*The Big Lebowski*

The Unbearable Lightness of Being (Me)

Most people turn into complete morons when you put them in front of a camera, and thank God for that.

Today I've got the digital trained on the two guys in my driveway—one on a unicycle, another on a tall bike. They're getting ready to joust. Their pages (pimply dorks with anime brain) hand them their lances (poles made from PVC pipe). Duct-taped to the ends of the lances are huge stuffed animals, an Elmo and a Hello Kitty. The object? To ride straight at your opponent and Elmo him right onto his Hello Kitty. And if you knock him hard enough to cause (a) bleeding, (b) broken bones, or (c) a humiliating, painful, and yet strangely hilarious groin injury, that's even better.

It's one of the dumbest things I've ever seen and I'm so happy. Watching these guys strap on bike helmets decorated with flaming skulls, I have to keep from doing my own moronic dance of joy.

"This is going to rock," Rory says, fiddling with the boom mike he's setting up to catch the walla walla of the crowd gathered in the garage and in the yard. We're shooting for our show, *Riot Grrl 16*. Our riot girl, Gina, is in full costume: black cherry lipstick, pink and black hair spiked as high as she could get it, striped shirt, and camos. Her feet are bare, but her pants are rolled up so that you can see the tiny tattoo of an ivy vine on her calf. (I told her once that it would be good for the show if she got a dagger tattooed somewhere; she said that the best place for a dagger was my heart.) In this scene, she's supposed to be partying at a tall bike joust when her drug-addicted brother shows up claiming to be in deep with the mob. Instead Gina's busy leveling her patented Death Glare of Obliteration at me. I'm not sure of the reason for this, but since the Death

Glare looks good on camera, I don't care.

Rory's still fiddling with the mike. "Are we going to get any sound or what?" I say.

"Keep your panties on, princess." He built a mile-long boom with multiple joints so we can get the thing almost anywhere, and we've never had it drop into the shots. He also built the steady cam. And we have a dolly that he rigged up from the Segway Gina's richer-than-J.K.-Rowling parents bought her, the one they said would help her be a more environmentally responsible human, the one she called "the Dorkway." But today, like most days, we're using handheld, held—of course—by me.

"Okay," Rory says. "We got sound."

"It's a revolution in filmmaking!" I say. He gives me an obscene gesture that he's given me so many times in the last six years it's ceased to have any meaning at all. I blow him a kiss. Joe, who had moved quickly to Gina's side to talk her out of any psychotic breaks she might be contemplating, rolls his eyes at both of us. Joe's the third member of our production company. If Rory's job is the technical stuff, Joe's job is the human stuff. He mostly works with Gina and the other actors, giving them suggestions, motivations, pretensions. He's an actor too, one of those fanatics who believes in immersing himself in roles, the kind of guy who would spend six weeks living in Beulah, Alabama, to deliver one line of dialogue with an authentic accent. For *Riot Grrl 16*, he dropped twelve pounds he couldn't afford to lose so that he could be more convincing as Riot Grrl's drug-addicted half brother. His face looks like a carved pumpkin. A *pissed-off* carved pumpkin. I can't understand why he's not more excited about this. It's our ticket. Our big shot.

To quote Matt Damon in *Dogma*: Somebody needs a nap.

A groupie hovers to my left. She's standing so close I can feel her breath on my arm. She's a junior at my school, but I keep forgetting her name. She's hot, if you like legs that go up to there (and who doesn't)? She's been hanging around our shoots for weeks now.

"It's so cool that you guys are in this contest," she says. "I mean, MTV! Can you believe it?"

Yes, actually, I can. "It's pretty sweet."

"What will you do if you win?"

"We're just trying to make the top five and get on the prime-time broadcast," I tell her. "That's enough visibility for us." This is the standard answer I give so I don't sound too full of myself, even though I think *Riot Grrl 16* is the best in the contest and people would be insane to think otherwise.

"Oh, you'll totally make the top five," Groupie says.

"You think so?"

"I know so." Groupie's lips are nice. Puffy and full. Lips you could use as throw pillows. "I've been watching you," she says. "You know your way around a camera."

I shrug. "I should. I've been doing it for long enough."

She nibbles at her puffy bottom lip and flutters her lashes. "I heard you know your way around a lot of other things, too." It's a lame line, but her voice is low and scratchy and hits me right in the fly. I calculate how fast I can hustle twenty-five tall-bike-riding geeks out of my yard.

"Jeez, can you focus for three seconds?" Joe says. Joe doesn't believe in fame, commercial success, or groupies. My mom told me that one day Joe will be forced to do TV ads for foot fungus cream just to have the work and then he won't be so proud.

"Hello?" says Joe, doing that slow-blink thing he does when he's annoyed.

"I'm focused, I'm focused," I say. I can't help it; my eyes are drawn back to Groupie's up-to-there legs.

Joe snorts and whispers something to Gina. Gina is making some kind of snarling sound and jabbing fingers in my direction, so I hurry up and center the shot.

The two jousting goons start racing toward each other, both of them wobbly as six-year-olds. I love it. For a minute, I forget about the groupie, I forget where I am, I forget everything that's happened in the last year and revel in the idiocy that unfolds before me. Tall Bike completely misses his opponent, but Unicycle gets in one good whack. Tall Bike looks a little dazed, at least more dazed than when they started. They circle for another run. Charge!

Groupie wraps her hot little hand around my bicep.

And Gina launches a bottle at my head.

"Ed! Duck!" Rory yells. Too late, as usual. The bottle misses my face but bounces off my arm, ricocheting into the garage behind me. My father's tools explode off the Peg-Board where they'd been arranged like a row of exclamation points.

"Hey!" I say, not because she probably shattered all the bones in my arm, but because of my dad's tools. My dad hates when his stuff gets messed up. He'll kill me when he sees it. Okay, he won't kill me, but he'll make me pay for any damage, which might as well be killing me because I'm broke. I spent everything I had on the new video camera. Speaking of, what if she'd hit it?

It takes me a few seconds to notice that Gina's crying; she wears so much makeup that it's sometimes hard to tell if the effects are intentional. "You're such an ass," she says, her lips quivering.

Rory shakes his head, which tells me he thinks *Riot Grrl 16* isn't acting; she's running riot for real. Behind her, the jousting continues. It's not looking good for Unicycle.

"What?" I say, reframing the shot so that Gina's in the foreground with the joust behind her. "Who's an ass?"

"And you can put the stupid camera down," she says,

glancing around the garage for more ammunition. I lower the camera. My arm is throbbing.

Joe throws up his hands, picks up his Bible, and flops in one of the folding chairs in the garage to wait this little episode out. He hates any drama that we don't create for the screen. And Gina is drama personified. She's spitting out an array of impressive and colorful swearwords, which, if she wasn't saying them so fast, might have an impact. Right now, she sounds like she's shouting in Latvian: *mutherfushiheadasdik!*

I'm getting impatient. We do one episode of *Riot Grrl 16* a week. We have till tomorrow to finish it and get it up on the web; otherwise we'll be disqualified from the contest. We really don't need to have our star freaking out on us, not unless she'll let us post it on the internet.

"Gina," I say. "Can we talk later?"

"We can talk *now*!"

Behind her, Rory has pulled his own digital camera out of his pocket. I know he's filming this. It's wrong, but I don't mention it. I had to promise lots of screen time to these guys to get them to joust at my house instead of at the park; we should have something to show for today. Besides, I'm missing all the action in the driveway. Unicycle went down. No embarrassing groin injuries, but it appears he did fall on his face, which now sports a few racing stripes. Two new guys are setting up to joust, one of them with fat, matted dreads snaking down the middle of his back. White guys should never, ever, *ever* wear dreads, especially while riding a tall bike with a SpongeBob strapped to the handlebars.

"What's the deal with her?" Gina says.

"What's the deal with who?"

This is not the right thing to say.

"Her!" Gina bellows, pointing at the groupie. "Ms. If Her Shorts Got Any Shorter, They'd Be a Gynecological Exam."

This has got to be about what happened three or four weekends ago. We were rehearsing for *Riot Grrl 16*. Dad was out for the night, working late as usual. So, yeah, things got a little out of control, but not in a bad way. I thought Gina was cool with it.

I guess Gina's not cool with it.

She's really crying now, the black mascara or eyeliner or greasepaint or whatever it is that she puts on her eyes dripping down her cheeks and onto the striped shirt. I like Gina; we're friends. I don't want to see her so sad. And she *does* look sad. Small, slumped in on herself.

Rory really shouldn't be filming this.

"Gina, look, I'm sorry," I say. And I am. Yes, we hooked up, but I didn't promise her anything. I didn't think she needed any promises. I mean, she even hooked up with Rory once (if you can believe Rory).

Then something else hits me and for a second I can't breathe. I take two steps toward her and try to lower my voice (for all the good it does). "Wait. You're not, like, late or anything, are you?"

Gina's mouth drops open.

Joe's mouth drops open.

Even Rory's mouth drops open.

It would have been funny, if things weren't so very unfunny.

"Jesus," Joe says.

"Dude," Rory says.

Gina starts to laugh then. Some kind of crazy-creepy laugh. Sort of scares me, that laugh.

"No, I'm not *late*, you loser. But even if I was, I'm not sure I'd tell you anyway."

"So what are we fighting about?"

"You just don't get it, do you?" she says.

And you know what? I *don't* get it. What I do get is that the first episode of *Riot Grrl 16*, the one we did just for kicks even before the contest, was one of the featured videos on YouTube. It got more five-star ratings than the skate-boarding dog, the guy who stuffed a dozen olives up his nose, *Top Ten Ways To Die in a Video Game*, and *The Best Banana Phone Video Ever!* And what I do get is that Gina has completely lost it the way that girls always seem to, the way they do when you least expect it. It's like they wait until you're at your most stressed out and then they lay this weird trip on you, like you all of a sudden had more going on with them than you had.

What is up with this? I just stand there, staring at her, watching her cry and laugh at the same time, wishing I could maybe hug her or something, but I know I can't touch her.

Groupie pipes up. "Maybe you should go chill, Gina."

Gina shoots her a glare that could kill. I expect to see Groupie's guts fall out of her body right then and there, a big steaming pile of intestines all over the garage floor.

But my dad's always saying I play too many video games. Gina's expression goes from murderous to amused in under three seconds. She does that thing, you know that thing, where girls look each other up and down? Yeah. So Gina does the up-and-down thing to the groupie and smiles this schizo little smile. Then she looks back at me. "Someday some girl's going to rip your heart out and stomp on it. I hope I'm there to see it." And then she turns and marches down the driveway, but not before snatching Dreads's SpongeBob off his bike and drop-kicking it into the next yard.

"Tell me you weren't filming that," says Joe.

Rory shrugs and slips the camera back into his pocket. "We won't use it without her permission."

Joe stares at him for a full minute. I try to convince myself that he's simply stunned by Rory's new hair, which he's recently bleached snow white to set off his perpetual sunburn.

But that's not it. Joe's ex Joelle—I know, Joe and Joelle, kills you, doesn't it?—was friends with this girl named Audrey who graduated last year. Someone, we don't know who, took a picture of Audrey while she was hooking up with her boyfriend at a party and then sent the picture everywhere. Joelle was furious about it, which means that Joe was furious, too. Now that Joelle's gone, Joe's furious on principle. Joe's all about principle.

If Rory has principles, we haven't found them yet. Rory imitates Joe, blinking slowly and ominously like a hit man about to go for his gun.

A beater car pulls up to the curb and honks but has to park a ways down the road because of all the cars. "That's my ride," says Joe.

"We're not done yet." I fight to keep the whine out of my voice. "You can't leave."

Joe heaves his backpack onto his shoulder as if he were Atlas and the pack were the world. "In case you haven't noticed, our star is gone. We only needed a few more shots. If you weren't such a slut, we could have finished the episode already."

"Can I help it that I'm irresistible?" This is supposed to be a joke, but Joe doesn't laugh. Joe doesn't think anything is funny anymore.

"You do know Gina's been crushing on you for months, right?" he says.

"That's not his fault," says Groupie.

Groupie is officially more trouble than she's worth. I don't even look at her. "I never told Gina we were going out."

"That's what you always say."

"Well, it's true."

"What if she quits?" Joe says.

That's exactly what I'm worried about, but I'm not going to admit it. "She won't quit. She wants this just as much as we do."

Joe shifts his pack. "I still have to go."

"We have editing left to do."

"Not much. Do it without me."

He's been saying that more and more. "What's more important than the show?"

"I have a history project due."

"Give me a break," I say. "We're graduating in less than a month."

"It's a group project and I'm meeting some people," he says.

"What people?"

Someone is standing outside the beater car waving for Joe. It's a girl—a blonde—that much I can tell from here. She's backlit by the setting sun, making her white shirt and hair blaze like a chemical fire. Even the jousting nerds have stopped jousting and turned to look, tenting their hands over their eyes as if it hurts them.

"Who's that?" I say.

"Don't worry about it," says Joe.

"No, really," I say.

"No, really," he says. He jogs down the driveway toward the car.

Riot Grrl 16 is going to be big; we're all going to be big—I can feel it. I aim my camera and zoom in on the human sunbeam. I want to know who's so important that Joe would cut out on us.

"Eddy?" Rory says.

I zoom in. And zoom again.

I know this girl.

We have history.

As in *History*.

She's not a sunbeam.

She's a lightning bolt.

"Eddy!"

I'm too busy to notice that Dreads is operating a tall bike without the proper training and is coming straight for me.

About humiliating yet strangely hilarious groin injuries? Yeah. Mine gets 1,236 views on YouTube, which, funnily enough, happens to be the exact number of kids at my high school.

The Birds

Gina is not the only girl who's mad at me. Tippi Hedren is furious.

"*I think you're a louse,*" she says when I limp through the door. She's been in her cage all day and she is not happy about it.

"Sorry, Tippi," I say, opening the cage. "But there were too many people around. You would have bitten them all new nostrils." Her beak is wicked sharp.

Tippi Hedren says, *"I don't like to be handled."*

I put my hand into the cage and she snaps at my fingers, but she's not serious about it. She's never chomped down hard enough to hurt me. I pop her onto my shoulder, her favorite perch. She puts on a show of flapping her wings but then begins to groom my hair, combing through the strands. *"You don't love me."*

"Love means never having to say 'I love you.'"

"I'm just something you've caught. Some kind of wild animal you've trapped."

"You got me there."

I sit at my computer with Tippi still on my shoulder. Even though I just spent two hours editing the episode with Rory, I still want to see it again. I go to the MTV website where Rory uploaded it. And there it is: *Riot Grrl 16*, episode 8.

We lied to Joe. We used some of the footage that Rory took with his camera, the stuff with Gina screaming at me in her slurred Latvian swear speech. It had that weird, grainy look that made the show feel more realistic but surreal and dreamy too, just like a life spiraling out of control would look from the outside. Gina will be pissed, but she'll get over it once she sees the show, once the comments and video responses come pouring in. She'll see that it was the right thing to do.

Joe will also be pissed, but for longer. I can't worry about that anymore.

My cell buzzes.

"Are you watching it?" Rory says.

"Yeah."

"Awesome, huh?"

"Yup."

"Tell me we're going to win that contest."

"We are going to win that contest," I say.

"That will be $4.29."

"What will be $4.29?"

"I'm not talking to you. I'm at work."

Work is Rory's parents' video store. "What are we renting tonight?" By "we" I mean any person who risks going to Rory's parents' video store, World of Video, which is a dump and a fire hazard and a repository of strange and mysterious miasmas.

"Nothing good," he says. "Have a nice day, ma'am."

"Ma'am? A hottie, huh?"

"She's had about nineteen face-lifts," he says. "She looked like the Joker in a wig."

"Glad to see that you're respectful of your elders."

"She rented something with Denzel Washington in it. I wanted to tell her that just because Denzel Washington's in a movie doesn't mean the movie's any good. But the 'rents are still freaked out about that Robin Williams thing and told me that I should feel free to keep my opinions to myself."

"That's because you wouldn't let anyone rent a movie starring Robin Williams."

"*Nobody* should rent them," he says. "I'm trying to save lives here."

"And because you kept suggesting *Evil Dead* instead of *Night at the Museum*."

"*Evil Dead*'s a classic, man. Sam Raimi directing before he went all emo with *Spider-Man*."

"*Spider-Man* isn't emo."

"He's so emo he should wear a bra. Hey, I'm working on a new list for the Jumping Frenchmen MySpace."

Jumping Frenchmen is the name of our production company. The full name is the Jumping Frenchmen of Maine. Another thing my mom came up with. She was always our biggest fan. She says she still is, but I don't know how that's possible.

"What's the list?" I say.

"Top-five fight scenes."

"Too easy," I say.

"For me," he says. "For the rest of you butt heads, not so much."

"Yeah?" I say. I'll let Rory ramble on. He lists before he thinks, which is just one of his problems.

"Five is *Fight Club*. Edward Norton kicking his own ass."

"Obvious."

"That's not obvious at all! It's, like, all quirky and stuff."

"It's *obviously* quirky."

He ignores me. "Four, *Who Am I?* Jackie Chan. All the cheesy acting and amazing fight sequences you can handle."

I fake a yawn. "Did you say something? I was napping there for a bit."

"Three: *The Matrix*. Carrie-Anne Moss in wet leather."

Being a fan of chicks in wet leather, I say, "Okay, I'll go with that one."

"Next, the Bourne movies."

"That's only 'cause you have a crush on Matt Damon."

"No, *he* has a crush on *me*. Dude won't stop calling."

"What's number one?"

"Drumroll, please: *Enter the Dragon*. Bruce Lee."

I don't say anything.

"Well?" he says.

"As usual, you missed the interesting stuff."

"Like what?" he says.

"Oh, I don't know, all of it. Lord of the Rings movies. Jet Li movies. Anything directed by Sam Peckinpah, John Woo, or Martin Scorsese. *Crouching Tiger, Hidden Dragon*. *Kung Fu Hustle*. *The Princess Bride*, where Inigo Montoya has a sword fight with the man with six fingers and keeps saying, 'Hello, my name is Inigo Montoya. You killed my father. Prepare to die.'" I even do Inigo's overblown Spanish accent, just to rub it in.

"*The Princess Bride* is—"

I cut him off. "And what about *Aliens*, where Ripley beats up the bug queen wearing that big metal suit? And *Jaws*."

"There's no fight scene in *Jaws*."

"The last forty-five minutes of the movie is one long fight scene with the giant shark. And you also missed *Monty Python and the Holy Grail*. King Arthur and the Black Knight. 'Look, you stupid bastard. You've got no arms left.'"

There's silence on the other end, which means that Rory's kicking himself for that one.

"*Office Space,*" I say.

"WHAT?!"

"The nerdy office drones kick the crap out of the printer? While the gangsta rap is playing in the background? Genius."

"But . . ."

"And if you're looking for the typical fight stuff, what about *Kill Bill, Vol. 1*? There are so many scenes to choose from: The Bride vs. Vernita Green. The Bride vs. O-Ren Ishii. The Bride vs. Gogo Yubari. Say it with me: Gogo."

"I'm not saying anything."

"You know you want to: Gogo. Go. Go. Have I mentioned her schoolgirl outfit? Her kneesocks?"

"All right, all right," he says. "Just go, Gogo." And he hangs up.

I win.

As always.

I turn back to the website MTV set up just for the contest. This is how it works: anyone between the ages of eighteen and twenty-two could enter a short film or pilot. MTV execs picked the top twenty and put them on their website. Every week for twelve weeks, everybody in the top twenty, Jumping Frenchmen of Maine included, is required to upload a new video. Just like on YouTube, anyone can go and view the videos and vote on them. The five production companies that get the highest votes will be on an MTV reality show where they'll compete for $250,000 and a production contract. The show will be called *The Producers*.

I'm going to be on that show. I'm going to win that contract.

I watch the new *Riot Grrl 16* episode again. Even though Rory just uploaded it, the comments are already starting to pour in. Five stars, five stars, five stars, four stars (excuse me?!!), five stars. I scan the list of comments:

Love it!!!!!

Riot Grrl rocks so hard!!!!

Riot Grrl, will you marry me?

And then this:

Oh, look, another vast conspiracy of the brain-free. Come on, people! This is a total piece of crap. Lonely Girl *rip-off, anyone?*

"It's not a rip-off, bonehead; it's a satire," I say out loud. "Look it up." Everyone loves *Riot Grrl 16*. Except for this moron. I laugh when I catch his name: the Tin Man. Ha. More like the flying monkey. There's always a few of them in the comment sections, yammering on about saving the dolphins or peddling porn or just trying to inject a little excitement into their own pathetic lives by bringing everyone down.

"I think you're a louse," Tippi Hedren squeaks.

"You tell him, Tippi." I read somewhere that birds don't know what they're saying when they say it, but I'm not so sure about that. Tippi has her own birdbrained way of thinking about things, but most of what she says is vaguely prophetic, like spam.

I get up from my computer and go downstairs to forage for food. My dad isn't so good at the food thing. He works a lot and late, so there's never much in the house, and what there is goes to feed Tippi Hedren. If I'm lucky, there will be a can of chickpeas floating around a cabinet somewhere. If my dad's lucky, I won't die of scurvy.

I walk into the kitchen.

And see Meatball sprawled next to the kitchen table,

a fork stuck in his gut. There's red smeared everywhere.

Tippi squawks.

I gasp.

I drop to my knees and shake him. "Meatball! Are you all right? What happened? Meatball!" I pull out the fork and send it skidding across the tiles. I put my hand on his heart to feel for a beat and then I grab his wrist to check for a pulse. I shake him again. "Meat! Wake up! Please, wake up! Who did this to you?"

"I guess that's where everyone meets Mitch," says Tippi Hedren.

Meatball opens his eyes. "Who's Mitch?"

I stop shaking him and shrug. "A character in Hitchcock's *The Birds*. She loves to quote *The Birds*."

"Yes," he says. "But I've never heard Tippi say that before." He sits up. "I've been waiting a long time for you."

Matthew, aka the Meatball, has been doing a lot of dying. As his only brother—half brother, if you're being picky—it's my job to find and then revive him. The blood is a new thing. Up till now he's done the bloodless stuff: heart attacks, cancer, old age. I wonder if the special effects are a sign of something. "I didn't know you were here," I say. "How'd I do?"

"Not too badly," the Meatball says. "Except for the waiting. If someone had really stabbed me, I would have bled to death, you know." He nods at the red mess splattered all around him. "Tomato paste. I thinned it with some water."

"Nice trick," I say. "Have fun cleaning up."

"But really, you should have been quicker to get to me."

I help him to his feet. "Like I said, I didn't know you were here."

"And maybe you could have told me that you didn't want me to die."

"I'll remember that," I say. Even though he doesn't like it, I ruffle his hair. Today he lets me. "Where's Marty?"

"He's in the den watching TV. We brought you food."

"You did?" I fling open the fridge. "Food, glorious food!"

"That's a reference from the movie *Oliver!*" the Meatball says. He's only nine, but most of the time he sounds like a professor. He even looks like a professor in one of his favorite button-down shirts and round glasses.

"I know it's from *Oliver!*"

"I enjoyed that movie. I especially enjoyed the character of Nancy, the character of Fagin, and the character of Bullseye." As he's speaking, he counts things off on his middle finger, ring finger, and pinky. He's that kind of kid. A middle, ring, and pinky kid.

In other words, he's a meatball.

"Bullseye," he's saying, "is the dog that belongs to the bad guy."

"Yes, I know," I say, loading up on cheese and meat and mayo and lettuce with the full intention of making a sandwich bigger than my head.

"Mom liked that movie. It's a very old movie from her childhood."

"I know that, Meat."

"She's going to call on Saturday," he says.

"Mom calls every Saturday."

"I'm going to ask her when she's coming back."

"Okay," I say. I used to tell him not to ask her that, but he'd get upset and pound his head with his fists. Now I just let him ask her whatever he wants to. She'll have to deal with it. It's the least she can do.

The Meatball cleans up his bloody mess while I construct my sandwich, which, I must say, is a work of art. Marty shambles into the room, looking a shamble, as usual. He's my mother's ex, the second one, my father being the first. Even though the Meatball is legally Marty's, me and Marty and Dad pretty much share him.

Let's just say we're an unusual family. Or we've become one.

"Hey," Marty says.

"Hey," I say. "When did you guys get here?"

"Been here for a while. Figured you were upstairs glued to your computer. How was the shoot today?"

I say, "Great." And then I think of Gina and say, "Great."

Marty opens the fridge and fishes around inside. "So was it great or was it great?"

"Great."

"Great," he says.

I take a huge bite of my huge sandwich. "How's work for you?"

Marty comes up from the fridge empty-handed. Work is a sore subject. It would be for me, too, if I photographed babies for a living.

"Well, I've spent the last two months doing an insect series," he says. "Dressing the little ones as butterflies and bumblebees and dragonflies. That sort of thing. Very cute. I've even got a little snail."

Since when is a snail an insect? "Wow. A snail."

"Anyway, I've been working like a dog to get this calendar ready and then I find out a certain someone is doing her own insect calendar this year."

"Pam Meddes," I say.

"Pam Meddes," he says. "That witch." But he says this last so mildly that you know he doesn't mean it. Marty is just too nice to think anyone is a witch, even his arch-nemesis, Pam Meddes, a baby photographer who has published nine best-selling photography books, a gagillion different baby calendars, and just launched her own line of maternity clothes. Thing is, the woman is knock-you-flat-on-your-back hot. Hard to hate a woman like that, even if *she's* filthy rich with houses in New

York and Tuscany and *your* living room carpet still stinks of the old cat that died eight years ago.

"Pam Meddes is always copying your ideas," I say. I take another few honking bites of my sandwich.

"I photographed babies in flowerpots first," Marty says. "So why was her book a best seller and not mine?"

"I don't know."

"Celine Dion wouldn't even take my calls, but she lets Pam Meddes take her baby's pictures."

I wonder about making another sandwich.

"What is that about?"

I shake my head. "Life isn't fair."

"You always say that."

"It's true," I tell him.

Marty is silent for a minute. "He looks more and more like you every day."

He's talking about the Meatball, who's quietly scrubbing the tomato paste from the floor. "Yeah," I say. "Maybe." What we don't talk about: Marty is my mother's second husband and the Meatball's father, but the Meatball looks nothing like him. He looks like me. And I look like my dad. Some days it's hard not to wonder exactly who the Meatball's father really is. It's hard not to wonder if Mom stepped out on Marty with Dad, her first husband. And then she stepped out on all of us.

Tell me you don't think we should have our own reality show.

"Are you still hungry?" Marty asks me as I stuff the last bite of my sandwich in my mouth.

I smile. "Always with the dumb questions."

After my second sandwich, the Meatball informs us that he needs more tomato paste. Even though it's late, I volunteer to get it. If it involves driving, I'm your man. I have a black, gas-guzzling Ford Explorer that Gina's parents have informed me is destroying the ozone, and I practically live in it when I'm not at home. I've got extra everything in there: lights, camera, clothes. You never know when you'll get a good idea. You never know when you'll get a good shot.

I put the Meatball and Marty in charge of Tippi Hedren—or maybe it's putting Tippi Hedren in charge of the Meatball and Marty; I'm convinced that bird is smarter than all of us—and jump in the Explorer. Nothing like driving dark roads with the wind whipping through the windows. A lot of people like to blast music, but I like the quiet, when the only sound is the disgruntled purr of the engine.

I'm taking the long way around so that I get in more driving time, sometimes ducking into small developments and looping back. It's dark out, but that not very dark kind of dark, like the sun is pressed up just behind it, the light bleeding through the skin of the sky. I think about how it might look on video. My mind wanders to the idiot online, the one who said *Riot Grrl 16* was a rip-off of *Lonely Girl*. I bet he was one of those guys who believed *Lonely Girl 15* was real. I bet he was one of those guys who fell for the whole thing. We knew *Lonely Girl 15* was bull the first time we saw it.

"Of course she's lonely. Look at that stupid hat," Rory had said, sneering.

"I Googled the religion she keeps talking about," said Joe. "Couldn't find it. She made it up."

"Or someone did," said Rory.

I said: "This stuff's been edited. She has some skills."

"Or someone does," said Rory.

"This has got to be a teaser for a movie or a TV show or something."

"Doesn't look like that, though, does it?" Joe said.

We watched video after video. Way more interesting than the show, which was supposedly a fifteen-year-old girl's whiny vlog, were the comments. People really bought the whole thing. There were heartfelt video responses; there were heartfelt responses to the heartfelt responses. They wanted Lonely Girl to get back together with her boyfriend, they wanted her to leave her boyfriend, they hated her parents, they hated their own parents, they totally understood where she was coming from because it was exactly where they were coming from and wasn't it amazing that they all came from the same place, blah blah blah.

I thought it would be funny to do the same sort of vlog but with a whole different kind of girl. A punk girl. A *riot* girl. Someone who didn't necessarily hate her parents but didn't necessarily care about them either. Someone who lived as if she didn't even have parents. Someone who acted as if she were a whole lot of Courtney Love with a nice pinch of Johnny Rotten. A tactless, lawless, shameless girl. An anarchist, a hedonist, a Satanist, a you-name-it-and-she'll-try-it-ist.

"I don't want to copy somebody else's idea," Rory said.

I sighed. "It won't be a copy. It will be a satire."

"A what?"

Even Joe was totally on board then. "I like it."

The rest is history. Or at least, it will be.

I turn back out onto the main road. I see a girl hunched over a car on the side of the road. More accurately, I see a girl in a very short white skirt hunched over a car on the side of the road.

A very, *very* short skirt.

Just go, Gogo.

I pull over, get out, and walk up behind her. Whoever she is, from this angle, she smokes. I make sure to call, "Hey!" as I'm walking so that I don't scare her too much. "Are you auditioning for a part in a slasher film?"

She straightens up and turns around.

I stop short when I see who it is.

Lucinda Dulko.

The kind of name given to hot-but-monumentally-screwed-up Russian spies played on-screen by Nicole Kidman.

The kind of name given to human sunbeams.

But if you think that's how every scene is going to end, with Lucinda popping up like some gleaming, other-worldly princess, you're wrong. *I* was wrong. But that's how it seemed to me then. Everywhere I turned, there she was, even when she wasn't.

10 Things I Hate About You

"Oh," she says, about as thrilled to see me as she always is. "Eddy. Hi." She looks sweaty and annoyed, but that's sort of typical. The times she doesn't look sweaty and annoyed she looks cold and bored and too busy to care about anyone else. I think it's all the tennis. I guess if I had to bounce a little green ball around for thirteen hours a day, I'd be cranky too.

But since I'm already out of the car, I say, "Need help?"

She doesn't answer, instead reaching into the car and popping the trunk. She rummages in the trunk while I stand around like an idiot. Then she comes back to hand me a flashlight. "You can hold this while I check the engine."

"Great," I say. But I flip on the light and hold it so that she can inspect the wiring. She drives some sort of ancient Oldsmo-Buick. A total piece of junk. The engine is all gunked up with sticky black crap; some of the bolts are fused with rust to the components. She'd be better off driving a lawn mower. Or a tricycle. If it were up to me, I would leave the thing to rot on the side of the road.

"I don't know," Lucinda mutters, more to herself than to me. "I think it's the battery. At least I hope it's the battery. Won't know till I get a new one, though."

"Uh-huh." I think she needs a whole new set of wheels.

She's rummaging in the car again. She pulls out a cell phone, another old piece of junk, almost too big to be considered portable. As she dials a number, she says, "Thanks for stopping, Eddy, but you don't have to stay. I'm calling my brother." She waves a hand.

I'm dismissed.

Isn't she a peach?

But maybe because I'm still holding her flashlight, I wait to see if someone's going to come for her. As she's waiting for an answer, she frowns at the T-shirt I'm wearing, which has a picture of a pickle and the phrase *Dill with it.* Then she scowls at the phone. "He's not answering."

Great. "Look, let me give you a ride home."

"Let me try my other brother," she says.

When the other brother doesn't answer, I say, "I can still give you a ride."

"All I need is a battery. I'm sure of it."

"So I'll give you a jump. You can drive it home."

She plays with her enormous phone. "Then I'll have to find a way to get a battery tomorrow."

"Okay. I can give you a jump and you can drive it to Sears."

"I could."

"But . . ." I say.

"But then they'll charge me for the installation."

I'm thinking, *Now I have to drive Lucinda Dulko to get a new battery. Why don't I just hit myself in the head with this flashlight a few times for kicks?*

"Fine," I say. "Sears is open till ten. I'll drive you there so you can buy the battery. Then I'll drive you back here."

She pauses. It's a significant pause with lots of inaudible dialogue in it. She glances around as if God might show up to save her. Or maybe she's considering throwing herself into traffic; I don't know. For some strange reason, it strikes me as funny. "Don't worry, Dulko, I won't hit on you or anything."

She shoots me a glare that says, *Hit on me and I'll tenderize you with my racket*, which actually makes me laugh out loud.

"What's so funny?" she says, putting her hands on her hips.

"Nothing. Come on." I start walking back to my car. I can hear her sigh behind me, the sound of the trunk slamming shut. I get in and open the door for her from the inside.

"Thanks," she says grudgingly as she buckles up. When I laugh again, she says, "You're cheerful."

"Sometimes," I say. I shift into gear and pull onto the road.

She looks around the car. "This is nice," she says, as if I've forced her to admit it.

"Thanks. It was my dad's. I bought it from him."

We drive in silence for a minute or two. Out of the corner of my eye, I see her glancing from me to my stereo, me to my stereo.

"I like driving when it's quiet."

"Oh," she says, sounding surprised.

"What did you expect? Metal? Gangsta rap? Hardcore?"

"I didn't expect anything," she says.

"Sure you did."

"Okay," she says. "Whatever."

All of a sudden, I don't like the quiet. I get uncomfortable. "Well, I *do* like music. Metal, rock, some old punk. But I'm not stuck on any type of music." I see she doesn't care if I listen to rockabilly Klezmer bands with bagpipe solos; she's picking at her skirt, tugging at the hem, trying to pull it down over her thighs, even though the thing's short enough to be underwear (not that I mind). "What kind of music do you like?" It's a question I always ask 'cause so many people mention the most obscure indie bands they know just to be cool.

"Latin. Salsa. Tango."

Now I'm the one who's surprised. "Tango?" Classical maybe, but . . .

She nods. "My mom's Argentine."

Lucinda's skin is so pale it's almost blue, and her eyes *are* blue, a scary pale blue, like a Slurpee. There's no Salma in her Hayek. No Jen in her Lopez. No Sha in her Kira.

"I know I don't look it, but it's true."

"But your hair is blond," I say.

She puts her hands to her head as if she's just remembered that's where people keep their hair. "Yes, I've been dyeing it since birth. Does yours come from a bottle?"

"Of course. Loreal. 'Cause I'm worth it." Girls

always comment on the hair. They always want to know. "It comes from my dad. And his dad. And his dad."

"It's a weird color."

"Thanks."

"No, I mean it's unusual."

I shrug. "It's red."

"But it's dark red. Not a color you see often."

I smirk at the road. "Do you like it?"

She snorts. "Not as much as you seem to."

"That's harsh."

"Ha. You should play me sometime. I'll show you harsh." Then, like she thinks she's said too much or been too friendly, she clams up and doesn't say anything more until we hit the Sears parking lot. Okay.

We go to the automotive department and Lucinda prices out batteries. "Buy the cheapest one," I tell her. "That car's not going to last the spring anyway."

She ignores me and debates her battery options with the sales guy while I pretend to inspect car parts. I keep sneaking looks. Lucinda might be a hard-ass, but she's not bad. She's short and curvy but with muscles in all the right places. A big chest she keeps strapped down with ugly sports bras that climb up her neck. I try to remember who she's gone out with. Mike Connelly, goalie of the soccer team. Guy had legs so short everyone called him Stumpy. Jon Sanchez, baseball player, the kind of pretty boy all the girls think is sweet and all the guys think is a girl. There was a rumor that she'd gone out with some way older dude, a coach she met at tennis camp, but who knows if that's true or not.

Anyway, none of it matters because she's totally not my type. I like the tall cool ones, you know? I like red lipstick lips and long legs in fishnets. I like tiny tattoos hidden like gifts at the small of the back.

As she's talking to the sales guy, Lucinda slips out of her jacket. Underneath, she's wearing a sleeveless shirt. It's something, watching her slip out of the jacket. It's like she rehearsed it so that it looks completely effortless and without any intended effect. Her exposed shoulders are smooth caps of muscle, singed pink by the sun. I want to touch them, which bugs me. Why would I want to put my hands on Lucinda Dulko? I don't. I mean, not seriously. This is a girl that no one calls by her first name. This is not a girl with tattoos on the small of her back. This is not a girl who's cool with it.

After Lucinda decides to go with the cheapest battery just like any reasonable person would, the salesman rings it up. "Is your boyfriend going to help you install this, miss?"

"Who?" Lucinda says.

Because I'm annoyed that I had to wait for so long, because I can't figure why Lucinda Dulko is getting so interesting, I put my arm around those shoulders and squeeze. "I help her with all her, uh, needs."

She elbows me in the gut. "Get off."

The salesman raises his eyebrows, but Lucinda's already grabbed the battery and the receipt and is stomping away.

"Wait up," I say, jogging to catch her. "At least let me carry the battery." That thing has to weigh thirty or forty pounds.

"You've always been an ass, Eddy."

"Chill, Dulko. I was just kidding around."

She keeps marching along hugging her precious battery.

I hate when girls walk away from me.

I hate when they're mad.

I hate when they won't let me carry their car parts for them.

She drops her jacket. I pick it up and throw it over the battery she's lugging. She glares at me. I think she's going to blast me for what happened when we were twelve, but she says, "Even in the fourth grade, you were an ass."

"The fourth grade?" I say. "What did I do in the fourth grade?"

More marching. "Never mind."

"Come on, you have to tell me. Or I'll be forced to leave you in the Juniors department. They'll make you wear a tube top and a shorter skirt than you have on already. Probably with fringe. It'll be ugly."

She's still marching, but she slows a bit. "You poured

your milk over my head."

"Is that all? What was I, nine?"

"Right. A nine-year-old ass."

Girls and their elephant memories. "So you don't like me because I poured my milk on your head when we were little kids?"

We're at the car now. I open the trunk and she puts the battery inside. She says nothing until I unlock the car for her. Then she flops into the passenger seat. I get in the car and go to put it in gear, but she stops me by grabbing my wrist. "I lost," she says.

Her grip is strong. Almost immediately, my pinky goes numb. "Lost what?"

"Today. I lost. And I had to wear this stupid skirt to school."

Even though it means admitting I saw her by her car, admitting that I was interested enough to look, I blurt, "I thought you were studying with Joe today."

She turns those Slurpee eyes on me. "I did study with Joe, but that was after the meet."

"Oh," I say. Her hand is still around my wrist. "Don't you always have to wear that stupid skirt?"

"When we play at home, the coach wants us to wear our tennis clothes—skirts specifically—to school. Basically he thinks that if the guys see a lot of girls in short skirts wandering the halls, they might show up to see the matches."

"It's not a bad plan," I say.

"Except it doesn't work. They ogle us in the hallway, but they don't care that we can play." *Ogle.* Only a girl named Lucinda Dulko would say the word *ogle.*

She sees me ogling her legs and pulls her hand away. "Oh, forget I said anything."

"Don't mind me; I'm just being an ass again. Who'd you lose to?"

"A girl I always lose to. Her name is Penelope. Penelope! Can you believe it?"

"Have you forgotten that your name is *Lucinda*?"

"Lucinda's my grandmother's name. It means 'light.' Penelope means 'she-demon from hell.'"

"Really. Is that from the Latin?"

She smiles just a tiny bit. "The Greek."

"Of course. So, why do you always lose to she-demon from hell?"

Lucinda stretches her legs in my car. I wonder if she'd like a massage. I'm good at those. Massages.

"First time I ever played her was freshman year in division finals," Lucinda is saying. "Penelope comes up to me in the locker room and makes some crack about my tennis dress."

"What did she say?"

"I don't remember."

"You remember that I dumped milk on your head about forty years ago."

"Shut up and listen. She says something nasty about my dress, and then she tells me that she's going to bagel me."

"Sounds kind of kinky."

"To you. To everyone else, it sounds like breakfast. Means she's going—"

"I know what it means. It means you won't win a single game in the whole match. Your score would be zero, zero."

"Right," she says, charging ahead as if she's wanted to get this out since I found her on the side of the road. "I'm smaller, but I'm *quicker* and I'm *better*. It didn't matter. I lost. She didn't bagel me, but almost. I took only three games. I couldn't get anything to work right. I couldn't serve; I couldn't move. My forehand completely broke down. And it keeps happening. I thought that I'd gotten over my nerves, but I didn't. And she did it to me again today. This time she made fun of my hair. My hair! Who gives a crap about my hair? But then I go out and I lose, 6–2, 6–2. What is that about? Why do I keep losing to a twit who's more concerned about her nails than her game?"

She's looking at me in the dark of the car, as if I actually might have an answer to her choking problems. "Well, you're not really better than her if she's able to psych you out so easy."

Her eyes glow like an animal's in the dark. "Excuse me?"

"I'm no expert, but isn't tennis about the mind, too? Maybe she's got a stronger mind than you."

I can feel her gaping at me. "She does *not* have a stronger mind."

"You just told me she did."

"I . . ." she says, and then stops talking, thinking about what I said.

"So, next time you play her, here's what you do. Before the match, you walk up to her in the locker room and you say, 'Hey, Penelope. I knew I'd find you here. I could smell your BO all the way down the hall. This should help.' And then you dump your milk on her head. I promise, you'll wipe the court with her. Plus she'll stink like bad cheese."

Lucinda laughs. And stops tugging at her skirt as if she could make it longer. "That's the dumbest thing I've ever heard."

"My specialty."

"I know."

"Seriously. Sorry you lost today. Sucks."

"Yeah, well. It happens."

"Not to you, though."

She shrugs, but I can tell that I'm right.

"Penelope doesn't know what she's talking about. Your hair always looks good."

The hands fly up to the head again as she glances at me. Her lips move as if she might say thank you, but she doesn't say anything.

I win.

I think.

I pull up to her car—nose to nose so that I can keep the lights on. We jump out of the SUV. Lucinda sets the battery on the ground and pops the hood on her Oldsmo-Buick. Instead of getting her tools, she gets her ginormous phone from the front seat.

"Calling for a pizza?" I say.

"My brothers," she tells me. She tries one number, then the other. "No answer." She tosses the phone back onto the seat, moves around to the front of her car, leans over, and plucks at some of the wiring. Then she straightens up. "Well."

"Well," I say.

She pokes at the wires again. "I thought they would be home by now. Or at least answering their phones. I don't know why they're not answering."

"Okay," I say, not knowing where she's going with this.

"You don't have to stay, Eddy. I'm sure you have stuff to do. I'm fine here."

"What are you talking about?" Then it dawns on me. "Don't you know how to install the battery?" Surprisingly, I'm surprised. I just assumed she was that kind of girl, the kind of girl who does one-armed push-ups and repairs motorcycles and still finds time to knit her own socks.

Lucinda shuffles her feet. It is an amazing thing to see, Lucinda Dulko humbled to the point of shuffling her feet. "But maybe *you* know how to—"

"Oh, I get it. I'm a guy, ergo, *I* know how to fix cars."

She moves to adjust her skirt for the millionth time but stops herself when she sees her hands are greasy. "Well," she says. "Do you? Know how to fix cars, I mean? If you could, I'd—"

I fold my arms across my chest. "I'm not sure I appreciate this stereotyping."

"Cut it out."

"I wouldn't have thought it about you, Lucinda, but I think you're being really sexist."

She rolls her eyes. "Do you know how to install the battery or not?"

"I have *feelings*, you know. Thoughts and dreams and *feelings*," I say, making my voice quaver. "I'm not just some motor head with a Y chromosome."

"Eddy—"

"Some hairy caveman you can use and abuse. Just because I'm incredibly tall and muscular and have superior mechanical ability doesn't mean—"

"Stop it," she says, but I can see the smile twitching at the corner of her mouth.

"Fine," I say, marching over to my SUV to get my wrench and screwdriver from where they're buried under a mound of extra clothes and papers. "I'll install your precious battery. But I don't want you ogling me while I do it."

She shakes her head. "I'll try to control myself."

She leans in close while I work, so close that I can smell her hair—soap and apples. Unfortunately it's an easy job and doesn't take me long. I'm just hooking up the cables when Lucinda says, "Sorry to make you hang around and do this."

I glance up. She looks as if she'd rather swallow her own tongue than say she was sorry about anything. I decide not to mess with her.

"No big deal."

"I don't mind asking my brothers, but I didn't want to bother my parents with this. They go a little overboard. They would have sent a tow truck and possibly an ambulance. And they would have come, too. Probably with my entire extended family. It would have taken hours and then I'd have to deal with them worrying every time I got into the car. I wanted to handle this myself. I wanted to handle *something* myself."

Handle it herself? Okay, I'm going to mess with her. "You mean you wanted to stare at my butt."

"I'm not staring at your butt," she says, but, of course, her eyes flick to my butt. I snicker.

"I really hate you," she says.

"Didn't we have a conversation about using and abusing me?" I slam the hood shut and wipe my palms on the front of my jeans.

"You shouldn't do that," she says. "You've got grease all over your hands."

"So do you."

She inspects them, then wipes them on the front of my shirt. "That's better."

It takes me a few seconds to register that she (a) just ruined my favorite T-shirt and (b) her touching me might be worth the ruin of my favorite shirt. "Now I'll have to throw it out."

"What a shame."

"Have you got something against dill pickles?"

"No, just self-absorbed redheads."

While I'm wondering if she's seen *Riot Grrl 16*, what she thinks about it, she jumps into the car to test the new battery. The car starts right up. Her smile is like a flash-bulb going off.

She leans out the window. "Thanks, Eddy. I really appreciate this."

"How much?"

The smile dims and the I'll-tenderize-you-with-my-racket expression is back. "Not *that* much."

"Jeez," I say. "I didn't believe the other boys when they told me, but they were right: you girls really do have one thing on your minds, don't you?"

She throws her head back and exhales loudly. "If you didn't just fix this car, I'd run you over with it.

What are you talking about?"

"I'm talking about a game of tennis. I want to find out how harsh you can be. How's Saturday?"

She eyes me for a long minute, inspecting me, studying me. I think she's going to say no, and for a minute I worry that I've played this all wrong. Then she says, "I have practice till noon. After that . . ." She trails off.

"How about I meet you at the courts at twelve thirty? Unless you'll be too tired."

"No, no," she says. "I'm never too tired. You're on. Saturday. Twelve thirty."

"Good," I say. I turn and start walking back to my car.

She calls after me. "Hey!"

"What?"

"You know I'm going to kick your ass, right?"

I feel the goofy grin stretching across my face and hope that's not the only thing she's going to do. "I'm counting on it."

Clerks

It was my mom who got me into movies. We rented new ones by the dozen and her favorites over and over again: *Casablanca*, *Chinatown*, *Bonnie and Clyde*, *Harold and Maude*, *Rear Window*, and every other Hitchcock ever made. She ate movies like other people eat potato chips, one after the other, never getting enough. As soon as the final credits rolled, she was pawing through the stack she'd rented, saying, "What should we watch next?"

But it wasn't just the classics she wanted. She was hungry for independents, blockbusters, foreign, animated, you name it. It made sense. Ever since she was a little girl, she wanted to be an actress. My grandparents thought it was a waste of time. They wanted her to be a doctor or a lawyer or a teacher, something practical and steady and boring as hell. She told me that when she was in high school in the eighties, she used to take the bus to New York City on Saturdays to take acting classes. Her parents thought she was babysitting for the Rosenblatt family around the block. She did that for two years until they caught her, and by then she was eighteen and there was not much they could do about it. For the next nineteen years, she auditioned for every Broadway play, every TV show, and every film she could. Sometimes, in the middle of a movie, she would press pause and then act out the scene, playing all the roles herself. Sometimes, maybe most times, she was better than watching the film.

Movies were her life. Everything else was strictly cutting room.

Anyway, it was because of my mom that I got to know Rory. It seemed we were at World of Video every few days with a new list of movies she wanted to rent.

The first thing he ever said to me was: "Dude. Your mom's a hottie."

The first thing I ever said to him was: "Dude. Don't make me break your face."

"You probably could," he said mildly and with no fear whatsoever. He was so small he was probably used to getting the crap kicked out of him. I noticed that he had a fading bruise under one eye and that his glasses were taped in the middle.

He watched my mom browse the shelves in the drama section, her finger under her nose as if she smelled something bad. "I've seen her somewhere."

"Duh," I said. "We're here practically every minute."

"No, somewhere else."

I hadn't told anyone about my mom yet and I was bursting to do it: "She's in a movie."

"What? Get out!"

"I'm serious."

"Which movie?"

As soon as he asked, I got embarrassed. It wasn't out yet. My mom told me that they were still looking for a distributor. "You probably never heard of it."

He shook his head in disbelief. "You do realize that you're standing in a video store, right? I've heard of every movie ever made and every movie that is getting made. And if I haven't heard of it, my parents have."

"Where are your parents?" I said. "I've been in here

a million times and never seen them." Rory's parents were infamous around town for successfully blocking the opening of a giant Hollywood Video, mostly due to the fact that they were distantly related to the mayor. Because of them, World of Video was the only place around to get movies. Most of us were used to the strange smells in the store—new car smell in comedy, vomit in drama, lemons in foreign, baby powder in horror. The restroom smelled like a restroom—circa 1890. Most kids in school called World of Video Smellovideo and Rory's parents the Smellovidiots. No wonder Rory's glasses were broken.

"The 'rents are around somewhere," he told me. "Mostly they let me run the place."

"Really," I said. He was short and skinny and about thirteen years old, same as me. "They let a *seventh grader* run their store?"

He shrugged his tiny, bony shoulders. "Cheap labor."

"As in free?"

He shrugged again. "They feed me. I can't complain. So what's the movie?"

"She just had a small part," I said.

"There are no small parts; there are only small actors," Rory said.

"Where did you hear that? My mother says that all the time."

"See? We were made for each other."

"I can still break your face."

"Yeah, yeah. What's the movie called, Clint?"

"Clint?"

"As in Eastwood? As in, 'Go on, make my day'? *Dirty Harry*?"

I shook my head.

"You're obviously hopeless," he said. "A classic, dude, a classic. Clint carries a gun about a foot long and shoots everybody."

We were getting off topic. I would discover later that off topic was one of Rory's favorite places to go. "My mom's movie's called *Villerosa*."

Rory frowned. "Huh. That might be the one movie in the world I haven't heard of. What's it about?"

"The main character's this mob guy named Villerosa, right? But everyone keeps mispronouncing it because of the two *l*'s."

"What *l*'s?"

"The *l*'s in his name. *V-i-l-l-e-r-o-s-a*. It's a Spanish name. The two *l*'s are pronounced as a *y*. So that's the joke in the movie. That people keep getting his name wrong."

"It's a joke?"

"Well, yeah. Because he isn't a very good mob guy. He keeps getting stuff wrong, too."

"Okay," said Rory, still frowning.

I decided I wasn't explaining it right; I was making

the movie sound stupid. "My mom plays a hit woman."

"Sweet!" said Rory. "Does she carry a foot-long gun?"

"She kills people other ways. Like with household stuff. A plastic knife. A soda can. A nail clipper. Like that. It's a comedy."

"Have you seen it?"

I hadn't. "They're still looking for a distributor."

"But you must have seen it."

"She wouldn't let me," I told him.

"Why not?" he said. "Wait, I know. She must get naked in it."

"She does *not* get naked. She's my *mom*."

"Then she takes off her top or something."

I held up a video. "She also kills someone with a video cover. She showed me how to do it."

"All right, all right, so she keeps her clothes on. Why wouldn't she want you to see it?"

"She says she's too nervous. It's her first big role. She wants me to wait until the premiere."

"When is that?"

"I don't know," I said. "Because of the distributor thing." I tried not to sound too nervous about it myself, but it was hard. My mother was so anxious that it was rubbing off on the whole family. My dad couldn't eat. Marty couldn't sleep. The Meatball had taken to banging his head against the wall, something he hadn't done since he was in nursery school. And I was spilling my guts to the weird kid who worked at Smellovideo.

Rory pushed his broken glasses up the bridge of his nose. "Even if your mom's movie goes straight to DVD, it would still be really sweet."

"You think so?"

"Sure. Lots of actors get attention that way. If she's good, then she's good, right? No matter what she's in."

I exhaled, relieved. "Right." I was so relieved, I stuck out my hand. "I'm Eddy."

He looked at me as if I was crazy—I mean, what seventh grader shakes hands?—but he shook it anyway. "Pleased to meet you. I'm the Dalai Lama."

"Nice to meet you, Mr. Lama."

It became our standard greeting. When I see Rory at my locker the day after we posted the latest *Riot Grrl 16* episode, the day after my world was eclipsed by a moon called Lucinda, I say, "Nice to meet you, Mr. Lama."

"Llama, llama, duck," he shouts, performing one of his strange and awkward white guy dance moves that he should never do in public but insists on doing anyway. Two girls passing by whip around to stare at him. "Have you ever kissed a llama on the llama?" he bellows after them. Rory's a lot like Tippi Hedren, always quoting the videos he sees, this one a stupid song that whipped through the web a few years ago. But unlike Tippi Hedren, I'm not sure he always knows the right time to do his quoting. One of the girls gives him a dirty look while the other one tells him what he can do with his llama, which sounds pretty uncomfortable, not to mention illegal (though probably available for viewing somewhere on the internet).

But I'm spared the predictable animal abuse jokes that would normally follow because Gina is stomping down the hall and heading right for us. She's recently started wearing her Riot Grrl combat boots to school. Always the queen of fashion, she's paired them with an intriguing plaid kilt.

"Is she armed under that skirt?" Rory mutters.

"We'll find out," I mutter back.

Both of us instinctively shrink against the lockers when Gina gets close. "You filmed me when I told you not to," she says, stabbing me in the chest with her finger.

No sense denying it. "Yes."

She stabs me again. "And you used the footage in the show."

"Yes."

"I think you're evil. No, not just evil. You're the devil. Tell me, Ed. Are you the devil? The fallen one? Beelzebub himself?"

Her eyes are wide black pits. They're sort of mesmerizing. I'm thinking I could actually get sucked into them and land in another dimension. "I don't think so."

"I think so." Stab, stab, stab. After a minute she says, "The show was number three with the voters so far."

"I know," I say.

"It looked awesome."

"You looked awesome," I tell her.

She keeps stabbing, but softer now. It's like Shiatsu. "I still think you're a girl-using slut."

"So why do you keep touching me?"

"I'm trying to leave a bruise. No, scratch that. I'm trying to put my hand through your sternum, reach into your bloody viscera, and rip out your still-beating heart."

"Really. And then what?"

"Then I'm going to feed it to my dog."

"Ah."

"Okay, Riot Grrl, that's enough," Rory says. "Eddy's delicate. You'll hurt him."

Gina finally stops stabbing me. "Hurt him? He'd have to have feelings for that." She slaps me across the face, hard enough for me to feel the sting, light enough to tell me that she'll keep doing the show. The people around us start chanting, "Riot Grrl! Riot Grrl! Riot Grrl!" as she pushes through the crowd.

"I think you could file a complaint," Rory says after Gina disappears through the double doors leading to the other wing.

"Are you crazy? She's perfect."

"Hot, too," he says. "If you like the unpredictable and kilt clad."

"What's not to like?"

"True," he says. "Maybe we should write a scene for Riot Grrl with Gina doing that stabbing-the-chest thing to her boyfriend? *Are you the devil? Are you what's-his-name?*"

"Beelze . . ." I say, trailing off because it's Lucinda's turn to walk toward us. It must be a match day because she's wearing another tiny tennis outfit, a dress this time. Rory whistles at her and I smack him upside the head. Lucinda's mouth twitches. I almost got her to smile.

"Hey!" Rory says. "What was that for?"

"Don't whistle. It makes you look like an ass."

"Girls love it."

"Yeah," I say. "Like they love colitis."

"Don't get weird on me, dude. Joe's acting up too. Notice how much time he spends doing history these days? And what's with the Bible?"

I wait for Lucinda to look back over her shoulder, but she doesn't. "I hadn't really thought about it."

The bell rings and Rory scurries off to wherever llamas go to waste time till graduation. I have English, where we will be discussing *Crime and Prejudice*. Or *Pride and Punishment*. Or *This Book Is So Bloody Dull Nobody but High School Students Will Ever Read It and Then Only Because They Are Repeatedly Threatened with Unjust Detentions Even Though Graduation Is Near*

Enough to Taste. Once, my mother tortured me with a six-hour BBC production of one of those period dramas where all the characters are trapped by circumstance and they all sit around in dusty drawing rooms not allowed to do the things they want or say the things they think. High school is a lot like that.

I turned eighteen in April. The first thing I did was go down to the school office and ask if I could sign myself out. I wanted to do an afternoon shoot with Gina at the beach. The secretary didn't even look up from her computer screen.

"No, you can't sign yourself out. Your parents have to sign you out. And besides, we discourage that sort of thing."

"I turned eighteen yesterday. That makes me a legal adult. I shouldn't have to have anyone's permission to do anything."

"Really," said the secretary. "I assume you'll be moving out of your parents' house and paying your own bills, then."

"I just want to go to the beach. What do you have against the ocean?"

"When you're elected president of the universe, you can sign yourself out. Until the end of June, you belong to us. After that, you can spend the rest of eternity perfecting your tan."

In English, I slide into my seat and try to remember

which book I was supposed to have read. All around me, people are smiling and nodding. I hear, "Way to go, Ed," and, "Great show."

The guy behind me claps me on the back. "Yo, Rochester. *Riot Grrl* rocked."

"Thanks," I say.

"Better than anything else in that contest."

I nod. "Thanks. We liked it too."

"That girl's a freak."

He's talking about Gina, of course. She isn't, not really. She gets good grades; she doesn't drink or do drugs. But not many people see beyond the big boots and the attitude and the I'll-feed-your-heart-to-my-dog. Everyone mixes her up with her character. It's like they've totally forgotten that just eight months ago, Gina was just another drama nerd. Like they've forgotten that *Riot Grrl 16* is a total figment of my imagination.

Cameras do that to people.

He leans in behind me. He smells a little like lunch meat. Looks like it too—thick, red in the face. "You're doing her, right?"

"Who?"

"Riot Grrl."

See?

"No," I say. "Riot Grrl's a virgin."

"Too hot to be a virgin," he says. His first name is Attila, so of course everyone calls him the Hun.

"Plenty of hot girls are virgins, Hun," I say.

"Not that girl," he tells me. "That's a girl who likes to neuken."

"Neuken?"

"It's Dutch, I think."

That's where the name came from. "So you're Dutch?"

He frowns. "No."

I sigh. "Riot Grrl is a made-up girl, okay? I wrote her. And I wrote her as a virgin."

"Why would you do that?"

"You're still watching the show, aren't you?"

He blinks slowly, breathing heavily through his mouth. He's thinking about this. Or he's having a petit mal seizure; hard to tell.

Joe slides into the seat next to me. "Hey," he says.

"Hey," I say.

He opens a book and starts leafing through it. I wait for him to say something about the new episode. He keeps leafing. It's a Bible.

"How's the book?"

"Interesting," he says. "You ever read it?"

"Parts. In Sunday school. Years ago."

"I think it's interesting."

"Okay."

"Really. Did you know there are two creation stories?"

"No, I didn't."

"Well, there are. Nobody talks about that."

"Why would they?" I say.

He just looks at me. His eyes are huge and expressionless, like a bug's. You never know what he's thinking unless he wants you to. Mostly, he doesn't want you to.

"Did you see the new episode?"

"Yeah, I caught it," he says.

"The show rocks," Attila the Hun pipes up.

"Thanks," Joe says, as if he had something to do with it.

"You should have stayed," I say. "Helped us do the edits."

Joe keeps leafing, the thin pages making an impatient rustling sound. "I told you. I had a history project. You did okay without me."

I know what this is about. He's mad because we used the Gina footage without asking. "Gina loved the episode."

"Yeah?"

"Yeah. I just talked to her."

His bug eyes bug. "Would it have killed you to get her permission first?"

"Yes," I say. "It would actually have killed me. My liver would have exploded. Or my pancreas."

Attila the Hun: "What's the pancreas do?"

Joe doesn't even glance back at him. "Secretes insulin."

"Anyway," I say, "it all worked out for the best.

The show's number three."

"Hmmm," he says.

"Would it kill you to show more enthusiasm?"

There's a carved pumpkin smile. "Yes, it would actually kill me."

Attila the Hun: "I still don't get why she's a virgin."

"Who?" says Joe.

"Riot Grrl," I say. "He's having a little trouble with the whole make-believe thing."

Attila the Hun: "Wouldn't it be better if she had sex all the time?"

"How would that be different than porn, Hun?" I say.

"And don't you find enough of that on the web already?" says Joe.

"No." Attila the Hun laughs. If dogs could laugh, they would sound like Attila the Hun. I wonder what Attila the Hun thinks of *Crime and Prejudice*. His papers must be pretty entertaining to read.

"We have to work on the rehearsal schedule," I tell Joe. "I have the script almost done."

"Don't we always have the same rehearsal schedule?"

I decide that I'm not going to get much more out of him. Maybe all his Bible reading will teach him a little forgiveness and maybe some gratitude, too. Then again, all the books on Buddhism didn't help him achieve true enlightenment. And the Marx didn't help him understand the common man. Neither did all that stuff about Plato. Which reminds me . . .

"How'd did the history project go?"

"Good," Joe says. "Really good. We're almost done."

"Who's in your study group?"

He shrugs. "A few people. Max Blume. Ashley Davidson. Lucinda Dulko. That's who picked me up. Lucinda." As he says her name, his mouth moves oddly, like he almost can't get the word out, like he's stuck on the *Lu* and might have to sing the rest. A flush of pink tinges his ears and he ducks his head a little.

It's been a long time since a girl made him give himself away like that. The last one was Joelle Lipshitz, and she chewed him up and spit him out last summer, right before she left for acting school and a role in a tampon commercial.

Oddly, this makes me feel better. Like Joe's human after all. And that maybe I'm not so stupid for asking Lucinda Dulko to play.

Mr. Lambright, the teacher, strides into the room just as the bell is ringing. "All right, people. Settle down. Today we're going to talk about . . ."

I take out a piece of paper and scribble a note. When Lambright turns around to write something on the board, I toss it on Joe's desk. Joe reads the note, answers it, and tosses it back.

I wrote: *So, are we cool? Can we get back to it now?*

He wrote: *We're cool.*

I look at the note, at Joe's pink ears. I hear him trying to say her name through a mouth that seemed to belong to someone else. I remember the feel of my own mouth stretching into a stupid grin in the glare of Lucinda's headlights.

Yeah.

We're real cool.

I don't know why, but a line from *This Is Spinal Tap* pops into my head: "We've got armadillos in our trousers. It's really quite frightening."

Disturbia

After school, I drive to the pet store to stock up on Polly's Extreme Tropical Fruit and Nut Bites and Sassy and Sleek Bird Kibble for Tippi Hedren. I find her hanging upside down in her cage, gnawing maniacally on her wooden "robot" toy. The poor guy is now missing his head, a head that Tippi has dropped strategically in one of her food bowls.

"You're a man-eater, Tippi," I say. I open the cage and she steps out onto my finger. I'll replace the toy with another one later. She goes through them like a cheerleader through football players.

"Long yellow?" she says as I reach back in the cage for her bowls.

"I didn't buy any corn on the cob today. But I have your favorite fruit and nut bites."

"Long yellow."

"I'll get you some tomorrow."

"Long yellow!"

"You ladies are so demanding."

"I'm just a wild animal you've trapped," Tippi Hedren says, ruffling her feathers.

"Yes, you are. But you're my favorite wild animal."

Tippi purrs happily on my shoulder—she does a mean cat impression, along with ringing phones, sirens, static, and asthmatic wheezing—I strip out the paper lining the bottom of the cage and replace it with clean paper. I remove her bowls, go to the bathroom, wash both, fill them up with food, and put them back in the cage. After I'm done cleaning, I take a handful of the nuts and seeds and then me and Tippi sit at my computer. There's an instant message from Gina: *Karma, ass face. What goes around comes around. I totally hate you. What time is rehearsal?* I tell her to come over at four the next day, as usual.

I feed Tippi some sunflower seeds and click over to the MTV site. We're still number three in votes. Ahead of *Riot Grrl 16* is a show called *The Amazing Adventures of Emo Guy*, which is a sort of funny animated show. I don't have any animation skills, and this makes me laugh once in a while, so I don't mind so much. But the other show is an unbelievably bad jackass-type show in which a bunch of guys try to launch themselves out of cannons or shoot potato guns at each other's crotches or have cavities drilled without novocaine. Their most recent episode consists of them eating as many Mentos as they can and then drinking a vat of Pepsi. Projectile vomiting ensues. Truly inspiring.

Sometimes I fear for the future of America.

And then sometimes I don't. I page through more comments about *Riot Grrl 16*. Most of it's the same as before. *Rock on, Riot Grrl, I love this show. As much as it hurts I think riot grrl needs to stop helping her brother he's just dragging her down.*

I'm feeling really good about our chances, especially good now that I know Gina's not going anywhere, and maybe Joe will hang around too, when I see that the Tin Man has struck again.

I can't believe you guys are still talking about this show. It's lame, lame, LAME. You can tell that chick is no more punk than the nearest mall rat. I bet those tattoos are stick-ons. I bet she just went to a Justin

Timberlake concert wearing a thong hanging out of the back of her Juicy jeans. And the guy playing her brother has about as much charisma as a corpse. Where'd they find him? The morgue?

"What's wrong with this guy?" I say out loud.

"I have to get back to San Francisco," says Tippi Hedren.

And right after the Tin Man post, there's another one from someone else.

never thought about it but now that you said it i guess except for the hair and the tattoos there's nothing punk about her really maybe she's just a wannabe like those girls who shop at hot topic

"These people are insane," I say. Tippi helpfully does her impression of a cuckoo clock.

I find another negative from a third person:

I don't like the brother either. He's creepy.

"He's supposed to be creepy!" I shout. "He's a heroin addict!"

Tin Man adds: *And do I have to mention YET AGAIN that this is nothing but a total rip-off of* Lonely Girl 15*? And that show isn't even GOOD????*

"Great, Tippi. This dumb ass is going to poison the voting pool."

"I jumped in the fountain!" says Tippi. *"Meow!"*

"I'd like for this guy to go jump in the fountain," I say. I click on Comment and start to type, but then I think better of it and consult the dictionary first.

Satire: the use of irony, sarcasm, ridicule, or the like in exposing, denouncing, or deriding vice, folly, etc.

Duh.

"Duh," I say.

Tippi Hedren says, *"I think you need these lovebirds after all. They may help your personality."* She growls like a lion, and I give her another small handful of seeds.

I click over to the Jumping Frenchmen of Maine MySpace. Not a lot of comments there but a few desperate groupies who call themselves "hott" trying to be our "friends." Like Rory always says, their parents would be so proud. I friend them all anyway. "You can't have too many friends, right, Tippi?"

"I have to get back to San Francisco," Tippi says.

I click out of MySpace and flip to my *Riot Grrl* script. We have only four episodes left, and I want to make sure everything is leading to a big finale. That I haven't thought of yet. We've already had Riot Grrl get together with her manga-obsessed crush, break up with her manga-obsessed crush, try out for *American Idol*, become a Wiccan, attempt to cast love spells with dead ants and cinnamon, rescue her best friend from a fifty-four-year-old freak she met on the internet, and deal with her long-lost drug addict brother. I'm thinking that the one commenter was right: Riot Grrl has to cut her addict brother loose. She can't cover for him anymore; she can't slip him cash; she can't keep lying to her parents that he's still in the rehab clinic they spent their life savings to send him to. She knows it has to be done, but it's going to break her heart to do it. It might send her over the edge; I don't know. That could be interesting. Riot Grrl goes over the edge? What would *that* look like?

I'm writing for a while when the floor under me vibrates. The garage. I hear a car door slam. And then my name. I take Tippi and head downstairs.

My dad's holding a hammer and sighing. His sighs are long and expressive. So are his eye rolls. He's worse than a teenager.

"I was going to use this and I noticed that it's broken. Did you break my hammer?"

"It's not broken," I say.

He points to the handle. "It's cracked. You cracked my hammer."

"Gina cracked your hammer."

"How did she do that?"

"She threw a bottle at me and missed. It must have hit the hammer."

"Okay," he says. "*Why* would she do that?"

"How should I know? She's crazy."

He raises his eyebrows. They're expressive too. "Women can be that way, if you give them enough reason."

"And sometimes they're crazy all on their own," I say.

"So you didn't give her a reason."

"I'm just a wild animal," Tippi says.

"Hello, Tippi Hedren," Dad says. "Beautiful as ever, I see." He winks at her and she winks back. The first trick I ever taught her. She makes a sound somewhere between a giggle and a cackle.

"You'll have to pay to replace the hammer," he tells me. "I liked that hammer."

"Fine," I say, hoping that the rest of his tools are undamaged from Gina's rampage. "You're home early." Dad doesn't normally walk in till one or two in the morning. Sometimes I don't see him for days. I get the feeling I'm not supposed to care about this; I'm supposed to like it. Not sure what it means that I don't.

"We wrapped up early for once," my dad's saying. "You'd think my schedule would have turned you off the movie business."

"You're not in the movie business."

"I'm in show business."

I'm about to say, I don't think doing the sound for a cable TV show called *Cleaning House* in which middle-aged people have massive amounts of junk cleaned out of their houses by some annoying Australian guy qualifies as show business. But all I say is, "Dad."

He smiles in that aggravating way he has, that way that says he's been there, done that, seen everything, and wasn't impressed. "I know, I know, doing the sound for

Cleaning House doesn't count, right?"

"Dad."

"Depends what you think show business is supposed to do. Entertain people? Help people? Most of show business doesn't do either."

Tippi Hedren says, *"You Freud, me Jane?"*

"I didn't say anything," I protest.

"This week we went to see this couple downstate," he says. "I've never even heard of the town. Seems crazy to me that there are towns in New Jersey I've never heard of, but there it is. Anyway, this couple lives in a tiny house with two kids. You can't even get into the house, it's so jammed with stuff. You know what kind of stuff?"

He's waiting for me to guess.

"Car tires."

"No."

"Encyclopedias."

"No."

"Hair clippings."

"No, but that would be funny. He collects Barbies. Works for the company that makes them. Anyway, whenever the company offers the fancy expensive Barbies for sale, the ones dressed up like Princess Diana or Paris Hilton or Cinderella or whoever, he buys them because he thinks they're going to be worth something someday. Had hundreds in unopened boxes stacked everywhere. Not one was made before 1985, and not one of them was rare. Which means that they aren't worth a dime and never will be. Couldn't tell him that, though. Here his kids had nowhere to sit, but he cried when we told him he'd have to get rid of his Barbies."

I hunt around for a broom. "That's a very sad story."

"Well, there are very sad people in the world. Wally did get him to sell about half of them at the garage sale. Your mother probably could have talked him into selling them all."

"Probably." My dad and mom met while working at the same cable channel—he was a sound guy and she was a hostess for a design show. Then they both switched over to *Cleaning House*. They worked there until *Villerosa*. *Villerosa* changed everything.

Dad examines the broken hammer. "I don't see why you can't go to school to study film," he says. Doesn't bother with segues, my dad. Besides, this has been his favorite topic since the beginning of the school year, when I told him that I wasn't going to college.

"I have been studying film for years," I say.

"I mean really study it."

"I've *been* really studying it. Since I was a kid. The workshops? The camps? The classes? Ringing a bell?"

He picks up the rest of the tools on the floor and hangs them neatly on the wall, making sure they're completely parallel. "I'm not sure your mother did you a favor taking you to all of that stuff. And that was a long time ago."

I'm so tired of this.

"Success doesn't just happen. There's apprenticeship. There's practice."

"Dad, I'm working as hard as I can."

"Really? When was the last time you mowed the lawn?"

"I'll do it tomorrow."

"Sure you will. There's also maturity. Talent needs to be developed over time."

"Orson Welles was in his twenties when he did *Citizen Kane*," I say.

"He was twenty-six. Eight years older than you."

"That's just an example. I don't expect to be Orson Welles. At least not yet. I just want to make movies. Isn't making movies the best way to learn how to make them?"

"I just don't want you to get your hopes up."

"Thanks for the vote of confidence."

Even though I put as much sarcasm in my voice as I can, he doesn't seem to register it. "Oh, I have all the confidence in the world that you'll be successful. Absolutely. I'm not sure you're going to be successful *tomorrow*. Or the next day. Or the next day. Just be prepared for that."

"Again, *thanks*."

"You're welcome," he says. "Understand, though,

that you'll be getting a job as soon as September comes around."

"I have a job. My movies are my job."

"A *paying* job."

"Mom gives me an allowance." I put the emphasis on the word *Mom*.

He doesn't bite. "You're eighteen years old, Eddy. You need to earn your own money."

"The movies will pay."

And there it is, the smile, the resigned, the patient, the all-knowing, all-seeing, you'll-learn-your-lesson-eventually smile. Makes me want to break a hundred more hammers.

But then I think about his life. Maybe he can't help thinking the way he does. I mean, when he was my age, he thought he was going to be big in the movies. He didn't know he was going to be working for some crappy cable show. He didn't know his wife was going to leave him. He didn't know he'd be sharing a kid with another guy when he isn't even gay and therefore couldn't even enjoy it. Maybe that kind of stuff makes you want to smile like the Buddha just to piss other people off.

He rubs his eyes and I see how tired he looks. He shuffles to the door. "Are you okay?" I ask him. Even though he gets on my nerves in the worst way, I still don't like to see him moving like an arthritic octogenarian. My mom's seven years older than him, but it's like she's decades younger.

"I didn't get a lot of sleep last night," he says. People say that we look alike, and it's true. At least on the outside. I have the same red hair, the same height, the same long arms that make it easy to reach the highest shelves in the kitchen. But the man never expects anything good to happen. I can't imagine living my life wrapped in a wry little cocoon, expecting boredom and disappointment and even disaster around every corner and then being funny about it when it comes.

"You want something to eat?" I say.

He shakes his head. "Not hungry."

He's never hungry. "I'm going to make you something to eat," I say. I go to the kitchen and fill up a pot. All I can do is mac and cheese, but he could use all the calories he can get.

"Can't have Dad wasting away," I say to Tippi Hedren. "What will the neighbors think?" I put her on the perch we keep in the kitchen.

"Why don't you love me, Mama?" says Tippi. She spreads her wings to make the line more dramatic.

Dad stands in the doorway of the kitchen as I tear open the box. He gestures to the cuckoo clock we have hanging over the counter. "Marty and Matthew should be here soon. Why don't you make enough for them?"

I stop ripping. "It's Wednesday?"

"Yep," he says, and ducks out of the room. I have to

search for more macaroni and cheese, but Marty set us up right the last time he went shopping: there are at least a dozen boxes in the pantry. I make four. Three for me, one for everybody else.

Only takes me fifteen minutes to cook the pasta and stir in the nuclear-orange cheese product and an artery-splitting amount of butter and milk. I hear the front door opening, voices echoing in the front hall. Tippi Hedren makes the sound of a doorbell, then a buzzer, then a clock ticking.

The Meatball appears in the kitchen, followed by Marty. The Meatball says, in his grave way, "Hello, Eddy."

"Hello, Meatball."

"Did you know that a human head is the same size as a roast chicken?"

I glance at Marty. "He's reading that book again, isn't he?"

Marty throws up his hands. "He likes it."

"He's obsessed."

"He's passionate," says Marty. "Everyone needs their passions."

"He's passionate about a book called *Stiff*. My mom would say he should get back on the meds."

Marty peeks into the pot and pokes at the macaroni like a kid poking a particularly gross bug. "Your mother isn't here." He grins wryly, looking a lot like my dad.

"Besides, the whole thing's funny, don't you think? Rather appropriate, considering."

"More like weird."

"Weird is funny."

"Did you know that dead people are occasionally used as crash test dummies?" Meatball asks. "The dead excel at tolerating pain."

Marty grins wider. "Funny. See?"

I hand them bowls and they spoon themselves some mac and cheese. I fill a bowl for my dad and one for myself. I leave them on the counter while I scoop up Tippi and put her back on my shoulder. Then I pick up both bowls and head for the family room.

Dad's already got the TV on and the opening song blares from the speakers. Something by the Who. "Who Are You"? "Teenage Wasteland"? Who knows? The title appears in blood red: *Crime Scene: Miami*. The credits roll. Takes a while to get to her. She's billed as Shelby Graham. That's not her real name, of course. She told me that no one in Hollywood uses real names. That she never got to go to Hollywood didn't seem to be relevant. Anyway, her real name is Shelby Rochester Fishbone because she isn't quite divorced from Marty yet, but I suppose Shelby Rochester Fishbone isn't the best name for an actress.

We take our seats, always the same ones: me and Marty on the couch, my dad in the recliner, and the

Meatball sitting on the floor by the coffee table. I hand my dad the mac and cheese and he starts eating it absently, as if he's forgotten that he's not hungry. I eat the way I always do—like I'm in a food-eating contest. Marty frowns at the food—he makes his own Alfredo sauce with freshly grated cheese—but doesn't complain. The Meatball's fork hovers between his bowl and his mouth, two shiny limp noodles hanging from it. The Meatball has a hard time doing two things at once. We'll remind him to eat during the commercials.

We have to wait a while, at least ten or fifteen minutes, for her one and only scene. Takes that long to kill whoever's going to die in this episode, find the body, call the cops in, have the main cop guy march around in his oversize sunglasses threatening everyone, and then get back to the office, where the pathologist can scoop out the dead person's guts and compare them to manicotti or maybe hack the top of his or her head off while making bad quips about hats.

My mom is the pathologist.

I guess the Meatball's obsession *is* rather appropriate.

"I hope she's wearing an actual shirt this time," I say. "I'm pretty sure most pathologists don't walk around in tube tops."

"Shhh," says Marty.

My mother stands over the "dead" body in the eerie green room. She's wearing a lab coat opened to reveal a low-cut shirt. Once I made the mistake of watching the show with Rory. When my mom first appeared on-screen, he yelled, "Whoa! Your mom's onions are about to fall out!" I never made that mistake again.

She's moving around the table, holding up shiny instruments and pretending to do mysterious, medical things with them. Her hair is longer and lighter now, streaked with fat stripes of gold, piled high on her head the way a queen might wear it. I wonder if she thinks of us, any of us—Dad, Marty, me, the Meatball. I wonder if she worries at all, or if she just imagines that we'll all muddle along fine without her. That's what she said when she left, "Oh, I know you guys. You'll all muddle along fine," as if she'd just be gone for a day or two, as if she wasn't leaving Marty and Meat and me to work for the kind of TV show she said she'd never work for and move in with some too-tan media mogul down in Miami.

She says, "The victim was only a kid. Nineteen, twenty maybe. This kid should be hanging out with his friends, not lying cold on my table."

Cop guy says, "What else can you tell me, Kallendria?"

"I can tell you that he didn't die of that shark bite."

Cop guy: "He didn't? But his legs are gone!"

Mom: "Look at this." She turns the dead guy's head and points to a tiny hole behind the ear.

Cop guy: "A needle mark."

Mom: "I almost missed it."

Cop guy: "You never miss a thing."

The Meatball slowly lowers his fork to the table and stands up. He wraps his hands around his throat and starts to cough. Then he falls to the floor, writhing and wriggling, clawing at the collar of his shirt. He stops moving, his tongue hanging out of his mouth, still as the "corpse" on TV.

When I was eight years old, Mom took me for an audition for *Law & Order*. Just for fun, she said, but she was so excited I could tell how bad she wanted me to get the part. So, I got the part. I was the dead body. I described it to Meatball not too long ago, how still you had to lie, how quiet, until they said, "Cut." How hard it was to control your breathing, to let only a little air out and a little air in. How your arm itches or your back itches and you desperately want to move and you can't because you'll ruin everything. The Meatball never forgot it. And when she left a year ago, he started doing this. I think he thinks that one day he'll open his eyes and it will be her shaking him awake, her reviving him. And he'll die every day until it happens.

Marty and Dad know the drill. I get up, move around the coffee table, and kneel by Meat's side. I grab him by the shoulders and shake him a few times. "Meat!" I say. "Are you all right? Was it the food? Is it stuck? Can you breathe?" I lift him into a sitting position and pretend to give him the Heimlich.

After a few minutes of this, he opens his eyes and turns to me. "I was choking."

"Yeah."

"You saved me."

"I always do."

"I appreciate your speed," he says. "You didn't let me choke for long. That was a fast response."

"I try."

"When I'm dead, I would like to be a crash test dummy."

I say, "Okay."

"Death," he says, "doesn't need to be dull."

We all watch as cop guy smirks and looks down my mom's shirt.

Dial M for Murder

Saturday finally comes and begins how it always begins: breakfast at Marty's and a ringing phone.

Marty turns away from the phone and begins to wash the dishes. I take my time finishing off a piece of bacon before I answer it. "Hello?"

"Eddy!"

She always sounds different, like she's trying out characters. There's the casual, "Hey, Eddy." There's the emotional, "Oh, it's so good to hear your voice." There's the please-don't-ask-me-anything-serious-because-I-can't-handle-it, "What's up, hot stuff!" I'm not sure what today is.

I take the phone and walk into the next room. I can only go so far, though, because this phone is ancient and has one of those long twisting cords. A built-in leash. "Hi, Mom."

"How are you?"

"Good."

"Not just good. I've been following the show, you know. You're doing great! I knew you could. I'm so proud of you!"

I twist the cord around my arm like I'm preparing mountain-climbing equipment. "We haven't won yet."

"Oh, now you sound like your father. Everything doom and gloom and doubt. Of course you'll win. Your show is the best."

"There are other good ones."

"Not as good as yours."

Because I want to believe her, I don't ask if she's watched the other shows. I walk over to the living room couch. Hanging over the couch are family photos, the biggest a picture of me, Mom, and Meat with all of us, even Meat, laughing. "How are things going with you?"

"Fine. I've been in some talks down here. Trying to get them to expand the part a bit. But I don't have any complaints. I'm meeting so many people, Eddy, you wouldn't believe. You have to get down here. I'll introduce you around. Never too young to network."

"That would be great."

"Though you probably won't need me, once you win that contest."

"I'll come down soon. Maybe at the end of the summer."

"We'd love to have you anytime," she says. *We*. I always try to forget there's a *we* and she always manages to slip it in the conversation.

"Any chance you'll be coming up this way?"

"I'm sure I will. There's talk of doing a dual episode with the *Crime Scene: New York* crew."

"I meant to visit us."

"Of course I'd visit you. How's your brother?"

"Fine."

"Just fine?"

"Well, he's the same."

"Is he taking his meds?"

I let the cord drop and walk farther away from the kitchen, out of earshot. "They don't think he needs them," I tell her. "They think he's funny."

"That's my point."

"Ha ha funny, not crazy funny," I say.

"He isn't crazy. He's troubled."

"They say he's unusual. They say there should be room in the world for unusual people. That's what makes the world interesting."

"Is Matthew still reading that book about dead bodies?"

"Yeah."

"Tell Marty to take him back to the doctor."

In his brief life, the Meatball has been diagnosed with ADD, OCD, depression, anxiety, hyperactivity, autism, and vitamin deficiencies. The last doctor, a young guy wearing a Hawaiian shirt under his white coat, said that Meat was a nerd, but so was Bill Gates and look at what he did with his life. That was good enough for Marty. And since Mom wasn't around to make a big deal about it . . .

"You should probably tell him yourself," I say.

"He doesn't listen to me," my mom says. "He thinks he knows everything. That was always our problem."

I don't want to hear about their problems. I don't want to hear about "we." I pluck at the cord. "So, about graduation."

"I thought you said that you didn't care about it," she says.

"I don't. Not the ceremony, anyway. But I thought maybe you could come up and make a big fuss over me." I'm trying to make it sound like a joke.

"You better believe I'll make a fuss over you. Speaking of fusses," she says. "Any new girlfriends I should know about?"

I peek into the kitchen. The Meatball has finished his breakfast—one egg, sunny-side up, two slices of bacon placed in an X over the top—and is waiting for the phone. "Meat wants to talk to you."

"I wish you would call him Matthew," she says.

"He'll always be Meatball to me," I say, and hand the Meatball the phone.

"Hello, Mother," says the Meatball. "I would like to ask you to come home now, please."

I don't wait to hear the answer.

At twelve thirty, I park in the lot of the school and grab my old tennis racket from the backseat. Lucinda's waiting at the tennis courts. No white dress today—black shorts, blue T-shirt with the sleeves rolled up—all business. She has two cans of tennis balls, two bottles of water, and her racket. In her hands, it looks like a weapon.

She looks like a weapon.

I'm hoping she can whack my mom right out of my head.

"Hi," she says, handing me one of the bottles of water. "I wasn't sure if you'd show."

"Why wouldn't I show?"

"'Cause I'm going to work you till you fall over." She pokes me in the gut with the racket. "You're soft, Rochester."

I'm tempted to take off my shirt to show her how not soft I am, but she'd see through that in a second. "Are we going to play or not?"

She doesn't answer. She tucks her racket under her arm, reaches into her pocket, and pulls out a coin. "Heads or tails?"

Because of where my own head is, this sounds like a proposition. I say, "Heads."

She flips the coin and slaps it down on the back of her wrist. "Tails. I serve first." She pockets the coin and two balls and strides away from me, her pale legs gleaming in the sun. She waits until I'm in position on my side of the court. Bounces the ball a few times. Tosses it—not too high, not too low—coils her body, snaps her arm down. The ball hits the corner of the service box and slams into the chain-link fence before I have a chance to react. I've seen this before. Topspin slice. Lucinda and I spent two months at the same summer camp when we were twelve. She didn't learn the serve there, but she used it on me over and over again.

Needless to say, it's a lot faster now.

I stare at her across the net.

She waves back.

She's enjoying this already.

I crouch and flip my racket from hand to hand. Time to take this a little more seriously. What Lucinda doesn't know: my mom used to use me as a tennis partner when she had no one else to play with. And my mom's pretty damned good. Or at least she was, before she turned into a wisecracking pathologist who makes bad hat jokes.

I watch as Lucinda tosses, coils, and springs, whacking another to the corner. I catch a bit of fuzz on this one but hit the ball out. Her third serve is a smash straight up the middle. Another miss. 40–love. I wish I could film her serving in slow motion so I could watch it at home. I bend and wait for the next serve, one that bounces high up around my shoulder. This one I hit solidly. Lucinda's so surprised that she gets it late, hits a short, soft ball. I run up to the net and put it away.

My turn to wave.

She grins. And proceeds to take me apart.

This is not the first time. The first time I was dismantled by Lucinda Dulko was on the courts of Camp Arrowhead when I was twelve years old. It was some stupid field day, where everyone had to play different sports in rotation and the counselors just signed you up for stuff even if you weren't good at it. I was okay at a lot of things—at least, I managed not to humiliate myself most of the time—so when they signed me up for tennis, I wasn't worried. I figured that whoever I played wouldn't be that great either, and I would manage not to humiliate myself again, and the next day we could all get back to regular camp stuff. That is, getting poison ivy, trying to drown each other in the pool, and watching Renee, the counselor with the most enormous boobs we'd ever seen, jump off the diving board.

When I saw Lucinda on the other side of the net, I demanded to know what was up. I didn't want to play old Lucinda Dulko from school. I didn't want to play *any* girl.

"Boys should play boys," I told the counselor running the tennis matches.

He didn't look up from his clipboard. "You'll play who you're scheduled to play, Rochester, so quit whining."

"I'm not whining."

"You're whining. Get out there."

Lucinda waited on the other side of the court, tapping the soles of her shoes with her racket impatiently. I could hear the other guys whispering, could see them bumping and nudging one another. I walked onto the court and sized Lucinda up. She'd grown early, so was taller than me, but not by much. And she was pale and skinny, like one of those bugs you find living under rocks (even if she was sprouting a pretty nice set of boobs herself). I figured I was stronger and faster. I mean, I was a *boy* and she was a *girl*. So it would be fine, I thought. I would win this. And I would try not to embarrass her too much. I'd let her get a few points here and there.

Yeah.

Right.

She flicked my serves away as if they were gnats and ran me all over the court. I was grunting and running and sweating and even swore once, so the referee docked me a point. I managed to humiliate myself soundly, or Lucinda did. When the match was over, after I was beaten, stomped, trounced, spit out like a cherry pit, we were supposed to shake hands over the net. With the jeers of my friends in my ears, I took her hand and squeezed it as hard as I could. She squeezed back just as hard.

Something in my gut thrummed like a guitar string.

Later that afternoon, I found her by the water fountain. I told her that I needed to talk in private. She nodded, followed me into a dense wall of trees next to the locker rooms. I hadn't planned what I was going to say or what I was going to do, but when I saw her leaning against an oak tree with green vines twining around the trunk, when I saw the sunbeams that shot through the leaves and spiked her like javelins, I put my hands on her shoulders and kissed her. I'd never kissed anyone before, but I'd been thinking about it, wondering what the big deal was, wondering if I'd like it, if I'd be any good at it. After a few seconds, she kissed back. The guitar string in my gut twitched like a hot wire.

Every afternoon for two weeks, we stole away from the art shack or the locker room or the bingo game in the main pavilion, hid in the trees, and kissed till our lips chapped. The weekends took forever—I stomped around, slammed doors, and screamed at my parents and poor baby Meatball, who didn't understand the meaning of "leave me alone." My mother told Marty one Sunday dinner that I was officially going through puberty and that the whole family should expect me to behave like a rabid grizzly on roller skates for at least five years.

One Tuesday afternoon I sneaked away from my group to meet Lucinda in the woods. She was leaning up against the oak tree, but her arms were crossed and she was eyeing me as if I'd stepped in dog crap and she could smell it.

"What?" I said.

"I was talking to a bunch of the girls at lunch. Want to know what we talked about?"

I didn't. "Okay."

"We were talking about first kisses."

I said, "Okay."

"Out of ten of us, five of us had kissed a guy for the first time this summer."

"Uh-huh."

"Four of us had kissed the *same* guy. Wanna guess who the guy was?"

Lucinda wouldn't let me kiss her anymore.

Now we're sitting on the bench right outside the court. I'm dripping sweat onto the pavement, so Lucinda hands me her towel.

"Thanks," I say, wiping my forehead. "I'll wash it and bring it back next time."

"Next time?"

"I want to play you again."

She's in the process of bringing a water bottle to her lips when I say this, and it makes her stop midway. "I totally creamed you today," she says.

"Yeah."

"So why would you want to play me again?"

I shrug. "I just do."

"But *why*, Ed?"

I look her in the eye and she looks right back, just as hard, just as directly. And for a second we're back on the tennis court at Camp Arrowhead, grinding each other's knuckles over the net. We're back at that fountain seconds before I lead her into the trees and watch the sunlight give her a crown. I don't know what it is. There have been plenty of girls around since her. But she was the very first. I can still remember how she tasted. And here she is again.

One side of my brain says exactly what she said: But *why*, Ed?

One side of my brain says the opposite: Why not?

And this is what I say. "Why not?"

She says, "You know this is just tennis, right?"

I don't know that. "Next Saturday?"

Lucinda holds up that bottle of water, looking at me through it as if it's a magnifying glass. Then she takes a long drink before she nods.

Yes.

The Matrix

"I *don't like to be handled,*" squawks Tippi Hedren.

"But you like to be fed," says Joe, holding out another sunflower seed from the bag I gave him. Joe scares a lot of people with his Bible and his brain, his big bug eyes and bony pumpkin head, but Tippi sees right through him. She's making kissy noises in his ear. If I wasn't so sure I was Tippi's main man, I'd be jealous.

"Okay," says Rory. "While we're waiting for Gina. Top-five chase scenes."

"We've done this one," says Joe.

Rory doesn't take no for an answer. "Five. *The Road Warrior*. Mel Gibson before he started screaming at cops and directing films in dead languages."

"Retro, yet decent," I say.

"Four. *The Blues Brothers*. Car chase through a shopping mall."

"That's a good one," says Joe.

"Three: *Gone in 60 Seconds*."

"Original or the remake?" Joe wants to know.

"The remake," says Rory.

"Figures," says Joe.

"One word," Rory says. "Angelina Jolie."

Joe holds up his index. "Angelina." Then he holds up his middle finger. "Jolie." He pretends to count.

"Tarantino's *Death Proof*," Rory says. He's on a roll and can't stop. "Zoe Bell hanging from the hood of Kurt Russell's car."

"Okay, I'll concede that one," I say.

"*Ronin*. De Niro at his finest."

"That wasn't De Niro's finest," I say.

"His finest car chase," Rory says.

"No *Bullitt*? No *The Fast and the Furious*? No *Bourne Identity*?"

"Cliché," says Rory.

"You're cliché. What about *Casino Royale*, the incredible chase that opens the movie? Bond going all out after that guy through the construction site, up on a crane, and into the embassy?"

"That's not a car chase."

"But you didn't specify a car chase," Joe says. "You just said chase."

"Exactly," I say. "And then there's *Crouching Tiger, Hidden Dragon*. Zhang Ziyi chasing Chang Chen on horseback."

"Crouching meerkat and hidden iguana," Rory says in disgust. "What the hell was that movie even about? If you want to do chopsocky, do chopsocky. Don't pretend it's some grand romantic crap."

"You're getting too complex for Rory, Ed," Joe says. Today he's thankfully Bible free, but he is holding up a small mirror and checking out his emaciated face. I think he's contemplating having his cheekbones surgically sharpened.

"Fine. Let's simplify. How about *Terminator II*?" I say. "Arnold Schwarzenegger on a motorcycle gets chased by a molten metal head in a big rig."

"And then," says Joe, "*Indiana Jones and the Temple of Doom*. Mine shaft chase in carts. Or *The Dead Pool*, where Dirty Harry is chased through the streets of San Francisco by a remote control car with a bomb."

"And what about *North by Northwest*, where Cary

Grant is chased by a crop duster?" I say.

"He's not actually chased as much as dive-bombed."

"He runs away and the plane follows. That's a chase."

"I forgot that one."

"And you claim to work in the world's most comprehensive video store."

"I never claimed anything," Rory says. "And I never liked you people."

I say, "Mutual."

"Okay," says Rory. "Let's do the top-five non-porn sex scenes."

"One word: Angelina Jolie," I say.

"I am just a wild animal!" says Tippi Hedren.

Joe gestures at me with his chin. "Speaking of porn, where are all your girlfriends?"

I'm focusing the camera on an empty chair, because Gina still isn't here. "What are you talking about?"

"The chicks," Rory yells. He's drinking from a brown bottle he found in my fridge that I hope is root beer and not regular beer, because I really don't want to be responsible for Rory becoming an even bigger tool than he already is.

"Bring on the hos!"

Too late.

Now Joe glances up. "Stop calling people hos."

"Sorry, Mr. Sensitive. I was just kidding."

"Stop kidding," says Joe. He mostly thinks Rory's an idiot, but Rory either doesn't know or doesn't care.

But Rory's right. It's the first time in a while that there are no groupies to watch us film. I hope that doesn't mean Gina's going to stay home. I don't like to admit it, but we don't have a show without her.

Joe plays us some music he wants to use for the new episode.

"Jesus, it sounds emo," says Rory.

"Just because you don't like it doesn't make it emo," Joe says.

"It's emo. And even if it's not emo, it sounds emo. I hate emo," Rory says. "Plus it doesn't work for the character. What about the Meteors or the Distillers or one of those screamy chick bands?"

Joe pets Tippi Hedren. "I was thinking that maybe it's time to soften Riot Grrl a little bit."

"Soften her?" Rory says. "Why would we do that?"

"Well, she just broke up with the boyfriend. She's sad."

"You do know Riot Grrl is a fictional character, right?" Rory says.

Joe sighs. "Somebody thinks this show is called *All About Rory and His Tiny Little*—"

"*In case you're interested, I was pushed into that fountain,*" says Tippi Hedren.

"What the hell is that crazy bird talking about now?"

Gina says, walking into the garage. She's wearing denim cutoffs and black boots that come up to her knees.

"Nice of you to show up," I say.

"Fight with the parents," she says.

Rory says, "Again?"

"They didn't like my boots."

"I thought they were all about understanding you."

"They were. They are. But I'm tired of being understood all the time. I'd like to be surprising once in a while. Maybe even annoying or thoroughly exasperating. So I'm wearing my boots."

Rory nods appreciatively. "I enjoy it when you wear those boots."

Gina sits on a tattered velvet couch we keep in the back of the garage. "They want me to go to the University of Michigan. That's where they met," says Gina. "One of the top schools in the nation. Blah blah blah."

"So," Joe says. "Are you going?"

"No."

"Why not?"

"Why should I go halfway across the country? At home I have everything."

This is true. Back in the late nineties, Gina's parents made a boatload of cash when they sold off their dot-com business right before everyone else went broke. Gina's house out-McMansions McMansions. She has a swimming pool shaped like an organ complete with individual cabanas. A game room. A private theater. There's even "guest quarters" over the garage, which, of course, they call a "carriage house" and not a garage. The whole place is solar powered. They're environmentalists now. If, by environmentalist, you mean a person who has a private theater, an organ-shaped pool, a cleaning woman from Nicaragua, and enough money to buy an island.

"They got me a new car," Gina says. "A hybrid."

"You already had a hybrid."

"This is a better hybrid. Or so they say. They're thinking about taking it back. They're mad because I don't want to go to their stupid school and because I'm wearing boots made in China."

"Where are your boots supposed to be made?" Joe wants to know.

"Ideally? I'd travel by horseback out to the Dakotas, shoot a buffalo with my trusty bow and arrow, skin the animal, and make the shoes myself using an awl I fashioned from a shinbone. Then I'd be sure to cure all the meat, turn it into pemmican, and eat it for the next year. Only take from the earth what you really need and what you use. That kind of thing."

Rory says, "I'd like to see you with a bow and arrow."

I say, "I don't think we should give her any weapons."

"You mean, you don't think we should give her any *other* weapons," says Joe.

Gina smiles and holds out a boot. "I think I'll wait till these wear out." She lights a cigarette and coughs into her hand. She never smoked before Riot Grrl. Now she can't stop. Joe would tell me that I'm responsible for her bad health as well as her bad attitude.

I say, "She's quoting *The Birds*."

"Huh? Who?"

"Tippi Hedren," I say. "She quotes lines from Hitchcock movies. *The Birds. Marnie*."

"Why does she do that?"

"Because they're the only two Hitchcocks my mom doesn't like."

"That makes perfect sense," says Joe.

"What do you want? It's a goddamn bird," says Rory.

"I think you're a louse," Tippi Hedren says.

"What do you want? She's just a goddamned bird," Joe says, eyes glinting in his skeletal face.

Gina rolls her eyes and tries to get comfortable on the tattered couch. We picked the garage as our backdrop instead of, say, a girl's bedroom, because we wanted the show to look stripped down. Dark. Gritty. Kind of like Gina herself. Or maybe the Gina she's become since we started the show. It's getting harder and harder to tell them apart.

The episode we're working on is one I officially call

Episode Nine and, unofficially, Makeup Sex. In it, Riot Grrl 16 talks about the fight she has with her boyfriend, Weasel, at a Dresden Dolls concert. He walks out on her and she has to find her own way home. She breaks up with him, but just a few days later she sees him at a friend's house and they end up having sex in a closet. It's her first time. She's not sure what to make of it later.

At least, that's what I wrote in the script. I pass out copies and everyone flips through them. I take out a pen and wait.

Joe says, "Wait, what is this?"

Rory says, "Cool!"

Gina blows smoke out of the corner of her mouth as she flips through the pages. "No," she says.

I say, "Listen, Gina, I thought—"

"They can make out in the closet maybe. I'll describe that. But Riot Grrl does not have sex in closets, okay? Especially not the first time. Riot Grrl is not some stupid slut. Riot Grrl has dignity."

Rory says, "She does? Since when?"

"I think I know what Riot Grrl 16 does and doesn't do," I say.

"Like hell," Gina says. She grabs my pen and starts marking up the script.

I'm starting to get mad. "Look, we might get more votes if—"

"If we cater to Cro-Magnons like Attila the Hun?" says Joe.

I want to say, well, now that you mention it, yes. And I'm about to, but I get interrupted again.

"Think for a second," says Gina. "It doesn't work. After all this time, why would she all of a sudden have sex in a closet?"

"This is a satire. It's supposed to be making fun of other vlogs. It's supposed to be making fun of the whole video culture. The more outrageous we make her, the better the show will be."

"But that's the thing. This isn't outrageous. It's just really, really sad," Gina says.

Once, Gina and I did some grappling in a closet. I had fun. I thought she did, too.

"Fine," I say.

"Don't you agree?" she says.

"I said, fine."

"Don't be such a baby."

"I'm not being a baby."

She smirks and I feel like getting that metaphorical bow and arrow and shooting her in the head with it. "Let's just get this done. I'll rewrite as we talk." I grab my laptop and open up the document. I stay pretty quiet while the rest of them decide that Riot Grrl isn't going to get with her ex-boyfriend at the party. Instead, the ex-boyfriend will show up in one of her dreams in an evil bunny suit.

"And Riot Grrl will say to Weasel, 'Why are you wearing that stupid bunny suit?'" says Rory. "And Weasel will say to Riot Grrl, 'Why are you wearing that stupid girl suit?'"

Joe says, "Will anyone get the *Donnie Darko* reference?"

I say, "Who cares? If they do, great. If they don't, evil bunnies are funny." I don't even glance at Gina. "And I think they qualify as outrageous, too."

She laughs and then collapses in a fit of coughing.

"Maybe we should have Riot Grrl go on the patch," says Joe. "Before you die of lung rot and kill us with secondhand smoke."

"Eventually," Gina says. "Right now, it's too amusing to irritate my parents by polluting the body that Mother Earth gave me."

"I thought your mother was your mother," Rory says.

I'm still thinking that sex would bring in better ratings than an evil bunny, but I decide to keep it to myself. I print out the revised script and give out the copies. We start blocking the scenes, trying to pick the best location for the dream sequence. We work for another hour, then decide to take a break.

Rory says, "Can I use the laptop?" He whips it off my lap before I can answer. "Let's take a look at the voting results. *Riot Grrl*, *Riot Grrl*, now coming in at number six. That's still pretty good. Lots of lovely comments from some clearly brilliant people." He frowns. "And some not so lovely comments. A lot of not so lovely ones. Rear*Window13. Isn't that you, Ed?"

"So?"

"Did you post something?"

"Only once, because some dumb ass annoyed me."

"Bad idea."

"What do you mean?" I pull my chair next to him so I can look at the screen. There's my post:

Satire: the use of irony, sarcasm, ridicule, or the like in exposing, denouncing, or deriding vice, folly, etc.

Duh.

And here's the response from the Tin Man:

Aristophanes wrote satires. Molière. Swift. If you want, throw Jon Stewart or Sacha Baron Cohen in there, I don't care. But Riot Grrl 16 *ain't* Gulliver's Travels. *It isn't even* Borat. *You're pathetic. Derivative. Dull.*

Duh.

After this post, there are about, oh, a hundred more. Some want to add their favorite satirists to the list. Some purposefully confuse satires with satyrs. Some just want to debate whether Jon Stewart is (a) hot or (b) too old to be hot. Some want to include links to their own videos. But a whole bunch agree with the Tin Man. *Riot Grrl* is stupid. Boring. Not worth the ten minutes it takes to watch the episode.

The Tin Man is gleeful:

LOL. I can just imagine Rochester reading all this stuff. He's probably crapping his pants right now. His red hair's probably green. Hey, Rochester, your mom's whoring herself on a suck-ass TV show for geriatrics. And you make *suck-ass TV shows for illiterate teenagers. Like mother, like son. She must be so proud.*

"He knows you," Rory says.

"He doesn't know me." I have a weird roiling feeling in the pit of my stomach, but if I pretend it isn't there, it will go away.

"He talked about your mom."

"Everyone knows about my mom."

"He talked about you having red hair."

"So, he's seen a picture."

"But we don't have any pictures of you," says Joe. "Not on MySpace. Not on the MTV site."

"We have the one group shot," I say.

"That's black and white," Joe says. His look is hard to read. His cheek muscles are twitching, like he's fighting the urge to smile.

"Maybe it isn't a guy at all," Gina says. "Maybe it's some chick you screwed over."

I don't look at Gina. "I didn't screw anyone over."

Tippi Hedren squawks, "*I don't give a damn what you believe!*"

"Whoever it is," Joe says, "don't engage them. Don't post anything again."

"But he's an asshole!"

"So?" says Rory. "What do you care? Half these lunatics are babbling about the last time they got drunk. All we need are votes. We don't need a flame war."

"We don't need you turning them against us," Joe says.

I stand up and make a show of gathering papers. "All I did was define satire."

"And made yourself sound like an idiot. Made *us* all sound like that, because they'll all think we agree with you."

"But—"

"Just don't post anything else," says Rory.

"He's talking about my mother."

Joe says, "Even if you say something reasonable and totally intelligent, people won't take it that way. If you make any kind of comment, you just give this guy ammunition to go after us again. He knows you're there. He knows you'll see it. And now he knows it bugs you."

"So I should just let some jerk say whatever the hell he wants whenever he wants?"

Rory doesn't say anything, just flips the computer around and points.

One star, one star, one star, one star, one star.

Best in Show

Joe and Rory and Gina tell me that I shouldn't look at the MTV site anymore, that it will just piss me off. And it does. But days later I'm still looking. I can't help it. And the more I read it, the madder I get. Who *is* this guy? Why has he gone off his lithium? And more than that, why do all the flying monkeys come flying out to listen to him?

What if it's not a *him* at all?

The phone rings. I snatch it up.

"Hello?"

"Hello. I'm looking for a Mr. Edward Rochester."

"That's me. What do you want?"

"Hi, Ed! This is Erin Loder, over at MTV."

Right. "Are you the bitch who's been posting all that stuff online?"

There's a pause. "I might be *a* bitch, but I don't think I'm *the* bitch. And I don't remember posting anything online recently." She sounds amused. I'm not amused by her amusement.

"Listen, whoever you are, I'm not in the mood."

Some low laughter. "This isn't a crank, Ed. My name really is Erin Loder, and I really do work at MTV. If you want, we can hang up and you can call the New York offices and ask for me."

My guts go cold, but I'm still suspicious. "I'm going to do that."

"Great! Talk to you in a minute." She hangs up.

I call information and get the number for the New York offices. I ask to be connected to Erin Loder. I am.

"Um, hello?" I say. "Sorry about that."

"No worries!" she says. "Listen, we've been keeping an eye on the entrants in the contest and we just love *Riot Grrl 16*. We really think you have something there."

"You do?"

"Yes, we do. We want you to come into the office and have a chat with us."

"You want us to come into the office."

"Yes."

"To chat with you."

"That's the idea."

"About what?"

"Well, Eddy. We think we might be able to work with you. We might be interested in producing your show. We'd like to discuss some possibilities." Pause. "Ed? Are you still there?"

"Yes," I say. It's all I'm capable of saying. I think I'm going to puke.

"Great! How does week after next look for you?"

Somehow I manage to make an appointment and hang up the phone without pulling an *Exorcist* all over the room. I sit down at the kitchen table. I can't believe it. We're on our way. We don't need the contest anymore; we don't need anything. We're on our way.

Screw you, Tin Man.

I know exactly who to call first. I get her voice mail. "Mom. The MTV people want to talk to us about *Riot Grrl*. They say they're interested in producing the show. Call me back when you get this."

I call Rory and Joe and Gina. The only one who's not totally over the moon is Joe, of course. "Sounds good," he says. "But let's wait to hear what they say."

"What could be bad about this, Joe?"

"I don't know. What if they want to change Riot Grrl into a badger or something?"

"So, then we turn her into a badger." I practically throw the phone back in the cradle.

"What was that about?"

This is my dad talking. It's midnight and he's just gotten home. He's putting a casserole Marty left for us in the oven.

"MTV wants to meet with us about *Riot Grrl 16*. We have an appointment the week after next." I wait for him to say something critical.

"Huh," he says. "Well, that's great, Ed. Congratulations. Do you want me to go with you?"

"No, I can handle it."

"Are you sure? Some of those TV people can be pretty slick."

"It's fine, Dad."

"If you're sure," he says. He pats me on the back. "Just remember that this is only a first step. There's never a guarantee in this business."

I roll my eyes so hard that I think they might get stuck somewhere behind my pituitary.

"Nice eye roll. I can tell you've learned from the best," he says. He sets the oven timer one minute at a time.

"Why can't you ever say, that's great, Ed, and leave

out all the other stuff?"

"I just want you to be realistic."

"You're going to feel pretty stupid if they hand me a check for a quarter of a million dollars," I say.

He laughs. "That kind of stupid I can live with."

I meet Lucinda at the courts. I want to tell her about the MTV people too, but maybe my dad has gotten to me some. I decide to wait until I've actually met the MTV people and have a firm offer (and that check for a quarter mil). Besides, she's playing like she's had fourteen cups of coffee, like she's under a spell, like she has a date with Orlando Bloom right after the match.

Between points I say, "Are you in a hurry?"

"We've got somewhere else to be at one thirty."

"We?"

She serves to the body and nails me hard in the chest. "We," she says.

She beats me 6–1, 6–3. I don't do much better than the last time we played, but I go down a lot faster.

"Come on," she says. "I'm driving." She starts walking to the *Titanic* on wheels.

"I can drive," I say. I'm walking behind her because I like the view.

She glances back over her shoulder. "You don't know where we're going."

There are little drumbeats in my temples. I'm having

visions of motel rooms, bedrooms, backseats, and bathrooms. "Right. I don't."

Her car's unlocked. She tells me she's always forgetting to lock it but that it doesn't matter anyway. She says, "Who would steal it?"

"You never know. I heard there's a run on ancient rusting behemoths."

"Don't talk about Snuffleupagus that way."

"Snuffleupagus? That's so . . . adorable."

"Don't make me smack you around with my racket."

"You already did that," I tell her. "Where are we going?"

"You'll see," she says. She's driving as fast as the car can go, which means we're traveling about 2.5 miles an hour. Wherever we're going, it will be a long ride. Which is okay with me. I like riding in the car with Lucinda. I like watching her foot move from the gas to the brake; I like watching her fumble for the volume controls on the radio that seems permanently stuck on some talk station.

"You can't change the station?" I say.

"No, but that's all right. It's NPR."

"Oh," I say. I get the feeling I'm supposed to know what that is, but I don't.

"National Public Radio," she says, looking at me. "They have some great shows on the station. You ever hear *This American Life*?"

"No," I tell her. I can't imagine what kind of shows she's talking about.

She says, "It's a radio magazine, where there are reports on weird subjects like what kind of superhero you always wanted to be or what it's like to be a Christmas elf at the mall during the holidays. There was one story about this guy who had his car stolen only to spot it in his rearview mirror as he's driving along in a rental car and he decides to chase it."

"So, these are made-up stories?"

"No, true ones. Just weird."

"Okay," I say.

"Really, it's good. I loved this story about an apology line. A man set up an answering machine where other people could leave apologies about anything they wanted. Thousands of people called and confessed."

"What did they confess to?"

"Stealing from stores. Having affairs. Embezzling. Beating people up. All kinds of stuff."

"If you called the apology line, what would you confess?"

"I'm sure you'd like to know."

"I *would* like to know. That's why I'm asking."

For a minute I think she's going to say something really interesting. But then she says: "When I was six, I took all my mom's jewelry and buried it in the backyard. She never knew what happened to it and I never told."

"She never suspected?"

"Truth is, by the time she figured out the stuff was missing, I'd forgotten where I buried it. She blamed my brothers. They knew I did it but couldn't prove it."

"Why did you do it?"

"I was playing pirate treasure. And I think I was mad at her."

"For what?"

"The usual stuff, I guess. She kept telling me what to do. She still does. Your turn. Confess."

"What do you want to know?"

She glances at me out of the corner of her eye. "How many girls have you been with?"

I force myself not to smile. "I'm a virgin."

"Come on, you can tell me." She pokes me in the leg. "Hello?"

"I'm counting."

"You can give me a general estimate."

"It's higher than zero and less than one hundred."

"And speaking of dogs . . ." She turns into a big parking lot. A sign says, BILLETS ANIMAL SHELTER. "We're here."

"Are you getting a puppy?" I say.

"You could say that," she says. "Let's go."

We get out of her car and walk over to the building. Inside, it smells like disinfectant and wet dog and kitty litter and piss and a million other things you don't want to think about. I must have had a look on my face because she says, "This is a no-kill shelter. The only one for fifty miles. They operate on donations. I volunteer here about ten hours a month. It's not much, but it's all the time I have."

A middle-aged woman at the front desk smiles up at us with big horse teeth and peppers us with questions that she doesn't seem to need answers to: "Lucinda! Hi! Haven't seen you in a while! How's your mom? And your dad? And Puck? Does Mogget still have that funny patch of fur on his back? What about Mrs. Havisham? And who's your friend?"

This, Lucinda answers. "Bonnie, this is Eddy."

Bonnie says, "Hi, Eddy! Do you like animals? Dogs? Cats? Have you ever seen a sugar glider? We just got one in—with babies! Gonna need some names for those. You want to come up with names? It's fun! You pick your favorite book and pick some character names out of it and voilà! So will you be helping us out today?"

She pauses and we wait a few seconds to make sure she really wanted an answer to this. Lucinda says, "Yeah, he'll be helping me out today, Bonnie. Mind if we go back? We'll start with the dogs and work our way over to the cats."

"Sounds great!" Bonnie says. She turns to me, frizzy yellow curls bouncing. "I hope you're not allergic!"

I have a feeling that if I said I was, she or Lucinda

would hand me a box of tissues and tell me to suck it up.

Bonnie presses some sort of buzzer under the front desk. As we move around the desk, I look under it and see four or five dogs tucked away, sleeping. Lucinda tugs my sleeve and leads me down a hallway where the disinfectant stink is stronger.

"What are we doing here?"

"We're working," she said. "These animals need some attention and we're giving it to them. For some of these guys, it's the only real attention they'll get all day." At the end of the hallway is a large room with a row of cages. In each cage is a dog. Lucinda grabs a leash from a peg on the wall and walks to the row of cages.

Lucinda drops to her knees in front of the first cage. "Hello, you," she says. A muscular brown pug wheezes at her. She unlocks the cage and the pug waddles out. His black-marble eyes roll around in his head like they've been oiled. He barks at me.

"Shush, Oliver. This is Eddy. Eddy is a nice guy. Well, mostly." She attaches the leash to the dog's collar. "He's going to walk you today." She hands me the leash. The pug looks up at me as if he's not certain I'm up to the task.

"Well," says Lucinda. "Say hello to him."

"Bonjourno," I say.

The dog woofs and then sneezes. I'm not used to animals that don't talk back. And look like they've been chasing parked cars. And catching them.

"His name is Oliver Twist," Lucinda tells me.

"What else would it be?"

"Let's go for a walk," she says, more to the dog than to me. We pass all the other dogs in cages, who bark and whine and howl their displeasure. Behind the shelter, there's a fenced-in dog run where we can let Oliver Twist off his leash. Lucinda pulls a toy from somewhere, I don't know where. Some secret place where she stows all her dog magic. This one is a squeaky ball that Oliver Twist chases around the yard. I pick him up and he gyrates from both ends, his head twisting one way and his butt twisting the other. Lucinda laughs. I love the sound, even if it was the dog that did it.

So when we go back inside and get the second dog—a black poodle named Inigo Montoya—I don't protest. We slip the leash on his collar and take him outside for his five minutes of bliss. I play with him and Lucinda gathers him in her arms and kisses him and whispers in his ear. I can't hear what she says, but I want to know. When I ask her, she says, "None of your business."

We play with Inigo Montoya for a while. I keep saying, "Hello. My name is Inigo Montoya. Prepare to die."

"You read *The Princess Bride*," she says. I don't tell her that I didn't even know it was a book, only a movie.

We work our way through the cages: Lily Bart, Queequeg, Elizabeth Bennet, Boo Radley, Bartimaeus,

Huck Finn, Hermione Granger, Mary Poppins, Artemis Fowl, even Moby Dick (who is one of those wiener dogs; I tell Lucinda that someone at the shelter has a very literal sense of humor).

After we've walked the dogs, we go to the cat room. It's every cat for itself in here. They've draped themselves all over the place, on countertops and ratty furniture and those tall, carpeted cat motels. Cardboard boxes have been thrown into the corners and the cats pack them, stacked on top of the other. Lucinda gives them fresh water and pets all the ones that want petting and talks to all the ones who demand to be talked to. Her voice is low and soothing when she does this, like she's hypnotizing them. In response, they blink slowly back at her. I blink at her too, and she calls me an idiot.

I walk to the far side of the big room where there is a lone lump in a cage. "What's wrong with this one?"

"Oh," says Lucinda. "That's Frank. As in Stein."

Frank is crouched way in the back of his cage. He's missing one eye and his left ear has a notch taken—bitten?—out of it. He doesn't meow as much as moan as I approach.

"Hi," I say, bending and pushing a finger between the bars.

"I wouldn't do that," Lucinda says.

Frank hisses and spits, lashing out. He rips a few holes in my finger. I snatch my hand away and shake it.

"Ow," I say.

"I told you not to do that."

"I was trying to be brave."

"Nice try. I found him living under my porch. He was starving, so I fed him some table scraps. Scratched me up when I tried to catch him." She points to faint silvery scars on her forearm. "I had to use a trap."

"Do you do that a lot?"

"What?"

"Catch animals that don't want to be caught?"

"Enough," she says.

"Isn't it kind of dangerous?"

She eyes me as if we're talking about something other than what we're talking about. "Somebody has to do it."

Outside the cat room, Lucinda hands me one of those lint rollers so I can get the cat hair off my shorts and T-shirt. It doesn't work. We visit some of the odder denizens of the shelter—some floppy-eared rabbits, guinea pigs, one potbellied pig named Sherlock Holmes. There's a cockatiel named Charlotte, after the spider.

"Don't worry, she's pretty friendly," says Lucinda.

This I can handle. I feed Charlotte some seeds and she warms up to me. Delicately she dances up my arm and perches on my shoulder. Soon she's nibbling on my ear.

"I think she likes you," says Lucinda.

"Surprised?" I say.

I think she's going to say no, she's not surprised, she's

never surprised, but she says, "You know birds?"

"I have a bird," I say. "An African gray. Her name is Tippi Hedren. She was my mom's bird."

"Tippi Hedren. That sounds familiar."

I nod. "Mom loves movies, especially Hitchcock. But she never really got *The Birds*. Ever see *The Birds*?"

"No, not the whole thing. I know what it's about, though."

"Well, Mom never liked it. She thought it was anticlimactic. Hated *Marnie*, too. She thought it would be funny to name her bird after the actress who starred in both movies. And then she taught Tippi all these phrases from that movie and some others."

"How is your mom?"

"Fine. Happy down in Florida. She's on—"

"TV, I know."

"Yeah. Anyway, she lives down there with some freeze-dried creep. I guess she'll marry him. Or maybe she won't. Whatever."

"I'm sorry."

"Don't be," I say. "We're not."

Lucinda waits as if I'm going to say something more about this, which I absolutely won't. She takes Charlotte from my shoulder and puts her back in her cage. Then she leads me over to another cage that looks empty.

"Look," she says, pointing to an odd pouch dangling from the top of the cage. I peer into it. Two huge eyes peer out.

"What the hell is that?"

"The sugar gliders Bonnie was talking about up at the front desk. They're marsupials." She opens the cage and reaches into the pouch, pulling out this freaky chipmunk-mouse-monkey thing with a long tail and a stripe down its back. There's a smaller chipmunk-mouse-monkey thing clinging to the bigger one. Lucinda checks the swinging pouch. "One more baby in there." She puts the sugar glider on her shoulder and the chipmunk-mouse-monkey thing promptly pees on her.

"Nice," I say.

"I didn't like this shirt anyway," says Lucinda. She pets the animals. "Hello, there. Aren't you sweet?" She glances up at me with her frost-colored eyes. "So what do you want to call them? All you have to do is pick some character names from books. It should be a book that you love, though."

"I don't love any books," I tell her.

"Come on. Not one? Not even the one you were named after?"

"I was named after a book?"

"Edward Rochester? From *Jane Eyre*?"

"That's a movie. Mom made me watch it. The only reason the experience didn't kill me was because Orson Welles was in it."

"Who's that?"

"You're kidding, right?"

She's not listening. "You should read *Jane Eyre*

sometime. But there has to be a book you love. How about from when you were a little kid?"

"Well," I say, thinking, "there was one book. My mom read it to me when I was, like, eight or something. It was called *The Ear, the Eye, and the Arm.*"

"Don't know it."

"I liked it because it was set maybe two hundred years from now in Zimbabwe. It was about three kids, the kids of some very important general, who escape their dad's house only to fall into the hands of some crazy people. Detectives are hired to find them—the Eye, the Ear, and the Arm. All of them have special powers because they were exposed to radiation or nuclear waste or something. Anyway, the Eye has super-enhanced vision. The Ear has one ear as big as an elephant's and has supersensitive hearing. The Arm has long, spidery arms and legs and his special power is that he can feel all the emotions other people feel. He feels them so much it hurts him."

"Huh," says Lucinda. "Sounds interesting."

"It was good. The last book I remember really loving. Maybe because you can't love a story as much as you can when you're little. It's different when you get older."

Lucinda strokes the biggest sugar glider, whose nose twitches. "Maybe Mom is the Arm. Moms are always Arms."

I grunt. "Some, anyway."

* * *

We didn't do more than walk some dogs, pet some cats, and get scratched, hissed at, and peed on, but I'm exhausted, like the Arm when he felt too much. I can smell the sugar glider on Lucinda, this pungent musky scent that makes my nose sting. When we get back to Lucinda's car, she opens the trunk and pulls out a bag.

"I have another confession to make," she says as she rummages in the bag.

"What?"

"You remember when we were at Camp Arrowhead? Those two weeks we were meeting in the woods next to the locker room?"

"How could I forget?" I try to touch her arm and she swats at my hand.

"Remember that I got really mad at you for being such a slut?"

"I was not being a slut," I say.

"Sure you were. But my point is that I got mad at you for kissing other girls, but I was kissing another boy."

"What do you mean? What other boy?"

"His name was Pete somebody. I was meeting him behind the baseball field in the morning, you in the afternoon."

"I can't believe you!" I say. And I really can't.

She laughs. "Surprise."

"You said I was a dog!"

Her eyes flick to my face. "Are you saying you're not?"

I open my mouth to argue but can't quite bring myself to do it. Lucinda was kissing someone else that whole time? How did I not know? And why wouldn't she have told me that last day in the trees, if only to make me feel worse? That's what most girls would have done.

Like a guy, Lucinda reaches behind her neck with both hands and tugs the stained shirt over her head. For a few seconds, I see the thrust of her ribs against her milky skin and that huge, ugly contraption of a sports bra before she pulls a fresh shirt down over her body.

I nearly cry.

"Lucinda?"

She's putting the bag back in the trunk. "What?"

"Can you do that again?"

"Oh, shut up."

I take a step closer. "Make me."

She turns and puts a hand on my chest, right where she hit me with the tennis ball. Then her other hand is curling in my hair and she is kissing me and killing me with her warm pear tongue and I am definitely shutting up.

Some Like It Hot

After I leave Lucinda, I'm too wired to go home. It's like the sheer voltage of her has short-circuited my brain and I've been left drooling and useless.

So, I roll down the windows and drive. The sun is warm, but the wind still has a little kick. I don't have any particular destination in mind. I loop through the developments, wind around blocks, rev impatiently at stoplights. I'm heading down Alps Road when, in the distance, I see the top of a Ferris wheel. One of the elementary schools must be having an end-of-year fund-raiser and has brought in a carnival. Though it's only five in the afternoon and the sun will hang around for another four hours, the rides sparkle and beckon. I pull into the parking lot.

I grab my video camera and get out of the car. The air is thick with the smell of hot dogs and cotton candy cut with beer. I push my way through packs of kids. I stop at the ticket booth.

"How much for the Ferris wheel?" I ask the pimply kid manning the booth.

"Seven tickets for the wheel."

"Okay, I'll take seven tickets."

He stares at me blankly. "You can only buy packs of ten," he says, as if this is obvious. I aim the camera at him and turn it on.

"What?" I say.

He blinks at the camera, nervously picking at a pimple on his forehead. "You can only buy packs of ten," he says again. I like this guy. I will have Rory put one of those black lines over his eyes when we edit so we don't need permission.

"Ten, huh?" I say.

"What's the camera for?"

"Movies." I pay for the tickets and head for the wheel. There's no line. Everyone's waiting to ride the teacups or the ship or the rotor—the vomit machines. The attendant, a tattooed and leather-vested reject from a biker gang, locks me into my own metal car. It swings gently as the wheel begins to turn, just enough to make the ride feel a little dangerous, like I could be an article in the next day's newspaper if I don't stay centered in my seat.

I focus the camera on my own feet, then on the people below, all of them screened behind the blue, rusty grid. Packs of kids pinball from one ride to another. Groups of older kids mill, checking out the clusters of girls dotting the landscape. You can't blame them. The girls are so beautiful in their tank tops and shorts and artfully messy hair. They're fourteen and fifteen and whateverteen. They sense the summer is coming. Life is coming. Anything can happen. I feel like that, too. I zoom in on the clusters of girls, mouthing the name Lucinda.

I ride the Ferris wheel for a half hour, watching the moms herd their young, watching the boys and girls watch each other, till the attendant finally makes me get off. He eyes my camera suspiciously. "You weren't taking any weird videos, were you?"

"Depends on what you mean by weird," I say. I hold up the camera and tell him to smile. He does, showing me his gold tooth.

Weird.

Someone's selling ears of hot buttered corn at the carnival. I buy two, have them wrapped in waxed paper and foil, and take them home. I find Tippi Hedren hanging upside down in her cage singing "Some Like It Hot." She nearly loses all her feathers when she sees the corn I've brought her.

"Long yellow! Long yellow!" she shrieks. I suspend one of the ears of corn from the bars of her cage by the husk, tying it in a knot. She alights on the cob, cooing as she nibbles.

I unwrap my corn and sit at my computer. It chirps like it recognizes me. Automatically I flip to the MTV site and scroll. The Tin Man is still at it, but I'm on a Ferris wheel high above it all. I don't care what he says, I don't care who he is, I don't care if he's a he. I'm hanging from a cloud, so high that the flying monkeys can't ever find me.

A new instant message pops up on my screen.

$ugar<loves>Honey: hey, you there?

Sugar loves honey, sugar loves honey. I rack my brains. Nothing.

Lucinda?

Rear*Window13: Hey.

$ugar<loves>Honey: know who this is?

Rear*Window13: Cameron Diaz?

Sugar sends a MySpace link. I click on it. It's the

groupie, the one who pissed Gina off. Her name, it turns out, is Sonya. In her picture she's biting her lip. Next to the picture it says, *Hotter than you.* And she is.

I type:

Rear*Window13: Much better than Cameron. What's up?

$ugar<loves>Honey: nothing. wish i was there with you.

Rear*Window13: Surprised. I don't think I was very friendly at the end of the shoot.

$ugar<loves>Honey: yeah well you were working i understand.

Rear*Window13: Good. I don't like pissing off the ladies.

$ugar<loves>Honey: i hear that you're pretty good with the ladies.

Rear*Window13: Where'd you hear that?

$ugar<loves>Honey: i have my sources. so, you want company?

Rear*Window13: Now?

$ugar<loves>Honey: no time like the present.

I hesitate, my fingers hovering over the keys. I must have taken too long because she types:

$ugar<loves>Honey: if you need some inspiration, check out my pics.

I shouldn't.

I flip to her page and click on Pics.

I stare. And stare some more. I can't believe she put these up. And I'm thinking that HELL YES she's coming over RIGHT NOW when I see her face.

Great face.

Wrong face.

Rear*Window13: Love the pics, but it's not a great time. Parents.

$ugar<loves>Honey: : (

Rear*Window13: Sorry, Sugar.

$ugar<loves>Honey: another night. i'll be thinking about you.

Rear*Window13: Talk to you later.

$ugar<loves>Honey: hope so.

Now I feel like I'm sitting on an anthill. I search MySpace and Facebook and the whole web to see if I can find a site for Lucinda. No luck. I think about her taking off her shirt, about her kissing me, about her doing all sorts of things that I can't imagine anyone in their right mind agreeing to and the ants do a hard march through my blood vessels. I lunge for my bed and chomp into my pillow, my own heartbeat taking me down.

Later I let Tippi Hedren demolish most of her corn before I pull her from the cage to wander around the house. I feel old, but not in the bad way, in the adult way.

In the I-can-go-to-the-beach-anytime-I-damn-well-please way. Like every other red-blooded American old person, I grab a beer and crash out in front of the TV. *Raising Arizona*, an old Coen Brothers movie, is playing on a cable station and I say the dialogue along with the characters: "You take that diaper off your head and put it back on your sister!" and, "Gimme that baby, you warthog from hell!" After *Raising Arizona*, I find a station playing Hitchcock's *Vertigo*, Jimmy Stewart as a cop with a fear of heights who's in love with a woman pretending to be someone else. Kim Novak plays the woman. Hitchcock really loved his blondes. Can't blame him.

I must have fallen asleep because the next thing I know, Tippi's squawking something about San Francisco and my dad's looming over me.

"Hi," I say.

"What's with the beer?" he says.

"I fell asleep before I drank any."

"You know I don't like you drinking."

"I know," I say.

"So why did you?"

You gotta love parents. They always ask questions that they (a) know the answers to or (b) have no reasonable answers.

"I took the beer because the little voices in my head said so," I say.

"You're not funny."

"Oh, but I am."

Dad sits next to me, and Tippi climbs up his arm to his shoulder. He pets her gently and she nudges his fingers with her beak. "Your mom loved this bird."

I suddenly realize that Mom hasn't called me back yet about MTV. "Yeah, she loved it so much she left it here."

"I remember when we got it. We were in a pet store. Terrible place. Sad, sickly puppies everywhere. Your mother asked to speak to the manager. She wanted to sue. She wanted to have it shut down."

I've heard this story a million times. "I know, Dad."

"But before the manager could come to the desk, a funny little bird started to talk to her. It said, 'Hello, lady!' I remember that clear as day. 'Hello, lady.' Your mother was so surprised."

"Surprised to be called a lady?"

"How much beer did you drink?"

"Five cases, give or take."

"So, the funny little bird says, 'Hello, lady!' and your mother tells me that it's a line from one of her favorite movies, *The Princess Bride*. Fezzik the giant says it to Princess Buttercup at the very end."

"I've seen the movie." I don't mention that it's also one of my favorites. But then I don't have to, because my father knows this already. It's one of his favorites, too. He always said that mom looked like Robin Wright

Penn, who starred as Buttercup in the movie. Nobody else saw the resemblance, but then I guess it doesn't matter much if they did or they didn't. Dad swore by it.

"Anyway, the bird was so cute that your mother forgot all about suing the place and bought the bird instead."

"I have to get to San Francisco!" Tippi chirps.

"Too bad Mom had to get to Miami."

Dad goes silent and for a second I feel bad for ruining his story. He loves to tell this story; he loves to talk about the early years with Mom. But I'm annoyed. She should have called me back. She should have been the first one to congratulate me.

All this talking about Mom is ruining my good Lucinda buzz. I change the subject. "How was work?"

"Super," he says in that dry way he has so that people don't know if he's serious or if he's kidding. "Went out to Staten Island. Another tiny house. Not sure why all those people with those tiny houses end up collecting so much stuff."

"So what did you find?"

"Giant balls of tinfoil. They were everywhere."

"What were they doing with them?"

"Saving them in case of excessive leftovers? I don't know. Thing was, they had no problem getting rid of any of the usual stuff—extra furniture, weird lamps shaped like mermaids, four pairs of bronzed baby shoes, old records, whatever—but they refused to get rid of the giant balls of tinfoil."

"Why?"

"Sentimental value? General mental illness? Wally talked to them, the designer talked to them, the producers talked to them, but no matter what we said, they wouldn't get rid of them. The designers ended up having to design them into the décor. Hung them from the ceilings like disco balls."

"Some people are too stubborn for their own good."

"Yeah," he says. "Speaking of stubborn, have you thought any more about college?"

"Good night, Dad."

The Lucinda buzz lasts until the next rehearsal. We're all hanging in my garage listening as Gina goes over her lines. "*My mom and dad told me I couldn't go to the party, but what do I care what they think? After they went to bed, I climbed out the window. Josh had heard me and Weasel had broken up and he thought he'd move in, the little creep. I told him to bite me. He said, Anytime, sugar. Sugar? Who seriously calls a girl 'sugar' and expects to get any?*"

"Right here is where we'll cut to you pouring a bag of sugar all over the ground," Rory says.

"And we could play that old song, 'Sugar, Sugar,'" says Joe.

"What song?" says Rory.

"You know the one I'm talking about."

"No, I don't. I wouldn't ask if I did."

"It goes, *Sugar, ah, honey honey.*"

All this talking about Sugar reminds me of my personal triumph, that is, turning away a hot girl of my own volition. I must be some kind of superhero. I hope Lucinda appreciates the effort. I pet Tippi Hedren and she purrs.

"What's with you and the weird songs?" says Rory. "That one doesn't go with *Riot Grrl* at all."

"I don't know if we really need to go over this now anyway," I say. "We're meeting the MTV people in a few days. They'll probably give us some direction."

"You're talking like it's a done deal," Joe says.

"They said they want to produce the show," I say.

"I thought you said that they *might* be interested in producing the show. And besides, *we're* the producers."

"We're the producers of a video that is currently playing alongside clips of some double-jointed dude who can fold himself inside a suitcase," I say. "I'd rather be co-producers of a real show, wouldn't you?"

"How do you know that they'll even give us that much credit?" Joe says. "Maybe we'll get some lousy 'based on an idea by . . .' credit line and that's it."

"Can we go hear what the woman has to say before you go all apocalypto on us?" Rory asks. "I think you've been reading that thing way too much." He waves at the

Bible Joe is clutching. "You've got doom on the brain."

"I'm just trying to be realistic."

I snort. "You sound like my dad. This could only be what we've been talking about since we were fourteen years old. This could fund future JFM projects."

When I say that, Joe looks at the ground. "But maybe you're not planning to do any more JFM projects."

His head whips up. "I didn't say that."

"You're thinking it. Are you going to tell me that if we win this contest, you'll give up college?"

"I'll give up college," Rory says. "I'd give it up in a second."

"I'm telling you that I think the fact that we do everything ourselves will impress more people down the line," Joe says.

"Which people?" I say. "And when?"

"Why are you in such a hurry?" Joe says. "We haven't even graduated yet."

"That's just a technicality at this point."

"Darren Aronofsky didn't make *Pi* until he was in his mid-twenties."

Rory is getting annoyed. "So? Who the hell cares what Aronofsky did? And *Pi* was a mess. It's an insult to mathematicians."

"*Pi* was visionary," Joe says. "And you can't do math to save your life, so what's it to you?"

"Why can't we just go hear what they have to say? If

you don't like it, then we'll talk, okay?"

Gina narrows her eyes and peers at me through the slits. "What's going on with you?"

Tippi's purring is so loud she sounds like a tiger after eating an antelope. "Nothing."

"Yes, there is. You're way too mellow."

"I'm always mellow."

"You're too mellow."

"Yeah," says Rory. "Even Tippi is mellow. And she's never mellow."

"I'm fine, guys. Everything's cool."

"You've got a new chick, don't you?" Rory says.

"No," I say.

"Yes, you do. You have that new chick look."

"No chicks here," I say.

"I'm just a wild animal!" says Tippi Hedren.

"Sorry, Tippi. And, uh, Gina."

Gina stares at me. Her dark eyes make me feel creepy, like she can crawl around in my brain and see that there's someone else in there. I turn on the beat-up TV in the corner, the one that makes everyone look green. There's an Ultimate Fighting competition on. For a minute, I watch two guys try their best to kick the crap out of each other, their faces pink and pulpy.

"Whoa! Sam Stout can really take a punch!" says one of the announcers.

"You don't get to be a kickboxing champ by being

a wuss," says another.

Gina sneers. "When these guys have given birth, they can talk to me about wusses."

"You've never given birth either," says Rory.

"Fine. When these guys have had *a single menstrual cramp* and not cried like a baby, they can talk to me about wusses." She flicks her cigarette to the floor and grinds it under her boot. "I'm going to get a soda." She stomps out.

"Tactful as always, Ed," Joe says.

"What are you talking about? What did I do?"

He doesn't answer my question. It seems he won't be answering any questions. "Do you mind if I take a look at the camera till she comes back? I'm thinking of buying one."

"Really? What for?"

He shrugs. "For this thing I want to do. No big deal."

Rory, who had been sprawled across the ratty velvet couch, says, "Hey, if you've got any good ideas, man up and spill. We could always use some new ideas."

"It's nothing," Joe says. "It's not even a show or anything. Not for Jumping Frenchmen. I just want to talk about religion."

Rory frowns. "You want to what?"

"I've been reading the Bible a lot, right? There's all kinds of stuff in there. Lots of stuff that people don't talk about. I want to talk about it."

"You're going to give Bible lessons on camera?"

"No, I'm just going to talk about what I've read, that's all. What I think about it. Nothing intense."

"Right, Joe. Talking about the Bible is so not intense."

"It's not like that. Never mind. Like I said, it's nothing for Jumping Frenchmen."

For four years, we've worked together. Not once have any of us done an independent project. We didn't need to. We didn't want to. And now we're in this contest, we're going to meet with MTV about producing this show, and Joe refuses to answer my question about deferring college, yammering on about the Bible. What does that say about his commitment? What does that say about *him*? Makes me wonder. Maybe he doesn't want this to work out. Maybe he'd rather we go down in flames or just go down period and he can get on with his much more meaningful, artistic, and intellectual life.

"I don't want to talk about the Bible. I want to talk about Eddy's new chick," Rory says. "Who is it? Wait! I know! That groupie girl that Gina was so pissed about. She was hot."

I shake my head. "No, not her."

"Who, man?"

"Forget it," I say.

"You. Must. Spill," Rory says. He's bouncing up on the balls of his feet like the Meatball. There's nothing that Rory likes to talk about more than girls. His girls, your girls, that guy's girls, all the girls that walk the face of the earth.

"It's nobody you know," I say. "Or at least, nobody you'd expect."

"You're killing me," says Rory. Even Joe seems mildly interested.

A voice in the back of my head tells me there's just been the one kiss and I shouldn't say anything, shouldn't jinx it, at least not yet. And I know that Joe's crushing on her too, and do I really need the Carved Pumpkin Boy to be even pissier? But I *want* to talk about her, I *want* to say her name out loud. And who cares about Joe? He doesn't seem to be thinking much about us, either. Any of us.

I say: "Lucinda Dulko."

"Huh?" Rory says, screwing up his face. "Sports chick?"

"What?" says Joe.

Rory thinks about this for a minute. "I'd give that girl about a 7.69." Rory's always very precise about his ratings. "She gets credit for the onions but points off for covering them up. Nice face, but sci-fi eyes. Plus she's got big calves."

"She doesn't have big calves."

"Yeah, she does. Bigger than yours."

"You're an idiot," I say.

Joe says, “No way.”

“No way what?” I say. “The calves?”

“No way Dulko would go out with you, Ed.” His voice is low and quiet, but he’s smiling ominously, like he’s channeling Jack Nicholson.

“We just went out on Saturday. We’re going out again this weekend.”

“She’s not your type,” Joe says. “Give it up.”

“What’s my type, Joe?”

He says, “Why don’t you leave her alone?”

“Why?” I say. “You got a thing for her?”

“I don’t have to have a thing for her to know that all you’re going to do is . . .” He trails off.

“All I’m going to do is what? What do you know about what I want to do?”

At this, he shakes his head. “Are you sure Dulko knows about this? Are you sure this isn’t some fantasy of yours?”

“Screw you.”

“Why? You run out of girls or something?” He grabs his Bible and walks out the door.

West Side Story

I don't have classes with Lucinda, I don't have lunch with Lucinda, my locker's on the other side of the world, and though I would never tell anyone this, I don't have her number and the Dulkos are unlisted. I wait all week to play tennis. It's a long week. Joe is barely speaking to me, Rory won't shut up. Thankfully, nobody says anything in front of Gina, so I don't get any more bottles launched at my head.

Today Lucinda's wearing a white tank top and shorts. She has her racket and her water bottles. There's no lipstick or fishnets or tattoos or cleavage. No hair spray or eyeliner. No twirling of the hair or glancing out of the corner of her eyes or any of what girls usually do.

"Hi," I say.

"Hey," she says. She smiles. I want to kiss her hello, but I can't be sure she wants me to. I punch her on the shoulder, a little punch. She laughs and whacks me in the butt with the racket. Then before I can think to do anything more friendly, she jogs to the other side of the court.

She beats me again, but this time it's 6–1, 6–4.

"You're getting better at this," she tells me when we're done. We sit on the bleachers by the side of the court, drinking from the water bottles she's brought. She smells like baby powder and sweat.

"I let you win that time," I say. "Next time I won't be so nice."

"Who says there'll be a next time?"

"What do you mean?" I say it too hard and too fast and now she knows.

She *knows*.

I want to pour the water over my head.

But she says, "What are you doing for dinner?"

"No plans."

"Want to come to my house?"

"Are you cooking?"

"Ha! That's funny. No. Not unless you want a peanut butter and jelly sandwich. My brother's cooking. He's a chef. Well, he's studying to be a chef. But he's a great cook. And he loves it when I bring new people over to eat his food. There's always a ton of it."

I have no idea if she wants me to meet her family or if this is some kind of date or just an excuse to get rid of extra food, but I'll take it.

"Sure. I'm in."

"How's six?"

"That'll work."

She scoops up her racket and stands in front of me. I'm facing the sun and have to squint up to see her. She's still slightly sweaty from the game and her white skin gleams, searing my retinas.

She's there long after she's gone.

When I get home, the Meatball is sprawled in my bed with a pillow over his face. I'm not sure if he's asleep or dead. Dead, I figure.

I throw the pillow to the floor. "Meatball! Are you okay?" I put my ear to his chest and check for a heartbeat. Thump, thump, thump. I check for a pulse next, pressing my fingers on the side of his neck. And then I start CPR, knotting my hands together and pressing them into his breastbone, one, two, three, four times.

"You'll have me up on my poor paralyzed legs in the very next scene," says Tippi Hedren from her cage.

Meatball speaks without opening his eyes. "You're supposed to give me four short breaths too."

"Yeah, I know," I say.

Now he opens his eyes. "Don't you love me?"

"Forever and ever. But not in a kissing sort of way."

He sits up. "You're a funny guy, Eddy."

"That's what they tell me."

"You didn't talk to Mom this morning."

"I was busy this morning. Things to do."

"She was worried about you. You don't skip her phone calls."

"Like I said, Meat, I had some things I had to do. For work, you know. She should understand that."

"Maybe you could tell her about it next time," Meat says.

"Maybe."

"What are you doing?"

"I'm getting some stuff ready. I need to take a shower and get changed." I flip through my closet for a shirt. I pull out an orange one with stripes.

"Blue shirt," says Tippi.

"I don't want to wear blue, Tippi."

"Who cares what kind of shirt you wear?" the Meatball says.

"I care," I tell him.

"Tippi's the one who cares," Meat says. "*You* don't care."

"Today I care."

"Why?"

"'Cause I'm going out later," I tell him.

"Where are you going?"

"To a friend's house."

"Whose house? Rory's house?"

"No, not Rory's."

"Joe's house?"

"No," I say.

"So then whose house?" He goes quiet, folding his hands on his lap. "Are you going to a girl's house?"

"Maybe."

"Girls smell."

"Yeah," I say, ruffling his hair. "They smell good."

"I don't think so."

"Talk to me in about five or six years. You might change your mind."

He sighs. "I'm doomed."

"What do you think of this one?" I'm wearing a brown shirt that my mom sent me for Christmas.

The Meatball peers up at me. "I think it's a shirt."

"Does it look good?"

"No, it looks like a turd."

"Thanks, Meat."

He picks the pillow off the floor and puts it back on my bed. "I don't want you to go."

"Sure you do. That way you get Marty and Dad all to yourself." If Meatball was here, Marty was around somewhere.

"You haven't played Dance Dance Revolution with me yet. You said you would. I'm getting very good at it. Dad and Other Dad said so."

"Tomorrow."

"You have to promise."

"I promise," I say. "I will play video games with you tomorrow."

"Everything's always tomorrow."

"Until it's today."

"I don't know what that means."

"Never mind. I have to go now, Meat."

"To see the smelly girl?"

"Yes, to see the smelly girl."

He sits up and stares at me. "You're going to kiss her, aren't you?"

"I hope so."

"I'm just a wild animal," Tippi Hedren says.

"Well, it's nice to see you choosing some nice clothes. What's the occasion?" Marty stands in the doorway. He has a key to our house so he can show up with the Meatball whenever he wants.

"Eddy's going to see a girl," the Meatball says.

"You'll be back for dinner, right?" Marty says. "Your dad will finally be home for once; remember I told you I was coming over? I thought we'd all eat together. I'm making pasta. Four cheese."

I don't remember him telling me anything. I hold the shirt up and check the mirror to make sure my shirt's more chocolate than turd. "I'm sorry, Marty, but I already told my friend that I'd go over to her house."

He crosses his arms and leans against the doorjamb. "I'm sure I mentioned it. Just the other day."

"I don't think so. And anyway, I really want to go to my friend's house."

"Who's the friend?"

"Nobody you know. Someone from school."

"Oh," he says. I can see that he's all disappointed, but I don't know what else to say. There's no way I'm blowing off Lucinda so that I can hang out with Marty and my dad, who are so depressing that my brain cells threaten to fling themselves out of my ears.

"I can't convince you?" says Marty. "I'm baking a chocolate cake. You can bring your friend here. Your dad is a little sad. Today would have been his twentieth anniversary."

"You mean today would have been his anniversary if Mom hadn't divorced him to marry you and then left you to go to Miami."

"Well, when you put it like that," he says.

"There's another way to put it?" I say. I like Marty. I like my dad. But if you'd told me that they were going to become best buds after my mom dumped them both, I would have said you were out of your mind. It seems more like the kind of situation that lands you on daytime talk shows, swinging punches.

"We were also hoping that we could talk to you about your plans," he's saying. "Show business is so unstable. Why not at least go to school and study film? You could still make your own movies on the side."

"Et tu, Marty? I don't want to make movies on the side. I want to make movies, period. And I don't need to waste four years just to make everyone else feel better."

"Can't convince you of much these days, can I?"

"Marty . . ." I say.

"Never mind. Go. Enjoy yourself." He thinks for a second. "But not too much." He looks pointedly at the Meatball as if the kid is some kind of human cautionary tale.

"*I have to get to San Francisco,*" squawks Tippi Hedren.

Marty rolls his eyes. "And teach your bird some new lines."

The house is middle-sized and crowded all around with overgrown bushes and red and yellow flowers. I ring the doorbell. I'm nervous, the way I've never been around other girls, the way I always am around her. The door opens and a small woman with shiny hair like Lucinda's is smiling at me. "You must be Ed," she says.

It takes me a minute to say, "Mrs. Dulko?" 'cause this woman is too young and too amazing to be anyone's mom.

"Yes, yes, that's me. Come in."

I follow her into the house and down the hallway. "We're glad that you could make it," she says. "David has made so much food that there's no way we could eat it all ourselves." She pronounces the name David as Da-veed.

I don't know how she could say that there aren't enough people to eat the food, because when we walk into the family room, it looks like a party to me. There are at least a dozen people drinking wine and laughing or bobbing their heads to the salsa music that's coming from the stereo in the entertainment center along the wall. One wall opens into the kitchen, and I decide that Da-veed must be the guy stirring stuff on the stove and muttering to himself. The oldish guy in the easy chair has to be Lucinda's father. Couldn't say who the others were. There are two dogs using the people like obstacle courses and one white cat with a bald spot on its back sitting on top of the TV set. And where the hell is Lucinda?

"Everyone, this is Lucy's friend Eddy," says Mrs. Dulko. Before they can acknowledge me, there's a tap on my shoulder.

“Hey, Eddy.”

I turn around. Lucinda’s hair is tied back and she’s got a pink flower stuck behind one ear, which could have looked dumb but instead looks mad hot, like a pinup from the fifties. I think she’s wearing makeup, too, because her lips are glossy and her frosty eyes seem enormous. And then there’s the sleeveless black dress that dips in the front. My brain screams, *Tits!* but that’s too small and too ugly a word. These are firm and full, a nose-sized channel between.

No wonder she keeps them under wraps. It’s all I can do not to bury my face in them.

I must have been standing there speechless for a while, because someone says, “Cleans up nice, doesn’t she?”

“Yeah,” I say, and when I do, my voice cracks, which makes everyone laugh.

“You should wear a dress more often, little Lucy,” a woman with red, red lipstick says. “That one looks like he’s been hit with a baseball bat.”

“I’ll remember that, Aunt Carmen,” says Lucinda, two pink spots scorching her cheeks. She shakes it off and introduces me around. Her brothers—David, who waves from his spot in the kitchen, and Roberto, both older. Her dad, Andrew. Her uncles and aunts. A smattering of cousins. The dogs, Puck, some kind of terrier, and Mrs. Havisham, a Lab. The cat, Mogget, who winds himself around my legs but hisses when I try to pet him. I'm offered a drink and get raspberry iced tea with mint leaves crushed in the bottom of the glass. People squish on the couch to make room so that me and Lucinda can sit. Mogget perches on my lap, tense as a rabbit. I think maybe he's an attack bunny, so I don't make any sudden moves. I'm asked about my parents, about school, and about my hobbies and whether or not I'm a tennis player too.

"He's pretty good," Lucinda answers for me.

"Not as good as you, though, eh?" says Aunt Carmen.

"Nobody is," I say.

Aunt Carmen points at me. "Smart boy. Did you tell him what happened yesterday?"

"What happened yesterday?" I say.

"Oh, it's no big thing," says Lucinda.

"Is too," her mother says. "You beat that nasty girl with the horse face."

Lucinda laughs. "She doesn't have a horse face."

"She has a horse face," Mrs. Dulko insists.

"Who are we talking about here?" I say.

"Remember Penelope?" Lucinda says. "The girl who thinks she's all that? The one who kept psyching me out?"

I'm smiling already. "Let me guess. You poured your milk on her head like I told you to."

"Nope. She came into the locker room and gave me coupons to some tanning salon so that I, quote, didn't look like a sunspot on the court, unquote. I thanked her and told her that the extra weight looked really good on her."

"Brutal," I say.

"Serves her right," Mrs. Dulko says.

"What was the score?" I say.

"7–6, 7–6. Two tiebreaks," says a random uncle. "Amazing."

"Not so amazing," Lucinda says. "It was only a practice meet."

"Yeah, but now she knows and you know that you can beat her," I say.

"Exactly!" says Mrs. Dulko. "That's what I keep telling her. Listen to your friend, Lucy."

"*Cute* friend," says Aunt Carmen of the red, red lips, and I can feel my face get hot. "Oh, look at him blush, Lucy. He's modest. Él es tímido."

"Oh, yeah," Lucinda says. "Real modest."

"Él es mucho más lindo que el último," Aunt Carmen adds, still looking at me. I took three years of Spanish, but she says it too fast. Takes me about two days to figure out that she said, "He's much cuter than the last one."

The last one. Who the hell was the last one?

"Sí," Lucinda murmurs, agreeing with Aunt Carmen.

She takes my hand and she squeezes it.

I want to know if she speaks any more Spanish.

And I want to lean over and lick her shoulder.

Da-veed comes out of the kitchen with a tray of food, little fried, chopped meat pockets—empanadas, he says—but who cares? They're incredible. Even though I'm going with the polite guest thing, I eat about fourteen of them and drink three more glasses of the minty tea. That only gets me more compliments from Aunt Carmen and the random uncles, who apparently approve of serious chowing down. I'm starting to worry about Lucinda's father, who has his eyes closed and is bobbing his head to the music but hasn't said anything to me yet. I'm wondering if he's one of those crazy, overprotective, Don Corleone, Tony Soprano types who won't allow his daughter to see any guy alone, which is why we have to have the whole family chaperone. I'm wondering if he'll put a hit out on me. The next time David brings in another round of empanadas, I offer Lucinda's dad the plate, hoping to start up a conversation so he'll know I'm a friendly guy who isn't going to molest his baby girl.

Even if that's the long-term plan.

"These are great, sir," I say. I figure the "sir" shows I'm making an effort.

Lucinda's dad takes the plate and says, "Thank you," and stares at the stereo as if the salsa band is going to pop out of it. Then he closes his eyes again.

Okay.

So maybe the dad's not a big deal in this family. Maybe it's the women, who follow Lucinda with their eyes, who glance back and forth between the two of us, whispering. Are they marrying us off already? Or are they conspiring to have me run out of town?

I feel that heaviness, that weight you do when someone's really staring, and I look up. Roberto, Lucinda's oldest brother, is smiling at me. Maybe he's the scary one. Maybe he's the guy who's supposed to beat up all his sister's prospective boyfriends. He looks like he could do it. He's tall and torqued, with big, showy biceps. I'm six-one and weigh one-seventy, but this guy could probably bench-press me. He gestures me over. I have to slowly extricate myself from Mogget the balding bunny attack cat, who glares at me to let me know how seriously I've damaged our tenuous relationship.

"Don't worry about my father," Roberto says when I'm standing next to him. "He's kind of in his own world."

"I thought it was me."

"Nah," Roberto says. "When music's on, he likes to focus. Same thing at movies or when the TV's on. He'll talk at dinner. If he feels like it."

"Good to know."

"And you don't have to worry about David or me, either."

"What do you mean?" I say.

"We're not going to threaten to kill you if you hurt my sister or anything. David's more interested in making the perfect sauce. And I don't need to threaten people."

"Also good to know."

"Because my sister could kill you herself. She doesn't need my help."

I say, "Okay."

"If you're scared of anyone," he says, "it should be Lucinda. She's like my dad. Quiet but fierce. She's not easy to please."

"I'll remember that."

"No," he says, laughing. "You won't."

Dinner is some sort of amazing pork loin with fried plantains, beans, and rice I eat in massive and embarrassing quantities. All around me, the Spanish is flying and it's too hard to keep up. But I'm smart enough to compliment the chef, who claps me on the back so hard I nearly go flying face-first into my plate.

"¡Gracias, hombre!" he says, which I get.

And Lucinda's dad does talk, in English, asking me more about what I'd like to do.

"Make movies."

"Movies?" the random uncles say together. They laugh.

Lucinda's thigh presses hard against mine. "Eddy

already makes movies. Short films. They're on the internet."

I had no idea she'd even seen *Riot Grrl 16*. "I have a production company. We do one show a week." I see the blank faces all around the table and make a mental note to do an episode about Riot Grrl meeting her boyfriend's crazy family.

"I hear there's money in commercials. Maybe you should direct commercials," says one uncle.

"That's a possibility," I say.

Lucinda's dad says, "We rented a good movie the other day. Called *Pan's Labyrinth*. Complex interweaving of two separate tales, one historical, one fantastical. It was directed by a man named Guillermo . . . Guillermo something."

"Del Toro," I say. "That film got a lot of attention."

"Yes, right," Lucinda's dad says. "You know it?"

"Yeah. I thought it was really good. I saw in an interview that he took both storylines equally seriously so that you never felt that the fantasy was a fairy tale."

"Huh," says Lucinda's father. "Has he made any other movies?"

We keep talking. I relax for the first time that night. Lucinda seems to relax too. I feel her thigh pressing against mine under the table. I press back. She presses harder, and we have a leg war while trying to remain perfectly stationary above the waist. I like it that she's so strong. Fierce, her brother said. How could that be a problem?

After dinner there's more iced tea and coffee and brandy and an obscene amount of custard called flan. I don't think I'll ever be able to move again when Mrs. Dulko claps and says, "Let's dance."

Before I know what's happening, someone has turned up the music. Mr. and Mrs. Dulko get up from the table and twirl their way back into the family room. The rest of us follow to watch. Mrs. Dulko is tiny and light on her feet. Mr. Dulko is a lot taller and doughier, but he moves nearly as fast, spinning his wife till you'd think she would puke (but she doesn't). The dogs cavort around them, barking.

Lucinda whispers in my ear, "That's where they met. My mom's a Latin dance instructor. My dad was her student, if you can believe that. He's pretty good for a chemist, don't you think?"

"Yeah."

Aunt Carmen grips my arm. "Come on, cute boy," she says. "Danza conmigo."

I must have looked terrified at the prospect of danza-ing with Aunt Carmen because Lucinda says, "I don't think he can handle you, Aunt Carmen. I'm more his speed." She looks at me. "Don't worry. I'll be gentle."

Aunt Carmen laughs. "Don't be too gentle. Él está muy bueno."

I wonder what kind of hormones Aunt Carmen's on.

Lucinda drags me to the center of the room as everyone else pushes the furniture against the walls and starts to dance. Lucinda holds out her hands. I worry about my breath and then figure Lucinda's will be just as bad. I pull her close, but she pushes me away.

"I need more room to move," she says. She puts her arms over her head, backs up a step, shoots one leg between mine, and then drags it back. She does it again with the other leg. She takes my hands and puts them on her hips, closes her eyes. I watch her dance, hips swaying, lashes brushing her cheeks, lips parted, white teeth peeking through them. My head feels like a giant empanada. I don't understand how someone who can leap up and smack an overhead like it's a bomb can roll her hips like some kind of stripper. Especially with her family doing the same thing all around us.

God, this is weird.

I wish I had a camera.

I wonder if someone's filming us.

I wonder if I'm in a reality show right now.

Despite what Roberto said, my eyes dart around as I wonder if her father or one of her other relatives will try to cream me for touching Lucinda, for holding Lucinda when she's moving the way she's moving. It seems like something you should do in private.

Her eyes fly open, freeze me. "Carmen's right. Usted es tímido," she whispers.

"What was that, Lucy?" Aunt Carmen says.

"Nothing," says Lucinda.

Carmen watches us, smirking. "No funny stuff. Your family's all around you."

"How could I forget?" Lucinda says.

"What?"

"Nothing." She yanks me past her mother and father. Her mother stops dancing. "Where are you going?"

"We're going for a drive."

"But we only just started!"

"I'm tired of dancing. I want some air."

"Air," says Carmen. "Sure that's what she wants."

Her mom laughs, spinning away. "Okay. Don't be too late."

"Fine."

"Eleven."

"I know, Mom."

"Well, you've been forgetting lately."

"I won't forget."

We walk through the screened-in porch, where Lucinda stops to grab her bag, and out the door to the backyard. She keeps walking and I follow. All the way around the house to her car.

"Get in," she says. I do. After we've driven for a minute, she exhales loudly. "I hope that wasn't too bad. They're a little much."

"No," I say. "I liked them a lot."

"Yeah, well, they make me crazy."

"What do you mean?"

"I'm never alone, for one. There's always someone yammering at me about something. I love them, but sometimes I just want my own space."

I have so much space that sometimes I don't know what to do with it all. If I didn't have Tippi Hedren, I might lose my mind.

She says, "I'm done with this."

"With what?"

"High school. Childhood. This." She thumps the steering wheel with the flat of her hand. "Done being so young that everyone's up your nose about this or about that. When you coming home, Lucy, don't be late, Lucy. Dance, Lucy, eat, Lucy, sleep, Lucy. You know what I mean?"

Her family seemed so nice. "I guess."

At the tennis courts she stops the car. It's dark and deserted, the kind of place where movie couples get attacked by murderers with hooks for hands. I'm confused. "You want to play now?"

"Sí," she says. She twists a tiny fist in the front of my shirt and reels me in, kisses me. I can't breathe, I'm so happy. I curl my arms around her and slide her onto my lap. The pink flower falls from her hair to the seat. She kisses me again like she's sucking the juice from a peach so I turn my face so I can give her more. And more. And more.

She pulls away. She has my face cupped in her hands, a vise grip. "I just want to start my life, do you understand?"

I'm not sure what's going on or what she's talking about, but it's okay that she feels what she does because she looks so amazing when she's *feeling* it, her eyes flashing in the dark, pupils wide and bright, pulling in all available light, like she's draining the stars of their energy and using it all to electrify me. If I were filming this scene, I would start there, in the sky. She throws her head back and I bury my nose in her chest the way I've wanted to all night.

I'm saying something against her skin, but even I don't know what it is. All I know is that she can twist her fist in my shirt, she can push me away and reel me back, she can hit me with her racket and with her serve, she can make me dance in her own personal puppet show.

Rory would say she has me by the cojones.

That's okay.

The Player

"Are you really wearing that?"

Gina looks down at herself. "What do you mean? This is the kind of stuff I wear all the time."

"But usually not all at once." She's wearing a black lace corset with a jean jacket over it, acid-green miniskirt, pink fishnets, and boots as big as boats on her feet. She's just dyed her hair red but left the bangs black. She's got on so much makeup that a drag queen would tell her to tone it down. We're supposed to be going to the MTV offices. I'm excited, Rory's excited. Joe's sulking in the backseat and Gina looks like something out of a Tim Burton production: *Corpse Bride II: The Curse of Raggedy Ann. A Nightmare Before the Business Meeting.*

"I wanted to look good," she says.

"I think she looks good," Rory says.

Gina puts her hands on her hips. "Can I get in the car now, sir?"

"Whatever," I say.

She gets in and I pull out of the driveway. She starts screwing with the radio.

"Can you leave my music alone, please?"

"I am *not* listening to this," she says.

"I am." It's a song list Lucinda made for me. It's got salsa and some bossa nova tunes on it, including "Girl from Ipanema," which Lucinda likes to sing to me while she does all sorts of amazing things with her—

"Where'd you get this crap from?" Gina says. She's peering at my iPod, which I've got hooked up to the stereo.

"From his new girlfriend," says Joe. "Wait, she *is* a girlfriend, right? She's not just one of your little . . . diversions?" His voice is all casual, but his eyes are flinty in my rearview. This is the new Joe. The Iceman cometh.

I grit my teeth. I really needed for Gina to know that I had a new girlfriend right before we meet the MTV people. As soon as we get into the meeting, she's going to clock me with a coffeepot.

But all Gina says is, "Oh, okay. I guess we have to listen to it, then," and puts the iPod back where she found it. She sees me glancing at her. "What?"

"Nothing," I say.

"You thought I was going to freak out?"

"No," I say.

"Yes, you did," she says. "But I'm over that."

"Really?"

"Did you expect me to pine away for the rest of my life? Do you really think you're that great?"

There's no good answer to these questions, so I don't say anything. For about five minutes, no one does. And then Gina pipes up:

"I just hope you don't give her a disease."

"That's my girl," says Rory.

"Don't you want to know who it is?" says Joe. I want to jam on the brakes so that his big stupid face slams into the back of my seat.

"Not really," says Gina, "but I think you want to tell me."

He does. "Lucinda Dulko."

"Well, well, well," Gina says. "Eddy's decided to hunt

outside his species. Never seen her wearing anything but white. Does she put out?"

"This is going to be a long day," I say.

Gina laughs. She pulls out a pack of cigarettes.

"Light one of those and I'll throw you out, star or no star," I say. "Nobody smokes in my car."

She stops laughing. I keep driving. Every once in a while, my eyes flick to the rearview mirror. Joe has stopped glaring at me and is now glaring at all the other cars on the highway. I'm not even sure why he's coming with us. I told him that. He said, "This is my production company as much as it is yours." Which was true. Was. Until he started blowing us off to do history projects. I might be distracted by Lucinda, but she's not a fantasy. She's real. And she wants *me*. Tough if he doesn't like it.

Nobody's saying much. Too nervous, maybe. My mind wanders. I think about the first day I met Joe. Just like with Rory, it's because of my mom that I met him. She dragged me to a local production of Shakespeare in the Park, something directed by one of her friends. *Romeo and Juliet*. I wasn't into it. Shakespeare wasn't my thing. Movies were my thing. But Mom said that a director has to understand acting, and Shakespeare was one of the hardest for actors to pull off. She said even if it was bad, I'd learn something. So, we went. We got there early. Mom introduced me to her friend the director, a distracted guy with frizzy hair, thick glasses, and a round butt just like a woman. There was a boy about my age lurking around him. I'd seen him at school. Total drama geek. "This is my son, Joe. He'd be my Romeo, but he's too young. Even though he's exactly the right age. Go figure."

"Nice to meet you," the geek said to my mom. He shook her hand, holding it for just a couple of seconds longer than normal.

I thought he was the weirdest-looking guy I'd ever seen. When we walked away, I said, "He looks like a skull."

"I think he's got one of the most interesting faces I've seen in a long time," my mom said. "I bet he's a good actor."

And he was. Turns out that he was too young for Romeo, but his dad had given him some bit part with a few lines. As weird as he was to look at, he was also hard to look away from. You believed every word he said. Riveting, my mom said later. After the show, I asked him if he wanted to be in a film.

"What kind of film?" he asked.

"I don't know yet, but it's going to be awesome." We called it *The Strange Sad Life of Aquaman*. It was about a superhero who could swim underwater without oxygen. Only problem was, he lived in Kansas. When we uploaded it on YouTube, we got more than ten thousand views.

Now the only view is the one in my mirror, the one where Joe is staring sullenly out the window. People think we're best friends. Which makes sense—we do the show, we're always around each other. But there's always been something there, something weird. Like we're speaking the same language but slightly different dialects, and there's always something lost in the translation.

It takes about an hour to get into the city with all the traffic and a few wrong turns in Midtown, but we finally arrive. We park the SUV in a lot that cost 1500000000 dollars for a half hour. When we get on the elevator, my stomach is screwed up so tight that I think it's trying to bend me in half.

"I wonder if we're going to see anyone cool while we're here," Gina says.

"Joey Ramone is dead," I say. "But maybe we'll run into Justin Timberlake."

"Maybe we'll run into Paris Hilton," Rory says.

"And we can watch her blow you off," says Joe.

"Key word is *blow*," says Rory.

Gina snorts. "You have quite the imagination."

"That's why we're here," Rory says.

"No, we're here because of *Riot Grrl 16*. I happen to *be* Riot Grrl 16 in case you forgot."

"Soon you're going to want your own dressing room with a big star on it."

"And low-fat vegan meals."

"And your own Pilates instructor."

"And spring water imported from France," Joe says.

"The least they could do," Gina says.

The elevator opens and we step out. We tell the receptionist that we're there to meet Erin Loder. She doesn't burst into laughter and throw us out, which I take as a good sign.

"Have a seat," she says. "I'll call Erin for you."

She calls, we wait. We wait for ten minutes, fifteen minutes, twenty minutes, a half hour.

"Taking her time, isn't she?" Gina mutters.

"Shut up," I say.

Finally a woman with a spiky cap of bleached hair comes out into the reception area. She's wearing what looks like a lacy pink slip with short brown boots. I have never seen these articles worn together before. I would never have thought they'd look so hot.

"Hi! I'm Erin. And you must be Gina. Loving the outfit."

"Thanks," says Gina. "Eddy thought it was a bit much."

"Really?" Erin says. "I think you're perfect. A riot girl if I ever saw one." She turns to the rest of us. "And you must be Ed, Rory, and Joe, right?" She shakes all of our hands. "Why don't you follow me back to the conference room. I've got some people who really want to talk to you guys."

As Erin walks, she casually swings the long rope of beads she's wearing around her neck. Rory gapes at her ass wiggling under the slip. If I were filming this scene, I would draw the camera in tight to the wiggling ass and cut sharply to focus on Rory's slack lips and darting tongue, then back to the wiggling ass. Joe sees where Rory is looking and elbows him hard.

"Ow," Rory says.

"Dog," Gina says.

Erin glances back over her shoulder. "Sorry?"

"Nothing," Gina tells her. "Rory was staring at your butt is all."

Erin raises a brow and playfully swings the rope of beads at Rory. Maybe she has high school kids drooling over her all the time, I don't know, but she doesn't seem too upset.

She leads us to a conference room and has us sit around a big table. "There's coffee and soda over there if you want it. We'll order lunch in a bit. Have a seat." She grabs a phone and punches in some numbers. "They're here. The *Riot Grrl* kids. Yeah. We're in the conference room." She hangs up. "Just to get this out of the way. You're all eighteen, right? Otherwise we have to get your parents in." We assure her that we're legal—exactly what I told her on the phone but not exactly true. Gina's still seventeen, but since she's not officially a member of the production company, I figure it's not a big deal. Besides, she would have killed me if (a) I told her she couldn't come or (b) that her über-rich environmentalist parents had to come with us riding their Segways and demanding to know MTV's policy on recycling.

We're still sort of shuffling around, trying to figure out if it's really okay to take a Coke, or if that's something that you're supposed to offer to people just to be polite and those people are supposed to refuse politely and if they don't they will make asses of themselves and no one will want to produce their TV shows. But then Gina grabs a Coke, so we all do. We sit down and try to open the Cokes without getting fizz all over the table, which we all do, except for Rory, who has to get up and scrounge around for napkins. When he's sitting again, Erin starts talking.

"Like I said to you on the phone, Eddy, we're really impressed with your show here. Especially Manny and Paul, who you'll meet in a minute. We think you guys have shown a lot of creativity and imagination. You've taken a rather clichéd idea, the video diary, and made it interesting again. That is not easy to do."

"Thanks," I say.

"Thanks," says Joe.

"Thanks," Rory says.

We feel extremely stupid repeating each other until the door opens and two guys walk in. "Hey!" says one.

"Hey!" says the other.

"Hey!" says Erin.

"That's Paul," Erin says, pointing at a guy with dark hair gelled to stick up in all directions. "And that's Manny." This is a prematurely bald guy with a baby face. "Paul and Manny are some of our very top development people. Paul, Manny, this is Rory, Joe, and Eddy."

"We love your show," Manny says.

"We think it's amazing," says Paul.

"Totally awesome," says Manny. "Hey, are we getting lunch? You guys like Japanese? We know this place that has great bento boxes. You want to get bento boxes?"

"I'd love bento boxes."

I have no idea what bento boxes are and I'm not sure that Rory or Joe or Gina does either, but we all say yes because nobody is going to say no to Erin, who is still swinging her beads and smiling. There are calls to Japanese restaurants and orders for bento boxes. There are more comments about how awesome we are, how awesome *Riot Grrl 16* is, how awesome Gina is. How everyone at MTV wants to work with us. Then the bento boxes arrive. They turn out to be actual boxes with California rolls and rice and little clots of seaweed in them. I'd like to photograph them; they don't look like food as much as art. Everyone eats except me, because my stomach has screwed itself into a tiny fist. I poke at the California rolls with my chopsticks and say, "Thanks!" and, "Great!" and, "Wow!" when appropriate.

"We don't want to mess with a good thing," Erin is saying. "We like the show as it is. What Manny and Paul are interested in is having you expand it. Enrich it. More settings. More expansive scenes. We'd like our star here"—she grins at Gina—"to really dig into the character. To have more people to work with. More emotional territory to explore. Do you know what I mean?"

"Yes," we say.

Paul chimes in. "Like, for example, and I'm just throwing this out here, so don't think I think you have to do exactly what I'm saying, but what if Riot Grrl here was a victim of a terrorist attack?"

"Yeah," says Manny. "Like she's on the subway and someone releases a poisonous gas. Or maybe she gets a letter with anthrax in it. I mean, I wouldn't do anthrax exactly; it's been done."

"Yeah," says Joe. "By real terrorists."

"Right," says Manny. "So you don't want to do anthrax. But maybe something else. Like, not terrorism, but some other mass-scale kind of crime."

"Another angle might be to have her contacted by a government agency. Like, they want her to spy on people. Or infiltrate some group. Punks, maybe. Or bikers," says Paul.

"Bikers!" says Manny. "Love that. We could get into the whole tattoo thing." He turns to Gina. "What do you think about getting a tattoo on-screen? We could have her visit that celebrity tattoo show."

Erin shakes her head. "Another network."

"So? I'm sure we could work something out." Manny's still looking expectantly at Gina.

"Uh . . ." says Gina.

"Another idea that I'd like you to think about," says Paul. "Does Riot Grrl have superpowers?"

"That would be so cool," says Manny.

"I mean, not real superpowers per se, but subtle superpowers."

"Is there such a thing as a subtle superpower?" Rory wants to know. Erin frowns at him as if he's being snarky, but he's not. He just doesn't understand what's going on. Not sure that I do either. Gina's looking a little dazed. Joe just looks mad.

"Maybe she can read minds. Or move objects with her thoughts."

"Only little objects, though. Like pens," says Manny.

"What's the point of having her move a pen with her mind?" says Paul.

"Well, we don't want her to be throwing cars around, do we?"

"What if she's bionic?"

"We did have her explore being a witch," I say.

"Maybe we could do more with that. Voodoo or something."

"Great!" Erin says. "I'm glad we're all on the same page."

"What page?" Joe says, but either they don't hear him or they don't know what he means.

After lunch Erin takes us around the office. We're introduced to producers, directors, assistants, sound engineers, and a lot of other people whose names we wouldn't be able to remember even with the use of thumbscrews. All of these people say we're awesome. I'm still feeling sick, but it's a strange sick, a sick that afflicts those waiting to hear if they've won an Academy Award kind of sick. I can barely believe this is happening, that we're walking around the offices of M-freaking-TV, that we are *in talks* with MTV. Even Gina has a huge grin on her face that she can't seem to shake (luckily for all of us it makes her look even more riotous; nobody wants to watch *Wholesome Happy Grinning Girl 16*).

We're in the offices for exactly two hours when Erin decides to wrap it up. "So, what we'd like to see from you is some more expanded video, more characters in future shows. And Gina, we'd like to continue to see you being bold, larger than life, and real. We want you all to think about the possibilities and the risks you're willing to take with this character and with this show. And we'll see how you do in the contest. After that, maybe we can talk about a pilot."

"The contest?" I say. I didn't think the contest mattered anymore. Does the contest matter?

"Just so that I'm being up-front with you, we are talking to a number of contestants." She must see something on my face because she says, "That's the way the game is played, you know?" She pats me on the back. "But I'm rooting for you guys."

I can't help it. My tiny fisted stomach punches me from the inside. I mumble, "We won't let you down."

Erin shakes all of our hands, leads us to the elevators. She presses the button marked Down. "Guys," she says, nodding at us, "we really think you're going to be big. We really do. I'm being serious here. We can't wait to see what you come up with next."

The door opens and we step into the elevator. "Thanks for having us," we say as the doors frame and then obliterate her. It's quiet for about three seconds, because Rory can't hold it in any longer.

"Oh, man, that chick was HOT. Definitely a 9. Maybe even a 9.5."

"Can't you wait until we get out of the building before you go all horndog on us?" says Gina.

"She can't hear me. Did you see the ass on her?"

"We all saw the ass on her, Rory," I say. "We were worried you were going to bite it."

"She looks exactly like Scarlett Johansson. When we

get the pilot, I'm asking her out."

"First of all," Joe says, "we're probably not getting any pilots, and second of all, you have a better chance of getting abducted by aliens than getting a date with that woman."

"What do you mean, aliens?" Rory says.

But I don't care about that. "What do you mean, we're not getting any pilots?"

He looks at me as if I'm crazy. Maybe I am crazy. I don't want him to say what he's going to say.

The doors to the elevator open and we walk through the building and then to the parking garage. Joe makes us wait until we're in the car before he decides to explain. "Did you hear those guys? They kept telling us how great we were—"

"Yeah? So?" says Rory. "We are great. The show's great."

"Let me finish. They kept telling us how great we were, but they never said anything specific. And were talking about making Riot Grrl bionic! What kind of crap is that?"

"They were just throwing out ideas," I say.

"Stupid ideas. The reason that Riot Grrl is good is because we push the envelope, but we never push it too far. Everything that's happened to Riot Grrl could actually happen."

"The government could be working on bionics right

now," Rory says. "For all you know."

"Don't be an idiot. Think about it: What kind of 'risks' do Erin and her cronies want us to take with the show? What kind of risks does she want Gina to take? Like, if they want her to get a tattoo on camera, what else do they want her to do? Get wasted?"

"I'd get wasted," she says.

"Have sex?"

"Screw you," she says.

"Well, that's what I'm saying. They weren't really specific, and they didn't promise us anything. Why should we mess with the show if it's great? And why should we mess with it at all if they haven't promised us anything? They said they're talking to all the contestants."

"They mentioned a pilot," Rory says.

"What did they say, exactly?"

"About what?"

"About the pilot? About a contract? About money?"

Rory shakes his head. "That's your problem, dude. You're all about the money. You have to think about the big picture."

"I'm the only person thinking about the big picture," Joe says. "They didn't say anything about anything. We got nothing."

No one speaks for a minute. Then Gina says, "We got bento boxes." She cracks the window and lights a cigarette. "That was cool."

The Good, the Bad, and the Ugly

I tell myself it's fine. It *is* fine. The next episode of *Riot Grrl 16* gets tons of votes, putting us at number four overall. If we put together a killer finale, we'll definitely make the final group. We'll go on to do *The Producers*, win that quarter of a million. We just have to be patient a little while longer. We can do that. Nothing has changed.

Nothing. It's all good.

Also good, but different than any other good I've ever known: Lucinda.

With me, the girl thing usually starts with an accident. I mean "accident." I "accidentally" brush her arm or bump into her. Sometimes I hold her wrist and tell her how small it is, show her how I can circle it with just my thumb and index finger. Sometimes, if I'm really pouring it on, I use the word *delicate*. Other times I pick up a lock of her hair and rub it between my fingers while talking about something trivial, like the weather or a TV show, and watch as her breath gets shallow.

And it works.

They like it, I like it.

Everybody's happy.

But I don't do any of this with Lucinda.

I don't accidentally brush her arm. I don't tell her how small her wrist is or show her how I can trap both of her arms with one hand. I don't lift locks of her hair and pretend to chat about school or the weather. And I don't pick her up to show her how light she is or how strong I am. I don't have to do any of it, and anyway, it wouldn't work. She'd know I was following a script. It's like we're dancing all the time. I'm supposed to be leading, but then, just when I least expect it, she spins in close and rests her cheek on my cheek or lets go of me to dance alone and all I can do is stand around like a dumb ass and pant.

Or maybe it's more like tennis, where we're in this great rally that I think might never end and all of a sudden she wrong-foots me or finds some previously unimagined, wicked angle and she's queuing up another serve before I understand we're on to a whole new game.

I never know what she'll do next.

Everything is a surprise.

Not a surprise: the whole school has found us out. Not because we're like those slags who play tongue hockey in the hallways, but because I've been spotted at her matches. With anyone else this would have bothered me, but now I don't care who knows. I'm the guy with the show headed for MTV. I'm the guy with Lucinda.

One of Lucinda's old boyfriends, Jon Sanchez, the pretty boy baseball player, passes by my locker and says, "Heard about you and Dulko."

"Yeah," I say.

"Good luck with that," he says with all the sarcasm he can muster. Which is not much, he's such a wuss.

But I don't even say anything, not "bite me" or whatever, because he looks even more sad and pathetic and girly than usual, like he should just give it up already, put on a dress and some lipstick, and start dating guys. I feel sorry for him. I feel sorry for anybody who's been with Lucinda and had to give her up.

"I don't want to give you up," I say.

Dad is still out at work, and I've put Tippi Hedren in her cage upstairs so I have Lucinda's attention to myself. We're in my basement watching a movie.

Scratch that. She's watching the movie; I'm watching her.

"Who says you have to give me up?"

"Nobody. I just don't want to."

She squeezes my hand, but she's still focused on the movie. I can't concentrate. It's the first Lord of the Rings and I've seen it about sixteen times already, but that's not the problem. The problem's Liv Tyler, with the blue eyes and the pink lips that make you want to get a taste. Even though Lucinda doesn't look like Liv, I get all crazy for Lucinda's blue eyes and tasty lips and she's sitting right here next to me. So close I can smell her baby powder deodorant and the fruity smell of her shampoo. I want to dress her up in one of those long Elvish gowns and drop a fancy, glittery crown on her head and listen to her promise her undying love in a language that sounds like music.

And then I want to peel off the gown.

"This is pretty violent," Lucinda murmurs.

"What?" I say. I've shifted my weight so that I can look down her shirt. "Say something in Spanish."

"That's why I never saw this movie. I don't like violence."

"But it's sort of fake violence, right? More like a

cartoon than anything."

"I don't think so."

I tear my eyes away from Lucinda's breasts and look at the screen. Orcs are splattered everywhere.

"Feels pretty real to me," she says. "Even though they're just sporks."

"Orcs," I say. "But the fact that it feels real is what makes the movie good, right? It's a great trilogy. Third one has a thousand different endings."

She turns to me. "It does? Hey, pancho! Are you looking down my shirt?"

"No," I say.

"You were."

"No, I wasn't."

"Liar."

"You're beautiful."

"You mean my boobs are beautiful."

"That too."

"So what's with you guys and breasts, anyway?"

"Is that a serious question?"

"I mean it. You guys are, like, downright *weird* about them. I never wear low-cut shirts because none of you would ever focus on my face."

I focus on her face. "I don't know what you're talking about."

She laughs and nudges my shoulder. "Estúpido."

"That's what I wanted to hear."

"Freak."

"Yes." I sigh. "I don't know."

"You don't know what?"

"I don't know why we're, 'like, downright weird' about breasts. I can't explain it. It's not meant to be an insult, though. When we look. We can't help it."

"Half the population has breasts. Your *moms* all have breasts."

"I really don't want to think about my mom's breasts, thanks."

"It's pretty random," says Lucinda. "You might as well slobber over someone's ankles. Or elbows. Or collarbones." She takes my hand and puts it around her neck. "Feel the collarbones."

"Ummm," I say.

"Sexy, huh?"

I run my fingers all around her collarbones and the little bird bones that form a V in the front, lightly, as lightly as I can without tickling her. As I'm doing this, her lips part and her breathing gets a little heavier. Her irises glow in the light flashing from the TV set. Her pupils widen.

I think she's just surprised herself.

I press my fingers against the side of her throat to find her pulse. It speeds up when my other hand cups her shoulder and I push her back onto the couch.

* * *

About twenty minutes or twenty hours or twenty years later, I hear the sound of the garage door.

"Shit," I say against Lucinda's lips. "Dad's home."

Lucinda shoves me off the couch and sits up. Her hair is everywhere. Her clothes look like someone tried to tear them off ('cause, uh, someone did try). She fumbles with her buttons, but she keeps missing the buttonholes.

I'm on the floor where she's shoved me. I laugh.

"Don't make me kick your ass," she mutters.

Her lips are so red and huge and . . . "You look amazing."

She rolls her eyes. "Will you please put on your shirt?"

"I thought you liked me this way."

"I'm going to hate your guts in another thirty seconds."

I drag the T-shirt over my head as Lucinda closes up shop. She's snapping an elastic around her hair when my dad's voice echoes through the house. I hear other voices too. Marty and the Meatball.

Great.

"Eddy! Eddy, are you home?"

Someone opens the basement door.

"Ed," Lucinda whispers. "Your shirt."

"Eddy? Are you down there?"

"Yeah!" I shout.

Dad trudges down the stairs, Marty and Meat behind

him. "Oh, hi," he says. "I didn't know you were going to have a guest."

"Dad, this is Lucinda. Lucinda, my dad."

"Hi." She shakes my dad's hand. "Nice to meet you."

"And this is Marty, my stepdad," I say. Marty shakes her hand as well. He pulls Meatball out from behind him, but Meat shrugs him off.

"This is Meatball, I mean Matthew. My little brother."

Lucinda looks down at the Meat. "Hello."

"Hello," Meat says. "Are you the smelly girl?"

"Meat!"

"What?"

Lucinda laughs. "You can call me Lucinda."

"Did you know that in 1954, a man grafted the head of a puppy onto a healthy Siberian husky?"

"No, actually, I didn't," she says.

"He was trying to make a two-headed dog, but it didn't work very well," says Meatball. "The transplanted head bit the other head."

"Wow," says Lucinda.

My dad glances around the room, looking wildly for a way to steer this conversation in a less morbid direction. "What were you guys doing?"

I wave at the TV. "Movie."

He frowns at the screen. "Lord of the Rings? Haven't you seen that a million times?"

"I haven't," Lucinda says. "But I don't think I missed anything."

My dad grins. "My thoughts exactly."

Marty scans the coffee table in front of the couch. "Did Eddy offer you anything to drink?"

"No, now that you mention it," Lucinda says. "He didn't."

Dad sighs. "You try to teach them some manners, but they never learn."

Lucinda smirks at me. "That's true."

"Can I get you something?" Marty says. "Tea? Soda?"

"Soda would be great."

"I'm kinda thirsty myself," Dad says.

"I want soda," says the Meatball.

"You can have milk," Marty tells him.

"I don't see how that's fair," Meatball says.

My dad: "We'll be right back."

They disappear up the stairs. As soon as they're gone, Lucinda says, "Your shirt's on inside out."

"They didn't notice. Not with Meatball's two-headed puppy story."

"At least put it on right," she says.

I take the shirt off and fix it. "You just wanted to see my body again."

"You mean you just wanted to show me again."

My dad comes back downstairs with a six-pack of

soda, a package of Oreos, and a book tucked under his arm. Marty follows balancing a hot cup of tea. Meatball holds a glass of milk out from his chest as if he doesn't want to be associated with it. We all arrange ourselves on the furniture. Dad opens a soda and gives it to Lucinda. And then he tosses the Oreos on the coffee table. "I hope you like cookies."

"Sure," she says.

"I mean, I hope you like *stale* cookies."

Lucinda grins. "My favorite." She pulls a cookie from the package and unscrews the top.

"I'd enjoy a cookie," says Meatball.

"You can have two," Marty says.

My dad settles in the armchair. "So, what can we tell you about Eddy that will embarrass the heck out of him?"

"Let me think." Lucinda's eyes literally twinkle. "Do you have any baby pictures?"

"That would do it," says Marty.

Dad gets up and goes to the bookshelves, rummages a bit, and scares up a battered album. Lucinda takes it from him and opens it on her lap.

I pop a soda for myself. "Flip to the middle-school pictures with the screwed-up hair and the braces and get it over with."

Marty pats Lucinda's hand. "He hides it well, but he can be very sensitive."

"I see that."

Meatball goes over to the shelves. "Where are my baby pictures?"

I slump in a chair while they go through the whole damned album. *Oh, look at this one! He's potty training! It's so adorable!*

At the shelves, Meatball collapses and starts to shake, milk dribbling from his mouth. I go over and revive him. 'Cause of the milk, it's a messy job. Lucinda is staring.

Meatball sits up. "That was a seizure brought on by a brain abscess."

"What do we do about the abscess?"

"Oh, it's gone now," he says. "I think I found some pictures of me."

Marty gets up and peers over Meat's shoulder. "Those are more pictures of your brother when he was little."

"They look like me," Meat insists.

"Yes, I know," Marty says. He smiles apologetically at the rest of us. "I think it's time I got someone home."

"Who?" says Meatball.

Marty and Meatball take off, the Meatball protesting that he didn't get a chance to show the smelly girl his baby pictures.

After they've gone, my dad says, "If you liked the pictures, I have something even better." He gets up from the couch and pops the DVD. Then he starts digging around in the entertainment center.

"Dad, don't even think about it."

"Think about what? Aha!" He holds up another DVD and spins it on his finger. Then he pops it into the player.

"Home movies!" he says.

"Dad!" I say.

"I'd love to see some home movies," Lucinda says.

"Eddy, this lovely young lady says she wants to see some home movies."

This is so not a good idea.

"Dad, I don't—"

Dad grabs the remote and presses Play. On the screen a redheaded baby grins. A disembodied female voice says, "Come on, Eddy. Time for the binky trick."

"Binky twick!" the baby says.

Lucinda squeezes my hand. "Aw."

With fat sausage fingers, the baby stuffs pacifiers into his mouth. Seven all at once.

"That's my boy!" says the female voice. "Aren't you the most talented boy?"

The baby on the camera attempts to grin around the pacifiers.

"Yes you are, yes you are, yes you are!" the female voice coos.

"Oh, the voice belongs to Eddy's mom," my dad tells Lucinda, as if she hadn't figured that out. Dad hits fast-forward. "Let's find another good one." A redheaded boy drags a Radio Flyer wagon down a bumpy sidewalk. The wagon has a bird in it. The bird says, *"I have to get to San Francisco!"*

The boy turns to the camera and says, "Mommy, why does Tippi want to go to San Francisco?"

"She doesn't mean it, Eddy," the voice says. "She wants to stay with us."

Lucinda squeezes my hand again. I pretend I have an itch on my wrist. I pull my hand away to scratch it.

Another scene: Christmas. Wrapping paper everywhere. A different voice behind the camera, a man's. "What have you got there, Eddy?"

The redheaded boy holds up a box. "A video!"

"Which video is it?"

"*The Christmas Before the Nightmare!*" the boy says.

"You mean *The Nightmare Before Christmas*?" says the man, but the boy has already dropped the case and moved on to the next present.

The camera lingers on the boy another minute, observing as he tears open the package and frowns at the clothes he finds inside. Then the camera pans away from the boy to a woman sitting in a chair with her legs tucked underneath her like a cat. She has blond hair still mussed from sleep and she sips at a steaming mug. She turns her eyes on the camera, her face inscrutable. The camera draws in, closer and closer to the woman. She stares back, her big blue eyes flat, giving nothing away. In the background, the sound of tearing paper.

I watch my dad watching himself watch my mother and I get so angry that I want to shove him off the couch and kick him. Lucinda clears her throat. "I'd love to see more movies, but it's getting late. I think my parents will start to wonder where I am."

"Oh! Right!" says my dad. "Wouldn't want your mom to worry."

I don't even get to walk Lucinda out alone. My dad pretends to fix the porch light while I walk her to the car.

"Well," Lucinda says.

"Well," I say.

"Is your brother really sick?"

I think about this. "Define sick."

"He doesn't have a brain abscess, then?"

"No. He's a little weird. Sorry if it freaked you out."

"It didn't. I thought it was . . ." She trails off.

"What?"

"Surprising."

"Like I said, he's weird."

"That's not what I mean. I thought he was adorable. I think you're all great. Your dad and stepdad and you guys all hanging out together. I don't know. I didn't expect your family to be like that."

"What did you expect?"

She shrugs. "Honestly, I guess I expected your dad might be some middle-aged bachelor bringing home his nineteen-year-old girlfriend."

"Thanks. That's very flattering."

"Well. Your mom's an actress. I just assumed . . ."

"That we're all a bunch of creeps?"

"I'm sorry. I think I've seen too much TV or read too many bad novels or something." She stands on tiptoe to kiss me on the cheek and while she's doing it hooks a secret finger into my front pocket, tickling my thigh. She whispers in my ear. "I'm glad I was wrong."

I'm going to say, "You owe me," but I don't. Instead I say, "Me too." The front of my thigh burns.

We watch Lucinda back old Snuffleupagus out of the driveway and rumble down the street. My dad and I go back into the kitchen. I sit. My dad leans against the sink and stands there, grinning at me.

"Cut it out, Dad," I say.

"She's cute," he says.

"I know."

"Not your usual type, though, is she?"

"I don't have a type," I say.

"Of course."

He's still grinning.

It must suck to be old.

He takes a sip of lemonade. "Your shirt was on inside out. Now it's not."

Oh hell.

"You are being careful, aren't you?" he says.

"Dad, don't make me throw myself out the window."

"We're on the first floor, Eddy."

"You know what I mean."

"Look, son, I have to ask, don't I? I wouldn't be a good father if I didn't make sure."

"I'm careful, okay?" I say. "Can we stop, please?"

"You don't want to get that cute girl in trouble."

"The window, Dad."

"You have a lot of work ahead of you with your movies. You don't want anything to get in the way of that, do you?"

"Since when do you want me to make movies?"

He's genuinely puzzled. "Since when have I not? I want you to take yourself seriously; of course I do. That's why I'm bringing up the subject. You have to be responsible, for yourself and for that girl too. Plus there are diseases and—"

I bang my head on the table.

"That's not an answer, you know."

Bang, bang, bang.

"Okay, Eddy. I can see you don't want to talk about this. I'll let you off the hook. For now. Just don't do anything stupid."

Sure, he's one to talk. I follow him up the stairs and say good night. Tippi sings softly at me, so I pull her from her cage and sit at the computer. I'm going to have to come up with something incredible for the *Riot*

Grrl 16 finale. Something so amazing that it will blow people's minds. But my head is spinning. From Lucinda, for one, but also from all the things Erin and those other guys said at MTV. Should Riot Grrl be a victim of terrorism? A witch? A psychic? A bionic woman? Would that make the sublime ridiculous, or just sublime? I don't know. And I don't know why I don't know.

Even though I shouldn't, I go to the MTV website and read through the comments. Just a few months ago, reading through the comments made me feel like a genius. It was so easy to ignore anyone who didn't like the show, skip right over them to the fans, the groupies, the worshippers. But now I find myself scanning for the one-star ratings, torturing myself with the negative comments, looking for the Tin Man, dreading him.

And here he is:

> **Another piece of stinking**, rotten tripe from E. Rochester and his motley crew, this one even worse than all the episodes that came before (if that's even possible). Maybe Rochester's distracted, not up to his usual level of idiocy. He's got a new girlfriend. Big deal, right? He's got a new friend every

week—including, I've heard, his leading "lady"—but this time he's in over his head.

Way over his head. He better get used to *this*.

It's a link. I click on it. A YouTube video pops up. It's me at the tall bike shoot, getting hit in the nuts by a runaway bicycle.

Saturday Night Fever

"This guy *does* know me," I say.

"Hold on. I got a customer," Rory says. Muffled: "Your total will be $12.87. *Unforgiven*, *Girlfight*, and *Blade Runner* are due back in five days. *Pretty Woman* you can just burn in your barbecue. Yeah, I was kidding. No, I wasn't. Yes, I was." He gets back on the phone. "Okay, what were you saying?"

"The guy. Tin Man. The one leaving all the comments all over the MTV site. He knows me. He talked about Lucinda."

"He did? What did he say?"

"That I have to watch out for her. Or something like that."

"What does that mean? What's up with Lucinda? What'd she do?"

"Nothing's up with her. She's not doing anything."

"Then what do you care?"

"Because this freak is talking about Lucinda! Because he won't shut up about the show! Because people listen to him! Because he knows me! He could be anybody!"

"Dude, you need to chill. And *stop looking* at that website. Listen, I got more customers here. Why don't you call Joe?"

"I don't want to call Joe."

"That's why you should call Joe. You guys are freaking me out with this Silent Bob crap. And you need to get over this thing with Lucinda."

"You mean Joe has to get over Lucinda."

"Whatever. Bros before hos."

I don't call Joe. I can't talk to Joe. But I also can't stand to be in my house alone, even with Tippi Hedren for company. I decide to go to one of Lucinda's matches. I try to focus as Lucinda roasts a blonde in a pink headband, wristbands, socks, and sneakers. They've been battling on the court for an hour and forty-five minutes and now, in the last set, Lucinda seems to get sick of all the playing around and is quietly and systematically annihilating her. After a string of humiliating points at the end of which Ms. Pink nearly goes sprawling into the fence, Pink bursts into tears. Lucinda stands on her side of the court, blinding in her tennis whites. She plucks the strings on her racket as Pink wails at the umpire. It's pretty painful to watch, especially, I'm guessing, for the girl's parents, two perfectly coordinated, uptight Barbie dolls sitting in the front of the bleachers. I catch all the snickering of the audience on my digital, which I brought to record Lucinda's serve. I pan over the audience, over a few guys I don't recognize in the front. I wonder who they are and why they're here. I wonder if any of them is the Tin Man. Then I pan over the rest of the bleachers. A clot of girls sits in the back. I'm surprised to see Sonya. I put the camera down. Her eyes widen and she waves, waggling her fingers. The other girls nudge her and she shrugs, saying something that I can't hear.

On the court, Pink tries to get it together, but she can't. Lucinda finally takes her down with an overhead smash. When they shake hands at the net, Lucinda says something to the girl that just makes her cry harder. I hop off the bleachers to go meet the tiny terminatrix. On the way down, Sonya and her friends pass me.

"Hey," Sonya says.

"Hey, yourself," I say. "How are you?"

"Oh, same old," she says. She doesn't bother to introduce me to the bored girls standing around her. "I'd stay to chat, but I have to go console the loser."

Pink's crumpled next to her parents, sobbing. "You know her?" I say.

"Unfortunately. My cousin."

If it wasn't for Ms. Pink's impressive calves, I'd never believe that she and Sonya the sex goddess are related. "Get out."

"I know," she says. "I tried to talk her out of the pink socks; at least she'd have a little dignity left. But no, why would she listen to me? So now she's not only been annihilated by your, uh, girlfriend, but she looks like an ad for Pepto-Bismol."

"Heh. I bet she's feeling a little sick about now."

"So, she *is* your girlfriend, then?" Sonya says, jerking her head at Lucinda.

"Yeah," I say. "She is."

"Right," says Sonya. "So, I'll catch you online sometime, okay?"

"Sure. Whenever." I watch her go. I'd film her walking, but that wouldn't be cool. Still, the thighs are killer.

I turn away from Sonya and move toward Lucinda, who not only has killer thighs, but also killer arms, killer eyes, killer hair, killer lips. She's got a towel around her neck and she's reading a note.

I grab the towel and flip it at her butt. "Hey, you."

"Hey," she says, grinning, and shoves the note into her duffel bag. She doesn't tell me what the note says or who it's from. The Tin Man howls in my head. *He better get used to this*. I shove the thoughts away and stomp on them with my mental boots.

"What did you think of the match?" she says.

"You rocked it like you always do."

"I did, didn't I?"

"What did you say to her at the end?"

"Oh, that." She grins. "I told her to take up scrapbooking."

"You're kidding." Seemed a little mean, since the girl was already toast.

"Don't feel sorry for her. That was Penelope. You remember, the one I couldn't beat? The one who used to psych me out so bad until you gave me some advice?"

"I guess the tables have turned."

"Yes, they have," she says. She's glistening with sweat.

I kiss her. "You look tasty."

"Cut it out. I need a shower."

I kiss her again. "That sounds good to me."

"You realize we're in public, right?"

"What's your point?" I say.

She rolls her eyes and shoves her racket into her bag.

"Listen," I say. "I know we haven't talked about this, but prom's coming up. I was hoping we could skip the limo. Would you mind? I mean, if you're totally into limos, that's okay, but they're a little expensive, and . . . what?"

"Eddy, I'm really not the dance type."

"What do you mean, you're not the dance type? I've seen you dance."

"I'm not the *school dance* type. They're not going to have a salsa band at the prom. Besides, I've had enough of all these people. I don't need to hang around a bunch of stupid teenagers wearing bad bridesmaid dresses, trying to spike the punch." She sounds so sarcastic when she says this that I'm embarrassed.

She zips up her bag. "You're okay with that, right?"

"Yeah. I'm fine," I say. "Most girls . . . I just thought you might like to go."

"I'd rather not. But if *you* want to, I—"

"No, no. We don't have to. I don't care." I do, kind of. Not that I want to get dressed up in a monkey suit, but prom is something everyone does. And I want to show her off. I want everyone to see how beautiful she is. I want everyone to see her with *me*.

She sighs. "You're upset."

"I'm not."

"Yes, you are. But I think I can help with that. Come with me." She grabs my arm and leads me back to her car.

"Where are we going?"

"My house," she says.

"Is David cooking?" I say, getting in the passenger side.

"Helping out at his friend's Cuban place. He won't be home till after midnight."

"What about Roberto?"

"Hot date."

I feel a bloom of heat in my gut as Lucinda guides Snuffleupagus out of the parking lot. "Mom and Dad?"

"Helping Aunt Carmen look for a winter getaway. In Florida. They get back in a couple of days."

"Oh," I say.

"Oh," she says. She nods to herself. We've been alone lots of times, but something about this seems different. Like she's got a game plan.

By the time I'm sitting in her bedroom, waiting for her to get out of the shower, my whole body is humming. I get up and pace around. The room has green walls and carpet the color of Granny Smith apples, but there's a black-and-white comforter that I don't think should match but kind of does. Even with the tennis plaques and trophies on shelves on one wall, this doesn't look much like a teenager's bedroom. Looks more like a model of a room you'd find in a furniture store. Bookcases line one side of the room, and they're packed neatly with all kinds of books, some for school but mostly not. There's a desk with silver-framed photographs. Lucinda with Roberto, Lucinda with David, Lucinda and her parents, Lucinda with the dog and the cats, Lucinda with people I don't know and I absolutely hate because they're with her and I'm not. In one of them Lucinda is standing with an older guy—older, but not old. Twenty-five? Thirty? His arm is around her. They're both wearing tennis clothes. Probably just her coach, but . . . I stare at the hand gripping her shoulder. I know how good that shoulder feels.

I put the photo back on the desk. I sit on the bed, then jump up again, in case she finds me and thinks that I think that we're going to have sex, and what if that's not what she's been planning? What if she thinks I'm just another drooling horndog idiot?

"Hi," Lucinda says.

She's framed in the doorway. She's wearing a tank and a pair of those crazy short shorts girls wear as underwear that I'm sure are illegal in some Southern states. Her hair is still damp and her cheeks are pink. Her red toenails are like jelly beans.

"So," she says, spreading her arms. "What do you think?"

I can't say anything.

"Hello?"

I'm afraid that if I open my mouth, my heart will pop out.

Before I can spew my own guts like some strange species of deepwater fish, she saves me. She walks toward me. My brain is so frozen that she's in slow-mo, planting one foot in front of the other, the muscles of her thighs tensing, then relaxing, tensing and relaxing. She reaches out for me, kisses me. We shuffle over to the bed and topple into it. She's brushed her teeth and tastes both warm and cold, like a Creamsicle. Have I mentioned how much I love Creamsicles? Then something burbles to the surface of my mind. I've never asked her if she's done this before.

"Wait."

"What?"

"Is this, I mean, have you, uh, you know . . . ?"

She puts her hand on my cheek. "We're going to do this by the book. You'll be wearing all the appropriate gear."

I've been carrying something with me for a month, just in case. "Covered," I say.

"Good," she says. "Besides that, does it matter?"

Yes. No. Yes. "I just don't want to . . ."

"You won't hurt me if that's what you're worried about."

It is. But that's not all. What about the guy in the photograph? Who is he? Is he the guy people whispered about last year, the way older one? And what about the other people in the pictures?

"I'm okay, Ed. Really. Unless you don't want to."

"Are you kidding? Of course I want to." And I don't want to know about that older guy. Or any other guys. Do I? And why am I thinking about this stuff anyway? It's so stupid. I'm no angel.

I kiss her again. And again. If I keep kissing her, I won't have to eat, I won't have to drink, I won't have to think. She's running her hands all over me. It feels right, sort of hesitant, not someone with a lot of practice. So maybe she doesn't want me to know she's a virgin. That's it, she doesn't want me to know.

I kiss her harder. She sits up, pulls off her top, and smiles as she tosses it at my head. At that moment I would do anything for her, jump out of a plane, fight a band of ninjas, wrestle an alligator, swim with sharks, sign away every dollar I will ever make; I don't care. I want to make her forget about every other guy on the planet. I want to tell her what I'm feeling. There's a name for it, right?

"I-I-I," I stutter.

I can't say it.

But I can prove it.

Lucinda's worried that one or the other brother will show up early, which, she says, would be Double Plus Ungood. So we get dressed and forage for food. Mogget, attack bunny cat, sprawls in the middle of the table and glares at me. The Lab, Mrs. Havisham, lies across my feet like a seventy-five-pound rug. Lucinda makes me her specialty, peanut butter and jelly with Fritos on the side. I'm absolutely starving, so I wolf the sandwich in three bites. She makes me two more. I feed Puck the Tasmanian devil terrier some of my Fritos—one for me, one for him—while Lucinda scoops some ice cream. Strawberry. Normally I don't like strawberry ice cream, but tonight it tastes like the ambrosia of the gods.

"You trying to get me fat?"

"I want you to keep your energy up," she says.

"Don't even kid."

"Eat your ice cream," she says.

I eat my ice cream. I think about her tennis match earlier and wonder how much traveling she'll have to do when she turns pro. A lot, probably. It will be hard to coordinate schedules, but that's okay. Anything worth doing is hard.

Speaking of hard . . .

"Where are the big tennis tournaments played?" I say to distract myself. "Wimbledon's in England, right?"

"Yeah. And there's the Australian Open, which is in Melbourne, Australia. French Open in Paris. And the U.S. Open in New York. Lots of smaller tournaments all over the place. Why? Do you want to go to a tournament?"

"I guess I'll be going to a bunch of them," I say. "To watch you."

She licks her spoon. She shouldn't do that if she wants to keep her clothes on. "To watch me? Am I going to the U.S. Open or something?"

"Aren't you?"

"You're serious?"

"Yeah," I say.

She puts the spoon in her bowl. "Well, that would be nice. But it's never going to happen."

"What do you mean?"

"I'm not good enough," she says.

"Yes, you are."

"No, Eddy, I'm not."

"You got that scholarship," I say.

"Yeah, but St. Joseph's is Division III. It's not one of the top tennis schools. It's not Stanford. I'm pretty good, but I'll never be great."

"You're wrong," I say.

"I wish I was," she says. "But I'm not. It's okay, though. I figured that out a long time ago."

I don't believe her. She can tell.

"Look, I'm going to major in biology and then I'm going to apply to veterinary school," she says. "That's the long-term plan. And that will be difficult enough, believe me. Tennis is just a hobby."

"You play a million hours a week!"

"So?"

"And you love it!"

"So? I don't have to be a pro to play. Besides, I'm going to be really busy. This summer will probably be the last vacation I'll have for the next ten years. God, I can't wait to get out of here."

I don't want to talk about her getting out of here. "But what if you win every tennis match?"

"It's still only Division III."

Division III, Lord of the Rings III, I don't care. "Well, what if the number-one tennis player in the world comes to your school for an exhibition match and you beat her?"

"Okay, okay. If I get the chance to play the number-one tennis player in the world and I beat her, maybe I'll rethink my decision."

"That's what I thought," I say.

"What about you?"

"What about me?"

"What are you going to do with your life?"

"I'm already doing it," I say, waggling my eyebrows at her.

"I mean with the rest of your life."

I shrug. "I'm already doing that, too. I'm going to make movies."

"Just like that?"

"No, not just like that. But I've been doing the movie

thing since I was thirteen."

"Five whole years?" she says. "Wow."

"Cut it out. It's a long time. *Feels* like a long time. I just want to get to the next step already. We're doing well in the contest. Really well. And we even had a meeting with MTV."

"I know," she says. "Joe told me."

"Joe? When did you talk to him?"

"I talk to him every day, Eddy. He's in my history class. You know that. Gina's in my classes, too."

I knew this, but I didn't think about Joe and Lucinda talking every day. Why would they have to talk every day? What would they talk about? And what would Gina tell her? "How come you didn't say anything?"

"About Joe being in my classes?"

"About MTV."

"I figured you'd tell me about it when you wanted to tell me," she says. She says all this like she found out I got good SAT scores or threw the winning basket at a game. The strawberry ice cream makes a slimy pool at the bottom of my bowl.

"Well, it's no big deal," I say.

"Joe says you think it's a big deal."

"Again with Joe."

"What are you talking about?" she says. "You're not jealous of Joe, are you?"

"Do I have reason to be jealous of Joe?"

She gets up from her chair and sits in my lap. "You're really a romantic, aren't you?"

"Absolutely not," I say.

She kisses me. "That's so sweet."

Double Indemnity

It's funny which memories come to you and when, interrupting the flow of your life like weird, jarring flashbacks in a bad film. I'm sitting in my garage with Rory. Joe and Gina are AWOL. Normally I would be annoyed that they were late. Normally I would have a pile of scripts and I'd be in a big hurry to go over them. After five minutes

I'd be calling their cells and if they didn't answer texting: WHERE R U???

But I'm not texting anyone. I'm remembering how we got our name. I remember a sheet of paper where we'd written *21-Inch Thumb*, *the Pirates of Destiny*, *Booty Call*, *Caffeine Dreams*, *Boys of Summer*, and *Three*. Joe liked Three. Rory liked 21-Inch Thumb. I didn't like any of them.

"Well, then, let's go with 21-Inch Thumb."

"I don't think anyone will know what it means."

"Who cares?" Rory said.

"Okay, *I* don't know what it means," I said.

Rory said, "I don't know what it means, either. That's what's cool about it."

My mom was washing the cookie trays in the sink while she listened to us. She dropped one of the trays and it made a loud noise as it hit the counter. We all jumped as if someone had just sprayed the room with BBs.

My mom laughed. "What about the Jumping Frenchmen of Maine?"

"The Jumping Frenchmen of Maine?" I said.

"I read about it. It's a disease kind of like Tourette's. It causes people to have an excessive startle reflex. Also echolalia."

"Echolalia?"

"Repeating every word that's said to them."

My mom was good at that. Coming up with the fresh

idea when all the other ones weren't working. I thought I had that talent, but it turns out that I don't. I don't have any fresh ideas. I don't have a script. I haven't been able to write anything. Truth is, I don't know what to do with Riot Grrl. I don't know if she should become a tweaker like her addict brother or join the Russian secret police or discover psychic powers or get attacked by a genetically altered shark or take up voodoo or dye her hair blond and pledge a sorority. I don't know what the right answer is, the ending that will get us the attention of Erin Loder and the rest of the people at MTV or, at the very least, the ending that will get us on *The Producers*.

"I think you're thinking too hard about this," Rory says. "What's your gut tell you?"

"My gut's a mess."

"I told you not to go to that stupid website and read all those comments. They've destroyed your brain cells. It's just like in *The Thing*."

"Huh? What's like in *The Thing*?"

"You know the part where the guy's head falls off and grows spider legs? Kind of scuttles around? That's you. You're a head with spider legs scuttling around."

"Vivid," I say.

"Accurate," says Rory.

"You're a big freaking help."

"What do you want me to do?"

"Maybe you can find the Tin Man and blow up his computer."

Rory shakes his head. "Dude," he says. "It's just some pathetic slob who has no life and absolutely no sex and spends his time trolling the internet."

"You're describing yourself."

"Funny. Not. You have to let the work speak for you."

"What work? We don't have any work; that's what I'm trying to say."

"We will."

"He knows me, Rory."

"He just thinks he does."

And that gives me an idea. I can't even believe it. It just pops, like it's been sitting there for years. I'm thinking of Gina, who started out as just another drama nerd. "Wait a minute. What if Riot Grrl wasn't really Riot Grrl?"

"What do you mean? Who is she?"

"She's actually a . . . a . . . a . . . twenty-six-year-old woman who has been hired to pose as Riot Grrl. Like Kim Novak in *Vertigo*."

"Okay, *Vertigo*. The mysterious woman. The guy with the fear of heights. Jimmy Stewart as the whiniest man in history. Totally overrated. Connection?"

"Look, the drug-addict brother's been gone for years, right? While he was away, he got in with the wrong people. The mob. Like, the Sopranos. We already hinted about that in earlier episodes, right? So, he doesn't have any idea where his family is or even what they look like."

"This is your brain on drugs," Rory says.

"Right. We can call the mob the Sopranos—or maybe we can call them something weird or funny, the Pianos, maybe . . ."

"The Pacinos . . ."

"The Tarantinos. So the Tarantinos hire these people to live in his childhood home and *act* like his family, including this wild girl who's supposed to be his sister. Her job is to get close to him, find out where he's hidden, I don't know, money? Drugs? Drugs and money? Diamonds?"

"What about a statue with some microfilm in it?"

"And then when she finds out where the statue is, she whacks him."

"Riot Grrl is a hit woman."

Rory's grinning so hard he's going to split his face in half.

"It's great, isn't it?" I say, nearly as hopeful as I was when I was standing in Lucinda's bedroom. "Tell me it's great."

"It's totally awesome. It freaking ROCKS!" He does his horrible white guy dance all around the garage.

"Where the hell are Gina and Joe?" I say.

We both leap for our cell phones.

* * *

We spend the rest of the week working on the two-part finale. Gina dyes her bobbed hair jet black and cuts the bangs high on her head. During the climatic chase scene through dark streets slick and glinting with rain, she wears a short tight dress with heels. She looks both sweet and deadly, a gorgeous assassin straight out of a French film. We film the whole chase in one long shot, following her on the Segway.

Joe is the best drug-addicted dupe in the history of drug-addicted dupes, his face drawn and gray and hollowed out. He's a scarecrow. He's a tortured jack-o'-lantern. He digs into the part like he'll never have another acting role in his life. During the scene in which he's about to die, he ad-libs the dialogue, telling the story of the prodigal son from the Bible, crying and slobbering the whole time he's telling it.

"A man has two sons. The younger son demands his share of his inheritance while his dad's still alive. The kid takes the money and goes off and wastes all his money doing whatever, you know, partying and whatnot, and eventually has to take a job tending pigs. There he comes to his senses, so he returns home to his father. But when he gets home, his dad isn't mad at all. He celebrates the kid's return. When the older brother gets pissed off about it, the father tells him that he's just happy his son came home safe. You see? We all sin. Just living is the constant weighing of sin. Like always picking the lesser of two evils every minute of every day."

Riot Grrl cocks her head like a weapon. We catch it from above, where Rory and I are perched in one car of the Ferris wheel filming through the grate and Riot Grrl and her drug-addicted brother swing in the car below.

"That's a sweet story," Riot Grrl says. "Too bad you're the lesser evil." And then she pushes him out of the Ferris wheel car.

When we watched the completed episode, we actually cheered.

At the tennis courts Lucinda has a present for me. From the trunk of her car she drags a huge box wrapped in silver foil.

"I don't remember telling you that I played the guitar," I say, tearing the wrapping paper off.

"You deserve a reward for finishing *Riot Grrl*."

"I thought you said it was too violent."

"Movies aren't my thing," she says. "What do I know?"

In the box is a new tennis racket that she put in an oversize box. I hold up the racket, toss it from one hand to the other. "Hey, this is pretty nice."

"Isn't it? I thought you'd play better with a new one."

The last match we played, the score was 7–6, 6–4, the best I'd ever played against her. "You *want* me to play better?"

"Sure I do," she says. "I can always use the competition. I'll even let you take some practice serves before we play so you can get used to the racket."

"Nice of you," I say.

"It is, isn't it? And I figure it might keep your mind off the whole voting thing."

"For a while, anyway." This round, MTV doesn't let you see the vote counts until the official winner is announced. People can still comment, but the results are up in the air. If I wasn't so sure that we killed it with the finale, I'd be out of my mind. Right now, the only thing that's driving me out of my mind is Lucinda in her tennis dress.

I practice serving for about five minutes, and then I'm ready. We flip for first serve and she wins the toss. She flounces back to the service line and bounces the ball three times. That's her ritual, three bounces, then the toss, then the snap of the racket on the ball. I know because I watched the video of her playing. I watched it over and over again, loving the way her arm muscles bulged and striated at the moment of contact. Something you can barely see in person, only on video. Press Play, and Lucinda is a ballerina. Press Pause, and she's a warrior.

She serves out wide, but I'm already there. I smack it down the line. Her eyes widen in surprise, then she smiles. "See? You're better already."

Her next serve is straight up the middle. This one I get

my racket on, but not as solidly as I'd like. She rushes up to the net and puts it away.

"Hey, we're tied," I say.

"15–15," she says, bouncing on her toes.

An hour later we really are tied, with a set apiece and three games each. She's not fooling around anymore. She's not grinning or flashing the short shorts under her skirt. She wants to win. And the more she wants to win, the more I want to win.

She whips a ball past me. I can only stand there and watch it. "Out!" I say. "Game."

"What?" she says. "That was in."

"No, it was like a mile outside the baseline," I say. It *was* a mile outside the baseline.

"Come on," she says. "That was my point."

"No, it wasn't," I say.

"Eddy! I've been playing this game since I was three."

"So?" I say. "That doesn't mean your ball wasn't out."

She has her hands on her hips, her racket tucked underneath one arm, the handle sticking out from her body. Her brows are furrowed, her face and neck are flushed and blotchy, and she taps her foot in annoyance. Then she grabs the racket handle and swings at the air. "Fine. Your point."

"It's okay. We'll play the point over."

"No, let's just move on. Your game. 4–3."

"Serve it up, Lucinda. I want to play the point over. Maybe I didn't see it right."

"You said you did."

"So, maybe I was wrong."

"You said you weren't."

I don't know why she seems so mad. We're just fooling around anyway. "I don't want to fight about this."

"Neither do I. So let's finish, okay?" She crouches and waits for me to serve. Finally I do. She plays even more ferociously, if that's possible, but I've broken her serve and the match is pretty much over anyway. The last two games go by in about ten minutes. 6–4, 4–6, 6–4.

"Well," she says when she comes to the net. "I guess that racket was a mistake."

"Yeah," I say. I feel weird. I want to forget about the match.

I want *her* to forget about it.

I know how to make her forget.

"So, how about coming over to my house? Dad has to work today."

She bends and pours water over her hair. As she's toweling off, she says, "I can't today, Eddy. I've got a history project I have to do."

"You can't be serious. Graduation is next week!"

"Yeah, but I still have to do this project. It's a group project and I said I would meet someone later this afternoon."

I don't like the way she says *someone*. "Someone?"

"Someone."

"Who?"

She sighs. "Joe."

"You're meeting Joe for a project. What kind of *project*?"

"We're making a porno," she says.

"Ha," I say. "That's hilarious."

"I already told you, Eddy. It's for history."

"So why were you keeping it a secret?"

"I was not keeping it a secret. It's just that I know how jealous you get if I mention Joe's name. So I didn't feel like mentioning it."

"I don't get jealous."

She rolls her eyes. In the bright sunlight they look nearly colorless.

"Do you have to meet him today?"

"Yeah," she says. "It's the only time we both had free." She smiles a little, reaches out, and slaps me with the damp towel. "If it makes you feel better, it's not a sexy project. We're doing the Bible. Well, not really. Mary Magdalene. We have to do a PowerPoint presentation on it. Music, voice-over, pictures, the works. We almost weren't allowed to do it. One of the other kids said it was against separation of church and state." She laughs. "Joe took care of him."

"Great," I say.

"Eddy—"

"No, I mean it. That's great. I'm glad my friends get along." When I say the word *friends*, I spit a little.

She stares at me. Then she stands on her tiptoes to kiss me. "Thanks. I'll call you later?"

"Sure," I say. "I love . . ."

But before I can get it out, she's already gone.

I get home and find a brush, a screwdriver, a can of white paint, and a tarp on the kitchen table. Taped to the paint is a note: *Make yourself useful. Paint the garage.* Dad didn't sign it.

I don't bother showering. I drag the stuff outside. I try to pry the can open, but the screwdriver keeps slipping in my hand. "Bitch," I say. Next door, Mrs. Winston is pruning her bushes with a pair of gardening shears big enough to take out a redwood. She glares at me.

"Not you, Mrs. Winston," I say. "The can. I can't get it open."

She shakes her head and lops off a branch with one snap of the shears. I almost say, "Actually, Mrs. Winston, I *was* talking about you," but I don't. I don't care about Mrs. Winston. I don't care about anyone except for Lucinda, and she's off reading the Bible with some bug-eyed pumpkin head who's supposedly my friend. What's up with this? She's already gotten into college, she doesn't need the grade anymore, so why would she choose to spend time with Joe over me? I slap the paint on the garage, spraying it all over my arms and T-shirt. Joe was hot for her even before we started going out. He tried to talk me out of being with her. Maybe he's still mad about it, still trying to get her.

I keep painting, the sun beating down on me, burning the back of my neck. I try to think about movies. My favorite shots, my favorite scenes, my favorite lines of dialogue. *Fight Club:* "First rule of Fight Club: You do not talk about Fight Club." *Clerks:* "There's nothing more exhilarating than pointing out the shortcomings of others, is there?" *Rear Window:* "Why would Thorwald want to kill a little dog? Because it knew too much?" But all I keep seeing is Joe touching Lucinda, Lucinda touching Joe. Joe saying something sensitive and caring and creepy like, "I really respect women," or, "I think players get what they deserve," or, "The Bible says that women and men were both created in God's image," and then unzipping her dress. I blink hard to erase the visuals, but I can't.

The phone rings inside. Nobody but telemarketers call on the house phone. Nobody except . . . I drop the paintbrush in the bucket of paint and run inside.

"Hello?" I say.

"I'm looking for Ed Rochester."

"This is Ed," I say.

"Ed! Erin Loder here. How are you?"

"Good! Great!"

"So, listen. We watched the finale of *Riot Grrl 16* and I have to say, that was some brilliant work. Totally surprising and yet totally logical. Joe and Gina were amazing. We loved it. We really loved it."

I realize that I've been holding my breath. I exhale. "Thanks."

"I'm calling all the contestants to let them know the final results before we put them up on the web. After you guys worked so hard, you deserve that much."

"I'm glad," I manage, though my tongue is practically glued to the top of my mouth. *This is it, this is it,* my brain hums. *We're on our way.*

"Eddy, I'm really sorry to say that while we loved it, our audiences didn't take to it the way we would have hoped. *Riot Grrl 16* finished outside the top five."

"It . . . what?"

"You didn't get the votes, Ed. Such a shame. Maybe the finale was just a little too complex. A little too over the top."

Over the top? "But you said that Riot Grrl should be a spy."

"Well, not exactly. We were just throwing things out there." I hear papers shuffling. "I know this is really disappointing news. I understand it, Ed, I've been there myself. All I can say is that you got a ton of exposure and maybe there'll be opportunities down the line."

I force myself to croak: "You loved *Riot Grrl 16*. Is MTV still interested in the show? We could take it in a new direction."

"The thing is, Eddy, my bosses feel that this has been done before."

"What's been done before?"

"The video diary format."

"But Manny and Paul—"

"I'm afraid Manny and Paul are no longer with us," she says, her voice crisp as a piece of paper. "They left to pursue other opportunities."

"But when we first talked, you said we brought something fresh to the format."

"And you did, you absolutely did," she says. "But some of our new people think we need something even fresher than that. *Truly* fresh, if you know what I mean. Downright minty."

My brain is now scrabbling around like a gerbil. "What if we came up with some other ideas? Brand-new ones? Minty ones." I can't believe I'm using adjectives normally used to describe gum.

"That's the spirit, Ed! Just what I wanted to hear. Go ahead and pull some pitches together and give me a call. Who knows what could happen?"

"Yeah," I say. "Great. I'll do that. Can I ask you a question?"

"Shoot!"

"Which show got the most votes?" Please be *The*

Amazing Adventures of Emo Guy, please be something good.

"*Bitchslap*," she says. "Our audience really loved the stunts."

"Stunts," I say. When did playing dodgeball with softballs become anything more than stupid?

"Just one more thing," she says. "Do you have Joe Meyerhoff's number? He didn't give it to us."

My brain stops scrabbling. My brain stands completely still. "Joe? Why do you need Joe's number?"

"I want to talk to him about his little show that's been running on YouTube, *Your Bible Fix with Brother Dude*? Is that a . . . a . . ." She trails off and there's more shuffling paper sounds. "A Jumping Frenchmen of Maine production?"

"No," I manage. "I've never seen it."

"You absolutely have to catch it! Fabulous stuff. The execs went nuts for it. I mean, absolutely over the moon. I haven't seen the execs so excited since *Real Life: Amsterdam* first aired. Joe is just so smart and likable and funny and engaging. And cute, too, if I don't sound too much like an old lady saying that. Can't take your eyes off him. We think it would be a great addition to our lineup. Religion is just so hot right now. Nothing hotter."

I say, "Hot."

"So, do you think you could give me his number? Eddy? Hello?"

Dr. Strangelove

I grab a beer from the fridge. If anyone in the universe deserves a beer, it's me. I have to do something to relax. I have to work up some ideas for Erin Loder. I have to come up with something brilliant. I can't believe they liked Joe's stupid Bible show. I didn't even realize he'd done it. I didn't know it was already up and running.

What else was he hiding?

Nothing, don't think about it, don't even think about it, I tell myself. Everything's fine, everything's good. So you lost the contest, so a troll ruined your goddamned life; Erin didn't tell you no. You still have a shot. I grab a yellow legal pad and a pen and settle into the couch. Tippi Hedren sits on my shoulder combing my hair with her beak. I tap the pen on the pad. I take a sip of beer. I have to think about what's hot.

> A TEENAGE BOY IS BEING BULLIED AT SCHOOL. HE SLOWLY GETS OBSESSED WITH THE WORLD OF ANIME AND MANGA. HE DECIDES TO COMMIT SEPPUKU, BUT BEFORE HE CAN DO IT, HE IS VISITED BY THE JAPANESE GOD IZANAKI, WHO WANTS THE BOY TO RESCUE HIS WIFE FROM THE UNDERWORLD. FANTASY-ADVENTURE MEETS GRITTY REALISM.

I cross this out. I take a few more sips of beer.

> A SHY, SMALL-TOWN GIRL IS DESPERATE TO BE A POP STAR. SHE TRIES OUT FOR AN AMERICAN IDOL-TYPE VARIETY SHOW ONLY TO BE SEDUCED BY THE SHOW'S MEGALOMANIACAL PRODUCER, A BRIT NAMED RICHARD SWALLOW. PROSPECTIVE TITLE FOR SHOW: SWALLOWTAIL.

I cross this out. I finish the beer. I get up and get another beer, making sure I bury the first beer bottle under the rest of the garbage in the can. I go back into the den. I drink the beer down first to make sure I'm really getting relaxed. But then I'm out of beer. I take another run to the kitchen and grab one more from the fridge.

Tippi Hedren says, *"I thought you knew! I want to go through life jumping through fountains naked!"*

I pet her with a finger. "That's a new one."

"Naked!" she squawks.

"You *are* naked," I tell her. I go back to my perch in the family room and pick up my pen.

> TWO BROTHERS LOSE THEIR MOTHER IN A MYSTERIOUS FIRE. THEY BELIEVE SHE'S DEAD UNTIL A BIZARRE LETTER ARRIVES IN THE MAIL, A LETTER FROM THEIR MOTHER. THE LETTER SAYS THAT SHE'S NOT DEAD BUT IN HIDING FOR HER SONS' PROTECTION. SHE WARNS THEM NOT TO TRY TO FIND HER, BECAUSE IF THEY DO, THEY'LL ENDANGER HER LIFE AND THEIR OWN. THE TWO BOYS SET OUT TO FIND THEIR MOTHER USING THE ONLY CLUE SHE LEFT BEHIND, THE FAMILY BIBLE. ALSO, THEY HAVE AMAZING SUPERPOWERS, WHICH ARE REALLY REALLY AMAZING.

"Well, it might have been good enough in Rome, but

it's not good enough now," says Tippi.

"Thanks. You're a big help."

"I have to get to San Francisco."

I'm feeling a little dizzy. I flip open my laptop and read all the comments on *Riot Grrl 16*, which seem evenly split between love and hate. The Tin Man is holding court as always, orchestrating the haters into a symphony of "this sucks!" The top five will be announced in a few days and it kills me to imagine them all feasting triumphantly on *Riot Grrl*'s once-magnificent corpse. It kills me to think about the Tin Man at all, this faceless enemy who could be anybody, anywhere, anytime. This guy who would never say this crap to your face but thinks it's okay to destroy your life at a distance.

Feeling truly ill, I flip over to YouTube and watch Joe's show: *Your Bible Fix with Brother Dude*. He's wearing a brown robe and yammering about the two different creation stories. After a minute I don't want to watch anymore, but it's like Erin said, you can't take your eyes off Joe. He's that good. And he'll probably be famous for it, whether he wants to be or not. Asshole.

I flip over to the MySpace page. I've got lots of friend requests. I approve 999 ways 2 say no 2 a horndawg, ! will kick your @$$, Principessa Peaches, G-Unit, and iNtErPlAnEt^^jAnEt^^. There are a zillion new comments, most of them "Thanks for the add!" or "I love your show!" or whatever. I friend them all. I need all the friends I can get. And then I see Sonya's picture. The little icon next to her name is blinking, which means she's online. I click on her profile and send a message.

Rear*Window13: Hey.

A few minutes go by. Maybe she's not talking to me anymore. Maybe nobody's talking to me anymore.

$ugar<loves>Honey: hey. didn't think you were talking to me.

Rear*Window13: Why not?

$ugar<loves>Honey: girlfriend.

Rear*Window13: Doesn't mean I can't talk to anyone else.

$ugar<loves>Honey: true.

Rear*Window13: So, how are you?

$ugar<loves>Honey: good. i thought you forgot about me.

Rear*Window13: You're hard to forget.

$ugar<loves>Honey: tease.

Rear*Window13: I never tease.

$ugar<loves>Honey: what are you doing now?

Rear*Window13: Work.

$ugar<loves>Honey: need a break?

Rear*Window13: I always need a break.

After that, nothing. I type another message, but she's gone. I stare at the screen. What was that about? And what did I just type?

I'm losing my mind. My eardrum is thumping. Why is my eardrum thumping?

Tippi wails: *"I have to get to—"*

"Tell me about it," I say. I slap the laptop shut and gather up the beer bottles. I shove them all in the garbage bag, tie it up, and haul it to the big containers outside, Tippi squawking on my shoulder the whole way. Then I go back inside and put a new bag in the kitchen can. I put a jar of pickles behind the other beer bottles in the fridge so it looks like there are more bottles than there really are. Dad will never know.

I decide to watch a movie. I go back downstairs and scan the DVDs. Not sure what I'm in the mood for. Not *Two Towers*. Not *Pulp Fiction*. Not *Dogma*, *Jaws*, or *Memento*. Scorsese, maybe? A little *Godfather*? No. *Miller's Crossing*, the Coen Brothers. I pull out the DVD and pop it into the player. I sit down and press Play just as the doorbell rings. Apparently nothing is supposed to go right today. I run up the stairs to get the door. I open it to find Sonya standing there.

"Hi," she says.

"Hi." I can't believe she's here. I didn't think she'd take me seriously. Not really.

"Who's that?" says Sonya, pointing at Tippi.

"I'm just an animal you caught," says Tippi.

Sonya smiles at this. She's wearing a tight red top and a black miniskirt that could have doubled as a headband.

"Can I come in?" She doesn't wait for an answer. She brushes by me into the house. She's put on perfume, or maybe deodorant. I don't know. Whatever it is, it smells like cake.

"I was just going to watch a movie," I say.

"That sounds good. What movie?"

"It's called *Miller's Crossing*."

"Is that about trains?"

"What? No. No trains. It's sort of a gangster movie. This guy is an advisor to the mob and—"

"I've got some time," she says. Her lips are pink and shiny, her white teeth peeking between them. "I'll watch it with you."

"Oh. Great. Let me put Tippi upstairs."

Tippi: *"Are you still in the mood for killing?"*

"What did she say?" says Sonya.

"Nothing." I run upstairs and stuff poor Tippi in her cage. I plug my fingers in my ears so that I don't hear her screaming and squawking as I walk out of the room and back down the stairs.

Sonya's still hovering in the hallway. "Um," I say. "Do you want something?"

She raises a brow and I realize how that sounds.

"I meant do you want something to eat? To drink? A soda?"

She shrugs. "I'm not a soda person. What else do you have?"

She follows me into the kitchen. I open the fridge. "I have the regular stuff. Juice. Water. There's a wine cooler here, you can have that, though it's probably from 1998."

Sonya starts opening cabinets. "Oh, I was thinking of something more like this." She pulls out a bottle of rum. "We could mix this with the Coke."

I look at the bottle. "You don't fool around."

"I don't?" She pushes me aside and gets two Cokes from the refrigerator. She has to bend over to reach for them. I understand Joe's obsession with religion. I want to say Jesus. Lord almighty. Hallelujah.

Then she straightens. "Glasses?"

"What?"

"I need glasses for the drinks."

"Oh," I say. I get some clean glasses from the dishwasher. "Here."

She mixes us the rum and Cokes and holds out a glass. This is not a good idea, especially not after the beer. But I take it anyway. What could it hurt? I'm not doing anything wrong. Lucinda's hanging out with Joe, working on their "project." I'll just hang out with Sonya and watch a movie. What's bad about a movie? Movies are good. Movies are art. I'm just trying to get inspired here.

I bring Sonya downstairs to the den. We sit on the couch. I even make sure there's a little distance between us so Sonya doesn't get any ideas. Who could say anything about it? Nobody.

I press Play.

The credits roll.

The movie opens.

I sip the rum and Coke. It tastes like something you might use to clean contact lenses.

After about a half hour, we press Pause and get another rum and Coke. The stairs seem to be tilting. I trip and hit my funny bone on the banister.

"Ow!" I say.

"Whoops!" says Sonya, hauling me upright. "Careful."

The second drink is better, killing the vicious throbbing in my arm. We sit down on the couch again. Sonya sits closer this time, her thigh touching my leg. I stare at it, at the way the muscle goes on for miles and miles and disappears up into the folds of her skirt. Her arm is resting on that thigh, her hand cradling the drink. Fine brown hairs dust her skin. On the round knob of bone above her hand she has a freckle. Just one, round and brown and perfect, too perfect, like an imitation of a freckle. My eardrum is thumping again. My fingers twitch. I can hear Tippi shrieking all the way upstairs, but I can't make out what she's screaming. My fingertips crawl across Sonya's thigh to her wrist.

"Your wrist is so small," I say, or try to say, because my tongue has gotten thick.

"Really?" she says. "I never thought so."

"It is. I can sss . . . circle it with my thumb and forefinger."

She looks down at my hand touching her hand, then back up. On the screen behind her, a man is on his knees begging for his life.

Sonya puts her glass down on the table. "So what else can you do with your thumb and forefinger?"

Apocalypse Now

After Sonya's gone, I clean up the evidence. Hide the rum bottle, scrub the glasses, throw the sheets in the wash, brush my teeth, brush them again. I pull Tippi from her cage so she stops screaming. My head feels like someone buried an ax in it. The audience would say it serves me right. I'm covered in a thin sticky layer of girl-who-isn't-my-girlfriend. She told me that I could tape her if I wanted. Why would she say something like that? What if I had? I could paste it all over the internet. I could bounce it off satellites and send it to other galaxies. Aliens could rent it on pay-per-view a million years from now. Do you want that stuff around a million years from now? Like that girl, Audrey, Joe hung out with last year, the one whose picture was taken and sent everywhere. Does she know it will exist forever? That she can never erase or delete it no matter what she does?

I feel sick.

The alcohol sloshes around in my stomach and I have to sit down. I don't know why, but I sit at the dining room table. It's where my mom always sat to do bills and stuff. I don't know how long I sit there. Awhile. My dad finds me still sitting there when he gets home. Tippi Hedren runs across the carpeting to greet him. Normally that makes me laugh, but I'm not laughing.

"Hey, Tippi," Dad says.

"I'm queer for liars," says Tippi.

"Really?" says Dad, holding out his arm so that she can crawl up to his shoulder. "What are you doing, Ed?"

"Nothing," I say.

"I see that. But why?"

"No reason."

"Uh-huh. Did you have someone over?"

"What? Why do you say that?"

"'Cause it smells like cake in here and I'm guessing that you didn't bake one," he says. He's staring at me suspiciously, as if cake isn't the only thing he smells. Beer. Rum. Deceit.

"Oh. No. Nobody was here."

"That's good," he says. "Because I'm still not completely comfortable with you having girls over when I'm not around."

I start to roll my eyes, but it sends bolts of pain back into my brain. "Okay, Dad."

"I do like Lucinda, though. How is she?"

"She's fine."

"Just fine?"

"Fine," I say.

"That's not too enthusiastic."

"What do you want me to say? That we're getting married?"

"You're in a mood," he says.

I have to tell him something. "MTV isn't taking *Riot Grrl 16*. I got the call today."

"Oh, so that's why you're sitting here." He sits down at the table. "I'm sorry, Ed. I know you were really hoping for that to happen."

"Thanks."

"How did Rory and Joe take it?"

"I haven't told them yet. I don't know how I'm going to explain it."

"It's not your fault," he says. "These kinds of things happen. You don't plan for it."

I could almost feel him fighting with himself not to say what he wants to say, the huge internal battle. An actor playing him would have to use every muscle in his face and jaw to portray it.

Dad loses, as usual. "This is one of the reasons why I think you should consider college."

"Dad, you work for a TV show. You're *in* the business. I don't know why you keep telling me that I shouldn't do it."

"Because this business sucks the life out of you. The hours are impossible. It costs things you can't even imagine. This business probably cost me your mother."

"Her again."

Great. Now I've wounded him. He's doing that rapid-blinking thing, the thing that would look totally studied if I didn't know him. "Yes, her again. You might not believe this, but I actually loved her."

"Maybe she didn't love you," I say. "Maybe she didn't love any of us. Did you ever think of that?"

"Your mother loves you."

My stomach rumbles, and not in a hungry way. "Forget it, Dad. It doesn't matter."

"I think it matters."

"Do we have any Pepto-Bismol or Tums or something? I don't feel so good."

He sighs, and I know he knows I've been drinking. But all he says is, "I think we have something in the medicine cabinet. Let me go see."

While he goes to see, I force myself to get up and to put the wet sheets in the dryer. I flip open the machine to find them bunched up into a big wad, as if the cheater fairies snuck into the house while I wasn't paying attention and tied them into knots. I yank and yank and finally get them out, but something lacy and twisted lands with a splat on the floor. It's Sonya's underwear. It lies there on the floor, wet droplets all around it like a murder victim. Something else I have to bury in the garbage can under the used tissues and old balls of lint.

I hope she doesn't want it back. I hope she doesn't call or write me anymore. I hope she was too drunk to remember what happened.

I hope she's the kind of girl who's cool with it.

"We should go out," Lucinda says. "Cheer you up."

We're talking on the phone. It's weird, because we never talk on the phone. She called me. I wonder if it's a sign that everything will be different from now on. The thought squeezes the breath from my lungs and I start coughing.

"Are you okay?"

"Yeah," I say. "Something caught in my throat. So, where do you want to go?"

"Where everyone else goes," she says. "The movies."

I think of *Miller's Crossing* and feel sick all over again. Right now the last thing I want to do is watch a movie. "How about we do something else? We could go to that miniature golf place."

"You hate miniature golf."

"I like it fine."

"You've been hounding me to go to a movie for ages. Come on."

"What's playing?"

"I'm sure we'll find something."

I'm not so sure. Hollywood churns out monstrosity after monstrosity and hopes that the public doesn't notice. Mostly, they don't. "If there's nothing out, we can just rent a movie."

"I want to go out in public for a change."

"We play tennis in public."

"I just want to see a movie with you. Is that so much to ask?"

"Okay," I say. "Let's see what they have." I pop online to check the local theater listings. "Oh, look! *The Stupid* is playing. And *Crap on a Stick II*."

"You're such a snob. Let's go see that one about the undercover cop. The one they're saying will win an Oscar. That's still out, right?"

"Do you know what a crock the Oscars are?"

"Pick me up in fifteen minutes."

A half hour later we're standing in line to buy tickets. Lucinda's wearing a plain white T-shirt, jeans, and red flip-flops with a ratty messenger bag she sometimes uses as a purse when she feels like carrying one. Nobody ever looked so hot in a T-shirt, jeans, flip-flops, and a ratty messenger bag. I wish she didn't want to go out tonight because I don't want anyone else looking at her the way I'm looking at her. I wish she hadn't gone to meet Joe. I wish she hadn't blown me off. Then the thing with Sonya never would have happened and I wouldn't feel like a bottle of soda that someone shook for a joke.

"How's the project going?" I say.

"Good. We got most of it done. We'll have to meet one more time and then it's all over."

"What's all over?"

"The year. High school. I don't know," she says. "It's the last major project before college. Isn't that freaky?"

"Not really," I say.

"Oh, come on," she says. "We're graduating, but I feel like I've already left. At least in my head. I just want to get on with the rest of my life already. Do you know what I mean?"

I don't have to say anything because she chirps all the way into the theater. I don't know what's made her so talkative; she's usually the strong silent type, at least with me. Maybe studying the Bible causes excessive chattiness. I wonder if it's guilt.

We find seats in the back row of the stadium and sit down to enjoy the 40000000 previews, most of them featuring lame chase scenes among a few semi-cool explosions. Then the movie starts. Out of the corner of my eye, I watch the movie play on Lucinda's face—darkness, brightness, day and night, the subtle flicker of movement carried out on her gleaming skin. I grab her hand and squeeze it. I think, if she squeezes back, she's mine. She squeezes back. I feel my lungs and heart and stomach settle back into their respective cavities, my breathing slow and deepen. I made one mistake, but it won't happen again, because she's mine, because she loves me.

After the movie is over, we take the back door out of the theater. It dumps us into an empty parking lot. I don't see my car and I freak a little until Lucinda reminds me that we parked in the other lot.

"Boys and their cars," she says.

"You'd be upset, too, if you carried around as much stuff as I do. I have a video camera in the trunk. It's not the expensive one, but still."

"So why do you carry around all that stuff in the first place? Why don't you leave the camera at home?"

"What if there's something I need to shoot?"

"Like what?"

"Like you."

She smiles. "You won't need to shoot me."

"Why not?"

"You'll remember me," she says.

"Will I?"

"Yes, you will, Edward Rochester. Oh! I almost forgot." She lets go of my hand and digs in the ratty bag. She pulls out a paperback. "Here."

"What is it?"

"*Jane Eyre*. You know, the book with the other Edward Rochester, your namesake."

"Ah," I say.

"I figured that you might want to read it. It's one of my favorites."

On the cover there's some painting of a woman in a frilly dress. "It looks like a chick book. An *old* chick book."

"It is an old chick book. But since you like chicks so much, that shouldn't be a problem."

Suddenly my back seizes up, like I've been sitting too long. "What's that supposed to mean?"

She stops walking a second, her foot hanging briefly in the air. It's long enough to know I overreacted, to know I just gave her a clue. "Come on, Ed," she says, giving me a sideways glance. "We both know how many girls you've been with."

"You don't know how many girls I've been with."

She closes the flap of the ratty messenger bag. "I can guess at least one of them."

"The only important one is you."

"What about Gina?"

"Nothing is going on with Gina," I say, relieved that I can sound so sure of myself.

"Okay," she says. She bites her lip. "What about Sonya?"

"Sonya?" My eyes feel gritty, like someone just hit me with a face full of sand.

"Sonya Powell. She's in gym class with me."

"What about her?"

"Do you know her?"

"No. I mean, I've seen her around school. But I don't know her."

"She called me an ugly dyke who couldn't hold on to a guy if I tried."

Shit. "What? When did she do this?"

"Last week," she says.

"Why didn't you tell me?"

"I didn't think it was a big deal, except that she said a bunch of other stuff this week too. I think I'm all that, I'm just a nasty bitch, blah blah blah. After going to school together for four years, all of a sudden she hates my guts?"

"You did cream her cousin at tennis."

"Her cousin? Who's her cousin?"

"Penelope? You know, horse face?"

"Penelope is Sonya's cousin? How do you know that?"

"She told me."

"Really. I thought you didn't know her."

We're at my car. I let Lucinda in the passenger side door and walk around to the driver's side. I take my time, trying to think. What the hell am I supposed to do now?

I get in the car and throw *Jane Eyre* in the backseat. "That girl is crazy. She has no right to say that kind of stuff to you." I start the engine. "I'll talk to her."

"*You'll* talk to her?"

"Yeah, I'll take care of it. Don't worry about it."

Lucinda nods. She pulls the bag from around her shoulders and puts it on her lap. She doesn't say anything for the longest time. She fidgets, smoothing the straps on the bag, brushing the hair from her face, tugging at her bottom lip. Just the kind of stuff a director would tell actors to do when they're supposed to be thinking about how to say something horrible so that it doesn't sound horrible, except that everyone knows it will.

"Okay," I say, putting the car back in park. "She has a crush on me. She's made some comments on my MySpace. That kind of thing. I didn't tell you because I didn't think that was a big deal either. I thought she would forget about me and move on."

Lucinda nods again. All she says is, "Yeah."

I don't know what that means, but I'm afraid if I ask, she'll tell me. I'm starting to sweat, so I open my window. Outside, other couples are getting into their cars, talking and laughing. I don't know why I was such an ass about going to the movies. Lucinda wanted to go. What was the big deal? I want to slam my head against the steering wheel.

She says, "Remember Camp Arrowhead?"

"Camp? Sure."

"The director called the other day. They need a sports coordinator for the summer. I'd be teaching tennis, softball, volleyball, golf."

"You play golf?"

"Yeah, I play golf."

"I didn't know that."

"There are a lot of things you don't know." She takes a deep breath. "Anyway, the job's full-time. Five days a week for eight weeks. I'll be staying at the campgrounds with the other counselors."

More stuff that I don't understand. "Okay."

"What I'm saying is that I'm not going to have a lot of time this summer."

"Yeah?"

"I'm not going to have any time, really. The weekends I'll want to see my family. Or they'll want to see me. The last summer before college and all that."

She has to shut up now; I have to shut her up. "Lucinda, I'm really sorry about the Joe thing. I am, I was jealous of him. But I know you wouldn't . . . you wouldn't do that to me. I was just being stupid."

"Eddy—"

"I promise I won't say a word about him again. You need to do your project, then you do your project. You do whatever you have to do. He's a great guy. Maybe we should invite him out sometime. Double-date or something. Maybe Sonya will like him." I try to laugh, but everything hurts: my back, my head, my skin.

"Eddy, we're really different people," she says.

"That's what makes this so great," I say. "That's what makes me love you."

"Eddy." Her eyes squinch up around her nose. "You don't mean that."

"Of course I mean it. I've never . . ." It's my turn to run my hand through my hair. My hair follicles ache. "I wouldn't say it if I didn't mean it."

"I'm so sorry, Eddy. I thought . . . Oh, I don't know what I thought." She clicks and unclicks her seat belt. "I just . . . I like you, Eddy, I really, really like you. You're funny and smart and I can totally see why every girl falls all over you. But I can't be serious with someone right now." She pauses, and in the pause I almost hate her. "And I don't think you can either."

"That's bullshit," I say.

She shifts in the seat so that she's looking directly at me. "Is it? How many times did Sonya write you? I bet you didn't tell her to stop, did you? I bet you strung her along a little bit. You like the attention too much."

"Stop it. She didn't mean anything."

She laughs, a hard, angry laugh, throwing up her hands. "Listen to yourself! She didn't mean anything! You're like a character in a movie. The husband who gets caught banging the baby-sitter. That's what those characters always say, *She didn't mean anything to me*. So why are you saying it, Eddy? What happened with Sonya?"

"What about you?" I say. "What about those notes you got in your bag?"

"Notes? What notes?" Her eyes widen. "You mean the ones in my tennis bag? Those were from my mom, Eddy. She's been leaving little notes for me in my lunch bags and in my stuff for years. Her way of making sure that I know I'm always being watched."

"Oh. Well, what about those other guys?"

"What other guys?"

"The ones in the pictures! In your room! That older guy, he had his arm around you!"

She shakes her head like she thinks I'm out of my mind. "Look, we both know that—"

"I don't know," I shout. "I don't know!"

"You do. This isn't going to work. I'm too focused on my future."

"I'm focused on my future!"

"You're dreamy about your future. You're in some big romantic la la land where all the children are famous," she says.

"So? A lot of people want to be famous."

"Yeah, but they don't expect to be famous *tomorrow*! They know it takes some time."

"You mean Joe knows it takes time."

"Fine, Joe does. And a lot of other people. You do, too. Or you would, if you thought about it for a second."

I feel like crawling the walls. I feel like reaching my hands down into my own body, ripping out my guts, and handing them to her. "I want to be famous for you."

"Stop it, Eddy."

"Sometimes I think I want to *be* you," I say. I'm breathing hard as if I'd been running. I don't know where this stuff is coming from, it's just coming.

"That's insane," she says. Her head is pressed to the passenger side window. It's like she wants to get away.

"You're perfect."

"Stop! Will you stop quoting lines from movies? Will you say something real, please?"

"But you are perfect."

"If you keep saying that, I'm going to throw up all over your car." She sounds so annoyed, so disdainful, so freaked out.

"Don't do this," I say.

She reaches out, pulls back, reaches out again. She touches my wrist, lightly, so lightly. "Eddy. I'm sorry. It's already done."

Lost in America

I drop Lucinda off. She tries to be nice to me, tries to kiss me good-bye, but I can't take it. I tell her to go. To get out. I call her a bitch. She is a bitch.

I'm going to drive home, but I don't want to drive home. I have no idea what I'll do when I get there. I don't have the MTV thing, I don't have

Lucinda, I don't even have stupid, big-headed Joe anymore. He'll be the famous one. I'll be left here with Rory, watching the same movies, making the same top-five lists, listening to Tippi Hedren repeat the same lines: *I'm just a wild animal you've caught. I have to get to San Francisco. I'm queer for liars.*

I go over the conversation in my head. How did Lucinda know about Sonya? Did Sonya tell her? But when? If it took a month for me to get Lucinda's number, it's not as if she'd give it out to random people in gym class. No, someone else had to tell her.

I make a U-turn, flipping off the idiot behind me, who lays on his horn. I punch the gas pedal, flying down side streets, yanking on the wheel so hard the tires squeal at every turn. I reach the development of McMansions and pull into the driveway of the largest one. I jump out of the car and march up to the back door. The door's half window, so I can see inside, but the huge kitchen seems to be empty. I pound on the door with my fist. When no one comes, I pound on it even harder.

Gina's face appears in the window. I almost don't recognize her because she's not wearing her *Cirque Du Soleil* makeup. She frowns and opens the door. "Are you trying to kick the door down, you idiot? My parents are trying to sleep."

"You told her."

"Huh?"

"You told Lucinda that Sonya was flirting with me that day."

"Rochester, I have no clue what you're talking about."

"That day you threw the bottle at my head! The bike joust! You must have told Lucinda something. You must have put it in her head. She never would have guessed."

Gina crosses her arms. "Are you on drugs? What would I tell Lucinda? And why would I tell Lucinda anything? I think I've talked to her all of five times in four years."

"'Cause you're obsessed with me."

"Somebody needs a nap," she says. The quote from *Dogma*. It makes me crazy.

I clench my fists and kick one of the rocks that edges the flower beds as hard as I can. It hurts like hell. When I swear, I bellow as loud as I can so that the whole world will hear it.

Gina shoves me backward and closes the door behind her. "Will you shut up! Someone is going to call the cops."

"So, let them," I say. I turn to walk back to the car, but I think I've broken my big toe. It feels like someone tried to saw it off with a spoon.

"You're such a moron," she says, grabbing my arm and steering me toward the picnic table next to the outdoor grill. "Sit!"

"I don't want to—"

"I don't care what you want," she says.

I slump onto the picnic bench.

"Wait here," she says. She disappears into the house. I look up at the sky. It's one of those really dark nights with only a sliver of moon to show for itself, like the rim of light you see under a closed bedroom door.

Gina comes back outside with a plastic bag of ice and a pack of cigarettes. She tosses the ice to me. She pulls a cigarette from the pack and lights it. "Go ahead," she says. "Take off your shoe."

"I don't want to," I say.

"You don't want to, you don't want to," she mimics. "You sound like a five-year-old." She sits next to me, bends down, and yanks at my laces with her free hand. She gets the shoe off with no help from me and plunks the ice on my foot.

"Ow!"

"Like I said, five-year-old."

I pull the foot and the bag of ice up to rest them on the picnic bench. Gina puffs on the cigarette, shooting smoke from her nose. My toe throbs under the ice. If I were shooting it, I'd shoot it as a cartoon, the throbbing toe the size of a ham, beating like a heart.

"She break up with you?"

"No."

"Yeah, she did. Because you screwed Sonya Powell?"

"I didn't."

She exhales a cloud of smoke. "You just can't help yourself, can you?"

"She was flirting with Joe," I mutter.

"That's a good reason to muck it all up."

"I didn't mean to," I say. "I got confused."

"Karma."

"What?"

She twirls the cigarette in the air. "What goes around comes around. You treat girls like shit and now you know how it feels. Sucks, doesn't it?"

I'm too tired to argue. "I love her."

"Uh-huh," she says, scoffing. "Don't expect *me* to feel sorry for you."

"I don't," I say.

"Sure you do. That's why you're here."

"I'm here because you told her. I'm here because you're the Tin Man."

"Don't be stupid."

She's right. Gina would never do anything anonymously. If she thought your show was crap, she'd tell you to your face.

She stubs out the cigarette on the picnic table and tosses it into the half-dead bushes. "Well, if you're feeling better and I can trust you not to break down anyone else's door, I'm going to go back inside."

I don't want her to go. I don't want to be alone.

"Come for a ride with me."

"Now?"

"Yeah, now."

She taps her watch. "It's eleven."

"So? Since when do you go to bed at eleven?"

She sighs. "A ride where?"

"Anywhere. I've got my camera and some lights in the back of the SUV. We can shoot some stuff. I've got some new ideas."

"What about *Riot Grrl 16*?"

I don't say anything.

She exhales sharply through her nose. "We didn't get it, did we? We're not top five."

"I didn't say that."

She crosses her arms. "What about Rory and Joe?"

"What about them?"

"You said you want to shoot some stuff. Don't you want to bring them along?"

"No. I'm the idea man. *Riot Grrl* was mine. I came up with the plots. I wrote all the dialogue. I was the one who wanted to cast you."

"You wanted to cast me because you wanted to have sex with me."

"Point is, I wanted to cast you."

She stares at me for a long time. She's kept her hair the same, all black with bangs cut straight across her forehead. If I didn't know her, I would have said she looked like a china doll. But I do know her. At least I know she doesn't break so easy. It's not fair of me, but it makes me feel better. To know I haven't broken her.

"I'll probably regret this," she says, "but okay. Let me get my stuff."

First, I stop at a gas station to fill up the tank, get some drinks and snacks, and buy Gina more cigarettes. Gina watches me load the two bags of stuff in the backseat of the SUV.

"Are we driving to Idaho?"

"I thought we should have something to eat just in case."

"Just in case what?"

"I don't know." I reach into one of the bags and toss her a pack of cigarettes. "Here."

"I can smoke in the car?"

"Yeah, you can smoke in the car."

With the back of her hand, she presses against my forehead, temple, and the side of my neck. I give her a look.

"I'm making sure this isn't a mask."

I knock her hand away. "Cut it out. I'm trying to be nice."

"Now you're really scaring me."

I ignore her and put the SUV into gear. I maneuver out of the gas station lot, turning onto the road. Since it's so late, we have the road almost to ourselves. The air is dry and cool. Perfect night for driving. I open the moonroof and let the night air flood the car.

Gina smokes quietly. Since I'm letting her smoke, I might as well let her fiddle with my iPod. She scrolls through the tunes until she finds one she likes, a retro tune. The Cure. "Why Can't I Be You?" It's fast and loud and the words hurt me a little, but I turn it up as I turn onto Route 46 east. I never wanted to be anyone else but myself, but right now I wouldn't mind being Tippi Hedren. I have a feeling that Tippi Hedren's pretty pleased with her lot in life.

"Where are we going?" Gina says.

"You'll see."

Route 46 turns into Route 3, which then turns into the Garden State Parkway. Gina smokes a few more cigarettes and then puts her seat back so that she can doze awhile. I keep myself jacked on Coke and Red Bull and the music that burns in my ears. Exit 149. Exit 119. Exit 80. Gina wakes for a minute to say, "We're going to the beach? But I didn't bring a suit," and then she's out again.

Three-plus hours after we left Gina's house, I've driven the length of New Jersey. After that, I have to pull over and consult a map to find the best route, but it turns out there's only one. I take 495 around Washington, DC, and get on 95 to drive through Maryland. After the bright lights of the city, the highway now seems deserted again. It reminds me of a two-minute film the Jumping Frenchmen made more than a year ago. We called it *Highway Man*. We went out late at night on the most deserted part of the Garden State Parkway and dropped Rory off on the side of the road wearing a zip-up suit and a mask. I drove down the highway with Joe, got off at the next exit, and got back on the highway again so that we could pass the place where we dropped Rory. We started filming about two miles away. Joe held the camera steady. There was no dialogue at all. Just the steady thrum of the engine, the passing streetlights, the empty highway rolling through the hills. Then, up ahead, you see the dim figure, someone standing under a streetlamp. You notice that he's standing oddly, with his arms hanging down by his sides but not touching his body. And then, as the car approaches, you notice the zip-up suit and the fact that there isn't a car or a house anywhere near the guy. By then you are so focused on this guy you couldn't look anywhere else even if you wanted to. What is up with this guy? you want to know. Who is he? What's he doing? Where'd he come from? Just as the car is passing the weird, zipper-suited man, the camera pans up to catch a glimpse of his face. That's all you want. To see his face. As if it will explain everything. Every question in the world you ever had. The camera pans up. He has no face. Just black holes where his eyes should be.

There is an audible gasp and the lens turns on the driver. The driver's own face is white and his eyes are huge. Both driver and cameraman start screaming. They scream all the way down the road. They scream until they don't have any breath left to scream. And then, just as the camera goes dark, a tiny voice: "Turn around. I want to go back. I need to see him again."

We put it up on YouTube and it was a huge hit. Everyone thought it was real, everyone thought there was a Highway Man. A local news team even did a story on it. Highway Man was what brought Gina to us in the first place. She wanted to know the truth about him. If he was real, she said, she wanted to see him for herself. She wanted us to show her. When we told her what we'd done, that it was a fake, she said, "Cool! Like *War of the Worlds*!"

I never told Lucinda about Highway Man. And even if I had, I don't think she'd understand why we did it. And if she didn't understand why we did it, then why did I care that she didn't want to go out with me anymore? Why did it feel like I'd swallowed one of Gina's lit cigarettes and it sat in the center of me, burning?

Gina doesn't wake up until we're in Virginia and the sun is turning the sky the color of bruises.

She sits up in her seat, surveying the landscape. Then she grabs the pack of cigarettes off the dash and lights one.

"Kansas?" she says.

"No. Virginia."

"Any particular reason we're going to Virginia?"

"We're only traveling *through* Virginia."

"So, you want to add kidnapping to your list of offenses," she says.

I shrug. "You're the genius who agreed to come with me."

"You were distraught," she said.

Her saying I'm distraught reminds me how distraught I am. Lucinda's words keep ringing in my head: *I'm sorry, Eddy. It's already done. I'm sorry. I'm sorry. I'm sorry.*

I'm tired of everyone being sorry and still screwing me over. "Top-ten favorite movies," I say. "Ten down to number one."

Gina puts her feet up on the dash. "I hate top-whatever lists. I always forget something or change my mind."

"Top ten as of right now, at this very moment, driving through Virginia, on the road to nowhere."

"I can't think of ten movies."

"Top five, then."

"I'm tired. And in *Virginia*."

"I'm distraught, remember?"

"Oh, all right," she says. She smokes carefully, rolling the cigarette between her fingers.

"I meant today," I say.

"I'm thinking." She taps the cigarette out the cracked window. "Number five. *A Room with a View*."

"I've never even heard of it."

"That's 'cause you're a heathen," she says. "It's a period comedy about a girl named Lucy Honeychurch who has to choose between two men."

"Lucy Honeychurch sounds like the name of a prostitute."

"See this? This is me ignoring you. Number four. *Edward Scissorhands*."

"Interesting choice."

"I think of it as a remake of the Frankenstein story but retold as a fairy tale. But I always go back and forth between that and *Beetlejuice*."

"Because it's goth?"

"Because it's good. Number three. *Pulp Fiction*."

"*Pulp Fiction* only gets the number-three spot?"

"Number two. *Amélie*."

"Ugh," I say. "What's with all the love stories? And a *French* love story? I thought you were a tough chick. A girl made me watch that. It was like being torn apart by the cutest kitten that ever lived."

She lights another cigarette. "And number one. *Eternal Sunshine of the Spotless Mind*."

"Another love story," I say.

"But an amazing one."

"I guess," I say.

She laughs.

"What?"

"You totally didn't get that movie, did you? When you really love someone, you really hate them, too. Or what you love turns into what you hate. Brilliant."

I think about kissing Lucinda, burying my nose in her skin, being inside her. "I don't hate anybody."

"Whatever," she says. I'm waiting for her to ask me what my top-ten list is, but she throws her cigarette out the window and then wiggles down in her seat. "Wake me up when we reach California, or wherever it is we're going."

She wakes up in North Carolina. "What time is it?"

"Time for lunch," I say. We stop at a truck stop filled with huge flannel-shirt-wearing guys sopping up egg yolks with white bread. We sit in the smoking section so that Gina can kill herself faster. Three cups of coffee, two sandwiches, and one, "Thanks, y'all," later, we're back on the road.

"Are you going to tell me where we're headed?" Gina says.

"Need-to-know basis," I tell her.

"Will I be back in time for college?" Gina's headed to the University of Delaware, where she got a full scholarship. Close enough to be close, she says, far enough to start fresh. She says she's going to quit smoking cold turkey, grow out her hair, and study psychology. Women are always leaving everyone and going off to reinvent themselves. There's a movie in there somewhere, but I'm too dizzy to figure it out.

"Yes, you'll be back in time."

She pulls off her sweatshirt. "You know, I really don't mind all this driving. I was kind of bored and looking for something to do. But I hope you realize that you're not getting away from anything."

"I don't know what you're talking about."

"You're going to feel the pain wherever you go. It will catch up with you."

"Thank you, Gina. That's really profound. I should have that printed on T-shirts."

She grunts. "You should have it branded on your forehead."

We drive through North Carolina, South Carolina, and Georgia. The air outside thickens with humidity. Gina asks if I'd like her to drive so I can get some rest, but I don't want her to drive. I really wouldn't know what to do with myself if I wasn't driving. It does feel a little like I'm trying to outrun something, but what's so wrong with that?

The last leg of the journey: nearly a thousand miles through Florida. There are palms everywhere. The smell of the ocean wafts through the windows and the late-afternoon sun bakes the tops of our heads. We stop for gas and then we're in the car again. The roads are dry with a thin sprinkling of sand that glitters on the tar. Around eight, we pass the signs that say Miami. The sky is an impossible shade of blue, but the buildings lining the roads look old and dingy, the color of dirty socks. I expect Gina to comment, but she doesn't. She's been quiet for the last hour, waiting for what's going to happen next. I can feel her anticipating it, like you do the key scene in a movie. Will he fire the gun? Will she figure out who did it? Will the ghost be put to rest? Will the birds fly away or stay to kill them all?

It's only after we cross a couple of long bridges that the buildings turn white and pink and yellow, like driving through a giant package of Smarties. I check the address again and then pull into a parking lot. We get out of the SUV. Gina stares up at the enormous wall of flamingo pink stucco, shaking her head. "We drove thousands of miles to get to the Shopping Network?"

Sunset Boulevard

"Not that building," I say. "That one." If Gina realizes where we are, she doesn't say.

We park in the lot and walk up to the security guard manning the gate. I tell him who I am and what I want. He's not impressed.

"I know they're taping," I say. "Tell her that her son is here to see her."

The security guard says, "You don't look like her."

"Do you want to take some DNA?"

"You don't have an appointment," he says. He has the jowls of a bulldog and they quiver when he shakes his head. "This is a closed set."

"I just want to talk to her."

"Come back tomorrow. And don't bring the video camera next time. We don't allow video cameras." He's staring at Gina as if he's never seen a girl before. Then again, she took ten minutes to put on her makeup this morning, and she's done an especially colorful job. Her lipstick matches her camo shorts. As in, green.

"It took me twenty hours to drive from New Jersey. It's an emergency."

The security guard grumbles something about uppity teenagers and picks up the phone. "I've got some kid here," he says.

"Kids," I say. The guard glares and turns away so that I can't hear the rest.

Gina taps her fingernails on the gate until I reach out and grab her hand to stop her. She pinches me, then tries to bend back my pinky, but I don't let go.

The guard slams down the phone. "Someone will be here to talk to you in five minutes."

We wait. Gina fogs the window of the guardhouse with her breath and draws hearts with jagged cracks through them. Under the hearts she writes, *Poor, sad Eddy.*

A skinny man in an orange shirt and slouchy brown pants heads to the gate, holding out his hand like a sword. "Bernardo, PA on *Crime Scene: Miami.*"

"I'm Ed. This is Gina."

"Yeah, nice to meet you." He turns to the guard. "Open it."

As we walk past, I salute the guard, who scowls at me. I raise the video camera and press Record, walking backward as I film. "Dirk had fifteen years on the force till the drink got ahold of him. This security gig is the only job he could get. His wife, Zelda, walked out. His kids only visit when they need money, and since he doesn't have any, they don't visit. He has a cat, but the cat doesn't like him either and pees behind the only chair in the living room. He goes home at night, gets Taco Bell, strips to his shorts, and drinks beer in front of computer porn until he passes out."

"Dirk" gives me the finger.

"That was mean," Gina says.

"But funny," I say.

Bernardo talks as he walks. "Shelby was surprised. She didn't know you were coming."

"I bet," I say.

Bernardo eyes Gina. "Are you in a film?"

"Yes," she says.

"You look like, uh, what do you call those, a Harajuku Girl? You know, from Japan? Except taller. And American."

"What a lovely thing to say," says Gina, fluttering her lashes.

"So, how long have you two been going out?" Bernardo says.

"We're not," Gina says, fiddling with the loop threaded through the top of her ear. "I'm his victim. He kidnapped me."

"She's kidding," I say.

"No, I'm not."

Bernardo smiles blandly. He looks too exhausted to keep his flirt on. My parents told me a PA does all the scut work on the set. If the stars want coffee, the PA coffees. If the director wants a sandwich, the PA sandwiches. If someone's cleaning has to be picked up, the PA picks. If there's glory to be gotten, well, that's when you can count the PA out.

We pass different sets: cop central, the courthouse, millionaire's mansion. The morgue must be tucked in some dark place somewhere. There are a few people milling around the craft service table and some lighting guys setting up a shot. There's a "body" covered with a sheet in the middle of the street. A guy who might be someone Important is yelling at no one in particular and waving his arms around. It looks like Hollywood, but in Florida. This is probably the only show on TV filmed in Florida instead of in California or New York.

Bernardo leads us to a small trailer. He knocks on the door. A voice says, "Come in!"

He opens the door and lets us into the tiny space. Inside, there's a chair with a big, lighted mirror in front of it. A rack of clothes. A small table with a plate of cookies and a half-drunk cup of tea in a china cup.

"Eddy," my mom says. "Baby."

I haven't seen her for a year. She's blonder now and thinner. Her skin is a shade of bronze not found in nature. Her pantsuit is Florida yellow, banana yellow. All of a sudden, I'm hearing the song "Banana Phone" in my head, blathering on about calling for pizzas and calling your cat, complete with visuals by way of video game characters.

She holds out her arms. I hug her, though it's kind of hard to do, because I'm still holding the video camera and because the table's between us. She smells of the vanilla-scented lotion she always used.

She steps back, still holding me by the shoulders. "Look at these muscles! You certainly don't take after your father," she says. "Bernardo, isn't he handsome?"

"Yeah, sure," says Bernardo.

"And you've brought your girlfriend!" my mother says. "What's your name?"

"I'm Gina, but I'm not—"

"Oh, give me a hug anyway." My mother wraps her in a bear hug. "Are you a fan of *Crime Scene*?"

"I've caught it a few times," Gina says.

"Just a few?" Mom says, like she doesn't quite believe

her. "You know, we might be able to use you as an extra. You have a very unique look."

"So I've been told."

"Shelby, I got to get back," says Bernardo.

"Thanks, B.," my mom says. "See you later."

Bernardo rushes off to do something vital like scaring up a taco for the best boy.

My mom smiles. Her teeth look bigger and whiter. I can't tell if it's because she's the color of an Oompa-Loompa or if it's because she had them bleached. She gestures to the small table. We sit around it.

"I'm thrilled to see you, Eddy. Surprised, but thrilled."

"That's me," I say. "Always surprising people."

"And thrilling them," says Gina.

"You told me you would never come," my mom says.

"Yeah, well. Things change."

"People grow up?"

"Some of us do," I say. My throat feels tight. My teeth feel tight.

She sighs. "Are you going to take potshots at me the whole time you're here?"

"I might," I say.

"And are you going to film said potshots?"

"I might."

She touches the camera. "Gina, he was always making little videos when he was a kid. Once, when he was eleven or twelve, he wrote a script about a mad ghost that haunted this suburban town. I," she says, putting a hand on her heart, "played the ghost."

"That turned out to be prophetic," I say.

"You're still mad. I don't blame you. Maybe you'll understand when you're older."

I'm so angry I think pieces of me might start randomly falling off. I don't even know what I'm mad at. I pick up the camera and aim it at her. "So, explain it to me."

"I don't want to end up in one of your shows."

"Pretend the camera isn't here."

"It's very hard to do that with you pointing it at me."

I put it down on the table, but I don't turn it off.

"How's Matthew?" she asks.

"He dies a lot. He'd like you to come home, please."

My mother downs her tea even though it has to be cold by now. "Eddy, I know I've made some mistakes. I know I've hurt you."

"Forget about me. You hurt Dad. You hurt Marty. You hurt Matthew."

"I'm trying to make amends."

"By moving to Miami?"

"I thought it was best."

"For who?"

"For everyone."

"Talk to the camera," I say, tapping it. "I want to

record this moment for posterity."

"You're not making this easy," my mother says. "Marty was more understanding. Your father was more understanding."

"What do you mean?"

"He made a few calls and told me about the audition. He knew I was miserable after . . . you know."

"*Villerosa*."

"What's *Villerosa*?" Gina asks.

"Why don't you tell her, Mom?"

"It was a movie," she says.

"A bad movie. Possibly the worst movie ever made, according to *The New York Times*. The *Chicago Tribune* said it was like watching a train wreck over and over again every day for a month straight. It was my mom's first major role."

My mom sighs. "I worked my whole stupid life to get that break. As much good as it did me. Didn't get another part until this one came up."

"What's wrong with this one?" Gina says.

My mom smiles again, this time without showing any teeth. "Nothing, honey. It's great." She massages her temples. "This is not going the way I'd like it to go," she says, more to herself than to me.

"You expected that maybe I wouldn't mention anything uncomfortable?"

"Come on, Eddy. We're not going to get this all

worked out in the next half hour. Let me introduce you around. You can take up your bad mommy lecture later. I promise I'll listen to the whole thing."

She's already up and outside before I have a chance to formulate a witty or even an unwitty response. She stops by the craft table, where a short, way-too-skinny woman is eating macaroni salad one noodle at a time by spearing it with a toothpick.

"Melanie, I want you to meet my son. Eddy, this is Melanie. She plays Officer Sasha DePonce on the show."

"Your son!" Melanie smiles, her teeth as white as my mom's. "You don't look old enough to have a son!" It's so obvious that she doesn't mean a word she says. Gina's mouth twitches.

"And who's this?" Melanie says, spearing a single noodle with the toothpick. "Your daughter?"

"Oh, no. This is my son's girlfriend. I'm going to talk to Bob about using her as an extra."

She scrapes her eyes up and down Gina's body. "We can always use hookers."

Gina giggles and takes a step closer to Melanie, breathing down on the top of her head. Melanie frowns, or tries to. Her forehead seems to be frozen.

"That's Dave, the cameraman," my mom is saying. "That's Rocco, he does some of the lighting. And that's Bob. The director. Bob? Bob!"

The man who had been yelling and waving his arms

around turns. "Yeah?"

"You have a minute?" My mom drags me over to the guy. "I want to introduce you to my son. Eddy, this is Bob Auster."

Bob has dark brown hair with a strip of gray roots at the part. And I thought only actors were vain. "Your son, huh? Hey, kid, how you doing?" The accent is pure Brooklyn. I wonder how he likes Miami. His skin doesn't like it. It's red and angry.

My mom clutches my arm. "Eddy wants to be a filmmaker, Bob."

"I *am* a filmmaker," I say.

Bob looks at the camera in my hand. "Oh, yeah?"

"Yeah. I'm in talks with MTV right now."

"Do you have any advice for him?" my mom says.

"Heh, sure. Those pukes at MTV will screw you over soon as look at you, so don't be surprised when they do, okay?" he says. "And then get yourself over to film school. Study. Graduate. Get some work on some sets. Like Bernardo over there." He points. Bernardo is helping Melanie select the rest of her afternoon snack, which will most likely consist of half a carrot, two olives, and a brimming cup full of air.

"Ed wants to make his own films," Gina says.

"That *is* how you get to make your own films, sweetheart," Bob tells her. "Work on other people's films first. After you get a little experience, you max out your credit cards and your parents' credit cards to finance something you might be able to get into Sundance or one of those other festivals. And then if you make a big enough splash, someone will let you direct a horror sequel, and so on. It's a food chain thing."

"Is that what you did?"

"Yep," he says.

"And look where it got you," I say.

My mom's hand tightens around my arm. "Yes! All the way to *Crime Scene: Miami*! Thanks for the encouragement, Bob. We really appreciate it."

She hustles me and Gina away, walking so fast that I have to break into a skip to keep up. "Okay, Ed. Was it really necessary to antagonize my director?" she hisses in my ear.

"Yes, Mom, it really was necessary."

We get as far as the millionaire's set when she stops. "Why did you come here?"

"You left."

"Yes, I left. And I'm a horrible person; is that what you want to hear? Fine. I'm a horrible person."

"That's not what I want to hear."

"Eddy, I was drowning in New Jersey. Drowning. Losing my mind. I'd quit my job at *Cleaning House* to take *Villerosa*. And after *Villerosa*, who was going to hire me? I'd have been lucky to get a job as a weather girl. And I wasn't lucky. Your dad refused to move. Not to Hollywood, not even to New York City. I had this one chance. Is it so wrong for me to want to be happy?"

"It's wrong to leave your six-and-a-half-year-old son."

"Don't you mean it was wrong to leave you?"

"We're not talking about me," I say.

"We're not?"

"No."

"Don't you think that was hard for me, too?"

"Not hard enough."

She lets go of my arm. "I left New Jersey. I didn't leave you. I'm still your mother. I'm still Matthew's mother." She makes an attempt to run her hand through her hair, but there's too much hair spray and it gets stuck. She has to yank it away. "I want to have both of you down for a few weeks in the summer, how about that? So that you could get to know Worth. As hard as this might be for you to hear, I love him. He's the first man who truly understands me."

At this, Gina snorts.

My mother looks at her. "You don't believe me."

"Oh, I believe you," says Gina. "But I bet you said that about Eddy's dad and your second husband, too."

"I . . ." My mother trails off, frowning. "I'm not sure this is any of your business."

Gina's mouth twists. "Right."

"Look," I say. "I just want to know why. I don't think it's so much to ask."

"You know why."

"But I don't!" My voice cracks and now both Gina and my mother stare at me.

Suddenly it occurs to me that this whole trip, this whole stupid, twenty-million-hour, hundred-bucks'-worth-of-gas trip, was a complete waste. I have no idea why I'm here. My eyes are filled with grit, my stomach feels like a shot put, and I'm never going to get the answers that I want. Didn't I believe that Marty and Matthew and Dad were worth staying for, no matter what? That *I* was worth staying for? Isn't that what I believe? And if I don't believe it, if I believe that there was some weird circumstance in which it was okay to leave us, do I really want to know what that is?

"Let me ask you something," my mom says quietly. "Did you come here because you wanted to understand why I had to come, or did you come here because you thought maybe I could do something for you?"

Blood pulses in my throat, I can feel it, like something in there trying to kick its feeble way out. "I don't know what you're talking about."

"Yes, you do. Because you're like me, Eddy. You want things. You want them so bad that it will eat you up if you don't get them. So even though you're pissed as hell at me, you'll still use me to move up in the world, right?"

There's a swift intake of breath. Me? Gina? I don't even know.

"You have a three-minute scene on a weekly TV show, Mom," I say. "You don't exactly have that much clout."

"At the moment I have more than you do. Your washed-up old mother in her funny yellow suit and her skimpy tops and her three-minute scenes has more clout." She absently buttons up her jacket. "I know what happened with MTV. Your father told me. We talk. I bet you didn't know that, but we do. And what I'm trying to say is that I understand why you came down here. 'Cause that's exactly what I would have done."

Rebel Without a Cause

Somehow I get from the studio lot back to the car. Maybe I ran. Maybe I floated. Maybe I grew wings and flew. I don't know. Gina's pulling on my elbow as I turn the key in the ignition, she's saying something about calming down or slowing down or whatever, but I don't care what it is. I just have to get away.

I drive. But I'm too exhausted to drive very far, so we find a Super 8 motel that's charging only twenty-eight dollars a night. When I put my debit card on the counter, the pimpled clerk taps his pen.

"She at least sixteen?" he asks, jerking his head toward Gina.

"Are *you*?" Gina shoots back.

On the way to the second floor, we stop at the candy machines and stock up on energy bars and cookies, as well as tiny toothbrushes and toothpaste also loaded in the machine. Then we drag ourselves through the door of our room.

"This is very nice," Gina says, bouncing on one bed. "I think we got the fleabag suite." She rips open a Twix bar and eats the whole thing in about three bites.

I sit on the other bed. "Sorry I dragged you down here. I don't know what I was thinking. I hope you don't get in trouble."

"If I didn't want to come, I wouldn't have gotten in the car. And I had a feeling it would be a long trip. I called my mom and told her I was staying with a friend."

I pluck at a loose thread in the bedspread. How many hundreds of people have sat here and plucked at this same thread? "There's something I should tell you," I say.

"Yeah? What?" She's moved on to the chocolate chip cookies.

"*Riot Grrl 16* wasn't picked up by MTV."

She washes the mouthful of cookies down with a swig of Sprite. "I know."

"You know? How do you know?"

"I guessed before, remember, back at my house? But Joe confirmed it."

"When did you talk to Joe?"

"I called him this morning."

"What did you call him for?"

"Oh, I don't know. He's your friend? You're out of your mind and he might know why? Anyway, he got a call from Erin Loder and told me about it."

Of course Joe would have gotten the call. Of course he would have told her. "That's why you asked about college in the car."

"Yeah."

"So, if you knew about the show, why did you come down here with me?"

She shrugs. "Because you're a pathetic, self-destructive, moronic ass face who couldn't be trusted to be by himself." She licks the crumbs from her lips, then the chocolate from the tips of each finger.

I can't stand it anymore. The thing with the show, the thing with Lucinda, the thing with my mom, the thing with me driving all the way down here. I want to forget it all. I'd do anything to forget.

I leap from my seat to kneel on the floor in front of

her. She raises both arms in surprise, which allows me to grab her around the waist. I kiss her. She tastes sugary and rich and smoky like cookies and chocolate and cigarettes and not anything like Lucinda, not even a bit like Lucinda, so I keep kissing her, pushing her up onto the bed, moving on top of her, trying to lose myself in her. She buries her hands in my hair, then slides them forward so they're cupping my face. I'm still trying to kiss her when she breaks the kiss. She pats my cheeks so gently when she says, "Eddy. I'm sorry. I just don't feel that bad about myself anymore."

I make a horrible noise, I don't even know where it comes from, that a body could make a noise like that without wanting to. Gina scoots out from under me, sits up, puts both hands on my shoulders, turns me over so that my back is to her. She wraps her arms around me and lays me down again. She says, "Sleep now, just sleep. Sleep now, just sleep," over and over until I do.

The sun is searing my eyelids when I wake up. Gina's not in the bed, she's sitting in a chair, dragging on a cigarette. Her hair is wet, her face is scrubbed clean, and she's changed into pair of ripped jeans and a black T-shirt.

"Morning, sunshine," she says and sends a plume of smoke into the air. Then she coughs. "I promised myself that I would quit by the time I graduated. Hope I can stick to it."

I push at the blankets. She must have covered me with them sometime in the night. "How long have you been up?"

"I don't know. Awhile. I slept in the car, remember? You needed a chance to rest."

"Thanks," I say.

"No worries. Not as if I had any big plans for the day."

I nod. I remember last night and swallow hard. I can't believe she's still talking to me. I don't know what to say. So I don't say anything. I stumble to the bathroom. I strip off my clothes and jump in the shower. I make the water hot as I can take, letting the steam and the soap clear my head. Then I jump out, try to dry off using a towel the size of a washcloth, and get dressed again.

Even though I've humiliated myself in a thousand different ways over the last two days, I have the nerve to feel better.

I'm astonished that more people don't hate my guts.

I open the bathroom door and step into the room. Gina's opened the ugly curtains wide and is standing in front of the window. The sunlight makes a blinding corona around her, like she's not even real, like she's a vision or a dream.

I take a step toward her.

She puts one shaky hand up. "I won't ruin it if you won't."

And for once, I don't.

* * *

I treat her to breakfast at a local diner and watch her plow through a spinach and cheese omelette, two sausages, two pieces of toast, and all of my bacon. While she gets coffees for the road, I check my cell phone. There are twelve messages: six from my dad, four from Marty, one each from Rory and Joe. I call my dad.

"Eddy! We've been out of our minds! I was about to call the police!"

"I took a little road trip with Gina. It's no big deal."

"No big deal! You're gone for days without telling anyone and it's no big deal? The only reason we don't have the FBI out hunting for you is because of your mother. She called last night to let us know where you were and that you were safe."

"I hope you don't expect me to thank her for that."

My dad sighs on the other end. "I expect you to be careful driving. And I expect you to get home in one piece, do you hear me?"

We set off. Fifty miles down. Only thirteen hundred more to go. Gina isn't in the mood to sleep, so we spend the miles talking about different things. Music, movies, why she wants to go to college, why I don't. How Rory and Joe and I became friends in the first place. The Meatball. Tippi Hedren.

"I miss her," I say.

"Lucinda?"

"I was talking about Tippi. But yeah, Lucinda."

"Why her? I mean, you've gone out with a lot of girls. So why'd you flip for her?"

"She's different."

"How?"

"She didn't flip for me, I guess."

"Typical."

"No, I mean it. She didn't try to impress me or anyone. She was impressive all on her own. Do you know she volunteers at an animal shelter? And she's an amazing dancer. She can speak Spanish, she can play tennis. She's beautiful without making a big deal about it."

Gina shifts in her seat. "She sounds perfect."

"Yeah."

She kicks off her shoes and puts her feet up on the dash. "I used to think you were perfect."

I laugh. "Right."

"I did, though, when we first started hanging out."

"Now you're just mocking on me."

"No, I'm not. Why wouldn't I think you were perfect? You're smart, you're funny, you're already making films when most people are just trying to get through earth science. You had that weird little brother who you loved so much. And that crazy bird."

I glance at her and remember the way she was before Riot Grrl took over. The long hair before it was cut and dyed pitch black, the lips before they were always painted red or green or blue. She was almost . . . sweet then. Almost. And now, with her hair tucked behind her ears and her skin scrubbed of makeup, I can just about make it out. That sweetness.

"But you're not perfect," she says. "I found that out."

I take a deep breath. "I'm sorry I was such a jerk to you."

She waves her hand at me. "Idiot. Keep your sorry. I don't need it. What I'm saying is that nobody's perfect. Not even Lucinda."

"I know that."

"But listen to how you described her. That sounds like a character in a movie, not a real person."

"But she is a real person. I saw her do everything I said."

"Yeah, but what about everything else, what about the real stuff? Was she ever a slob? A bitch? Did she chew with her mouth open? Did she pick her toenails? Make bad jokes? Hate her dad?"

I think about how much Lucinda wanted to get away. How she complained about her family. How she wiped the tennis courts with that girl Penelope.

"No," I say.

"But you said you loved her."

"I did. I do."

"But how can you say that if you only knew her a

couple of months? If you've never even seen her in a bad mood?"

I'm starting to get annoyed now. "What if she doesn't have bad moods? What if she's just a generally cool person who doesn't pick her toenails or chew with her mouth open?"

She pulls her feet off the dashboard and twists to face me. "People like that don't exist, Eddy. They're just figments of our imagination. You didn't know her. She just fit the picture in your head."

I glance away from the road to tell her that she's got it all wrong, that I'm not so bloody stupid, that I know Lucinda or at least knew enough to know I loved her, when Gina screams, "Look out!"

In the windshield, the truck looms. I know it's impossible, but I see the whole thing frame by frame, a series of snapshots, like I'm editing a movie.

The skid marks on the pavement.

The truck's red lights in front of me.

The white headlights in the rearview.

Gina with her arm thrown over her face.

My foot stomping down on the brake.

The truck in front getting bigger and bigger, filling the windshield a shot at a time.

I can't stop the crash, but I can turn the wheel.

And I do.

The Return of the King

I spent three days in the hospital. Mild concussion, broken nose, seven stitches in my forehead. I missed my own graduation. I don't consider it a big loss.

The cops said that I did something unusual during the crash. Instead of turning the SUV to the left, away from myself, I turned to the right.

"You took the hit instead of your passenger," the cops told me. "Usually happens the other way around."

"So my instincts are screwed up."

The cop looked at Gina, who was curled up in the chair next to my bed. "Or maybe your instincts are just fine."

When I got home from the hospital, there were a few messages from my mom. She loved me. She hoped I was okay. She'd call again Saturday. She promised.

And then there was a message from Lucinda. She'd heard about the accident, she said, she wanted to make sure I was all right. I don't trust myself enough to call either of them back.

The day I get out of the hospital, I go to the junkyard to get what's left of my life from my totaled car. (The place was called Nirvana, if you can believe that.) When I come home empty-handed, no one asks any questions. I guess no one was surprised I had nothing left. Maybe they thought I deserved it.

I get a job at Video World and Rory and I get through the boring summer nights pretending we're in a Kevin Smith movie, *Clerks III*. We make top-ten lists to pass the time. One night I'm giving my list of the best all-time car crashes when the bell over the door chimes. Joe.

"Hey," he says.

"Hey," I say.

Rory looks from Joe to me to Joe again. "Uh," he

says. "I have to take these movies to the back room. And then I, uh, have to stay there. To do stuff. So." He grabs a stack of DVDs and practically sprints away.

After Rory's made his escape, Joe says, "Smells better in here."

"Don't tell Rory, but I hid air fresheners in some of the DVD cases. They're everywhere."

"Smart."

"You would too if you had to spend twenty-five hours a week at Smellovideo." I grab the random receipts left by the customers and crumple them in a ball. "You gained some weight back."

He puts his hand to his cheek. "Yeah. Eating again."

"That's a good thing," I say.

"MTV. They didn't want me to look so . . ."

"Skeletal?"

"Dead."

"Ah."

He sets some movies on the counter. Bergman's *The Seventh Seal* and Branaugh's *Henry V*. Always the high-brow stuff for Joe.

I take the movies. "Any good?"

"Incredible," he says.

"Did Lucinda think so?"

I almost laugh at the look on his face. Almost.

"How did you . . . ?" he says, then stops himself. "Okay. You should know that I wanted it. But she didn't. So. We didn't."

"Oh."

"Not before, anyway. Not while you guys were . . . whatever."

He didn't need to add that last bit, but there it is. I suppose he figured he should be the one to tell me, be upfront about it. But I think he said it more because he wanted to, the way I wanted to say her name out loud a couple of months ago, not because I wanted to be honest so much as I wanted to grind his face in it.

I can hear Gina's voice in my head: *Karma's a bitch.*

"I hate your guts," I tell him. He starts nodding, but I say, "No, not for Lucinda. Not why you think. I hate you because you're better than I am."

He blinks his huge bug eyes. "I'm not."

"Yeah, you are."

He stares for a minute. "It's only because you're greedy."

"Thanks."

"It's true," Joe says. "*Riot Grrl* was great until you started dreaming about money and all that crap. Stick to the story."

"What story?"

"Whatever the story is. The story's the important thing. People forget that. They get distracted by sex and superpowers and special effects. But none of that works unless it fits with the story."

Easy for him to say. Mr. I'm-Going-to-Be-Famous-on-MTV. But maybe he believes this stuff. Maybe you need to believe in something.

He unfolds his arms and looks around the dusty and decrepit place that has become my home away from home. Emotions flash across his face: pity, guilt, whatever. "Listen, Ed. I'm sorry."

Now I do laugh. "Yeah, you should be."

"No, not about that. About Lucinda." He looks like he means what he says. He probably does. Mostly. And maybe the accident did more damage than I thought. I should want to rip his throat out with my teeth for being with Lucinda, but I feel sorry for him. He's a wuss. She'll roast his heart on a spit.

"If it makes you feel any better, she's leaving," he says.

"She already left," I say. "I mean, she's still here, but . . ."

"She's just killing time," he says. "I know that."

I don't think he does. "Okay."

"Well," he says. "I guess I'll see you around."

"Yeah. Good luck with school. And with your Bible show."

"Thanks."

"Don't let them mess with it."

"I won't." He jams his hands in his pockets and turns to go. Stops. Turns again. Says: "You know, *Riot Grrl*

16? That was the right way to end things. Even if some people didn't understand it."

I nod. "Thanks, man."

"See ya," he says.

"Yeah. See ya."

I watch that bony, brainy pumpkin head walk out the door and wonder if I'll ever see him again. The chance I won't makes my throat tight and dry, like I hadn't had water in days.

So, we're all a bunch of wusses. As soon as the door chimes again, Rory scurries out from the back like a small animal from its burrow. "So what happened? I didn't hear any noise, and it doesn't look like you guys used the displays to beat the hell out of each other."

"Nah. Lucinda sucked the fight out of both of us."

"I was going to tell you."

"You didn't have to. And I was the one who screwed it up anyway."

Rory fidgets with the stacks of videos lying everywhere, shuffling copies of *The Prisoner of Azkaban*, *Spider-Man*, *Sin City*, *Scary Movie 5*, *A History of Violence*, and *Eternal Sunshine of the Spotless Mind*.

"Who do you think it was?" he says.

"Who?"

"The Tin Man."

The Tin Man's been on my mind, too. After I got out of the hospital, I allowed myself one last visit to the

MTV site, but the Tin Man hadn't posted in weeks. Seems he was gone, off to see the wizard.

"That's the giant cosmic joke," I say. "I don't think I'll ever know who it was."

"Freaking internet."

"Yeah. If no one knows who you are, you can be as big an ass as you want."

"Stupid technology is taking this place down, too."

"What? What do you mean?"

"Well, not this minute, probably not this year or the next, but eventually. Netflix, Blockbuster, pay-per-view, YouTube, they're all killing us. Soon everyone will be getting their movies through the mail or through the cables or through the little chips Hollywood implants in our heads. Won't need us anymore."

Rory's folks have owned this store his whole life. "What will your parents do?"

"I don't know. They love this. I know it's hard to tell sometimes. If they loved it so much, why don't they get some new posters?" He gestures to a cardboard *Terminator* yellowing in the corner. "But I guess they'll have to find something else."

"Like us."

"Nah, we'll keep making movies."

I appreciate the "we." In August, Rory's going to school for film editing. I'll be the only one left here trying to figure out how I'm going to deal with the next seven decades. Dad says I can apply to film school for next semester, but I'm too depressed to look at the applications.

Rory sniffs the air. "Have you been spraying some kind of disinfectant stuff around?"

"No, why?"

"Funny. I'm not smelling vomit anymore."

I take *Eternal Sunshine* from the pile. "Is it okay if I borrow this one?"

When I get home, Marty's old Toyota's in the driveway. They've been over more and more since my accident. I've overheard some talk about all of us moving in together. Probably a good idea. The Meatball could use two parents. And Tippi Hedren would like the company.

I walk into the house. For once, the Meatball isn't dead. He's sitting on the couch in the living room, reading his favorite book, the one with the toe tag on the cover. Tippi Hedren is perched on his head. I don't know how he coaxed her from her cage without losing a single body part, but he did.

Tippi says, "*The human head is roughly the size and weight of a roast chicken.*"

"I taught her that," says the Meatball.

"No kidding."

"She was singing before. Something about liking it hot. It's difficult to concentrate when she's singing."

"And when she's standing on your head."

"I like her on my head. Makes me feel taller." He closes his book. "I decided not to die today."

"Why is that?"

"I didn't feel like it. But I think maybe you should try it."

"That's okay, Meat. I came close enough once."

He puts his fingers up to his head and Tippi steps aboard. He gets up from the couch and points. "Here. Lie down on the floor."

I'm about to argue, but if it's going to make Meat happy, what the hell. Besides, I'm so beat down that the floor seems like the perfect place for me to be.

"Now, close your eyes and be still. Don't even move your eyeballs. That's the trick. Don't even try to see anything. Breathe slowly, as slowly as you can so that your chest doesn't go up and down so much." He's so close to me and I can feel his breath on my ear and smell the Frito-and-pee smell of Tippi's feet. "You don't have to worry about anything 'cause you're dead, see?" he says. "There's nothing you can do but lie here. That's your only job. Being nice and still and quiet. Doesn't that feel good? Don't answer."

I do what he says, breathing slowly in and out, keeping my eyes unfocused under my lids. I remember trying the same thing all those years ago when I was on *Law & Order*, but this feels different because I'm doing it for myself. No one is standing there waiting to scream, "Cut!"

I'm so relaxed I'm nearly asleep when suddenly Meatball grabs me by the shoulders and shakes me. "Eddy! Wake up! Eddy! What's wrong? Did you have a heart attack? Did you hit your head? Eddy! Do you hear me?" He shakes me so hard my teeth rattle like dice in my already-bruised head.

"Ow," I say, opening my eyes. Marty and Dad are standing in the doorway, watching. "That's good, Meat. I'm okay."

Meatball smiles, something he does about once a year. "I saved you."

"Yeah, Meat. You did."

Marty lets me borrow his car. It's a warm night, raining just enough to jewel the windshield, not enough to need the wipers. I don't have to go far. A McMansion to top all McMansions. This time I ring the bell.

Gina answers the door. Her hair's in pigtails. She's wearing denim cutoffs over blue and white striped tights. "If it isn't my stunt driver," she says.

"Got some free time?"

She steps onto the porch and closes the door behind her. "Before you ask, I'm not going on another road trip with you."

"Nah. No more road trips."

"And I'm not sleeping with you," she adds.

"I don't want you to."

"Really," she says, not a question.

"You know what I mean."

She points to the chairs around the cold, ashy fire pit. We sit across from each other. It takes me a while to say what I have to say. Truth is, I'm feeling a little tired. Like I'm living my own personal version of *Lord of the Rings*—there are a lot of little endings, and this isn't even the last one.

Still, I show her the digital camera I just bought, a cheapie, about three hundred dollars. "I'm starting a new show."

"Yeah?" she says. "What's the show called?"

"I don't know yet. I was wondering if you wanted to help me with it."

"You know I will. When do we start?"

"How about now?"

"But it's dark. And you don't have any lights."

"That's all right," I tell her. "Doesn't matter."

"If you say so. Where do you want me?"

"Right where you are."

I size up our positions. Then I hand her the camera. Confusion flashes on her face, but for only a second. She's smart, that Gina.

She takes the camera and points it at me.

The End

Maybe you don't want to hear from me. Maybe you think I deserved everything I got. But I have one more story, and then I'll shut up. Forever if you want me to.

Let me tell you about Nirvana.

You can't miss it from the highway because a 1950s tow truck teeters like a toy on the roof.

Bodhi—short for Bodhisattva—is the official greeter. He's a border collie or maybe an old bath mat; it's hard to tell. Anyway, his job is to herd you into the front office, which he does by walking alongside you and leaning into your shins. I'm actually relieved—I don't have to worry about where I need to be; I have a guide. As I'm herded, I pass the Wreck of the Week, parked out front on the piss-colored grass. This week it's some kind of red truck twisted into an impossible L shape, its back end sticking up like a cat's tail. Guess the make and the model and you win an official Nirvana baseball cap.

That's what Tony tells me.

Tony runs the place.

"What's your guess?" he says. He's tall or medium or short and he's got black or brown or blond hair.

"What?" I say.

"About the wreck? What do you think it is, kid? A Chevy? A Nissan?"

"I don't know," I say, the answer to every question since the accident.

Tony shakes his head, tucks an unlit cigarette into the corner of his thick/thin mouth, and punches a number into an ancient computer. It makes a wheezing noise and belches up a location.

"Ford Explorer, model year 2003, registered to one Edward Rochester," Tony says. "Lot C, row 7, slot 43. Too bad for you. I bet it was a chick magnet."

"Yeah," I say. "Chick magnet."

Tony switches the cigarette to the other side of his mouth. "So, Ed. What were you doing? Looking at some girl crossing the street when you should have been watching the road?"

"What?"

Tony squinches his black/blue/yellow eyes at me. "What happened to your car?"

"I don't know," I say.

Tony stares as if I might be suffering from head injuries. (I do have that ladder of stitches on my forehead, the black eye.) But then he shrugs. Tony's only making conversation; Tony couldn't care less. He tells me if I can't guess the Wreck of the Week, I can buy a cap for $15.99 and a T-shirt for $9.99. The Nirvana tow trucks are $24.99, perfect for gifts. Do I have a little brother? Little brothers love them.

"Or," he says, "maybe you're interested in some earrings." He gestures to the wall behind him. Sure enough, there are rows of earrings pinned to a Styrofoam board. Some have teeny Nirvana trucks dangling from silver wire. "My wife makes them. For your mom, maybe?"

I say, "I don't have a mom."

Tony blinks. "Everybody has a mom."

"Okay, I have a mom, but she doesn't play one on TV."

"Huh. Well. That's . . ." Tony shakes his head in con-

fusion and then decides to cut his losses. He leads me outside and points. "Lot C, third lot on your left. Rows and slots are marked."

I see nothing but acres of mangled metal.

"Trust me. You'll find what you're looking for. Everyone does."

I start walking. I expect Bodhi the bath mat dog to herd me, but I guess his job is done. I pass a new Beetle, midnight blue, smashed on the front passenger side and missing both back tires. The right headlight has been plucked neatly from the socket, like a diseased eye.

I keep walking. A Honda Accord looks perfect from one side, but when I make it around to the other, I see that the back door has somehow been ripped off. There's an Infiniti with weird punctures all over the body, as if a pissed-off pro-wrestler had a tantrum with a pickax. A bunch of cars with no damage at all that I can see, ones that must be broken on the inside.

Nirvana is the place where cars go to die.

The place is a scene waiting to happen. I want to film it all. My fingers curl, itching for my camera. But I don't have my camera. It's in my car, along with the rest of my life.

I'm here to get it back.

Tony's right, the car's easy to find. The lot numbers are marked with signs, and the rows and slots are spray-painted in safety orange on the crispy grass. Lot C, row 7, slot 43. A black Explorer registered to one Edward Rochester, chick magnet. I thought that SUVs were supposed to get the better of car crashes, but not mine. The front end looks like a failed experiment with origami. The back end has the perfect imprint of the mattress truck that had done its best to crawl up my ass. Broken glass shimmers on the seats and floors. There are big smears of blood on the steering wheel and on the dash. At the hospital they told me that head wounds bleed more than anything else, which is why I looked like something out of a news report on Iraq.

I open the only door I can, the front passenger door. Amazingly, all my stuff's still here. My laptop's in three pieces, which can't be good. I peer into the backseat, at the piles of extra clothes, the shoes, now damp from when it must have rained (except I don't remember any rain). Pages from my show binders are everywhere, littering the whole interior with white. I see Riot Girl 16 *notes, scripts, equipment lists, all that stuff. I can't open the trunk without a crowbar, but I know what's in there. A microphone, spotlights, extra batteries for the laptop, about a thousand pens and pencils, blank cue cards, and the camera.*

I'm here for all of that. But I'm also here for a CD, the one with "The Girl from Ipanema." I want that book I promised to read but never did. And I'm here for the tennis racket, the good luck racket, the racket I used when I won that one time.

I have a duffel bag with me. I sit in the passenger seat, the empty bag on my lap. I should be cramming it with stuff, packing up the bits and pieces of my life, putting Humpty back together. But all I can think is: What will I do with a laptop in three pieces? With a tennis racket? With the lights or any of it? The video camera alone cost sixteen hundred dollars. I should go back to the office, get a crowbar, and get that camera. But I can't. I'm too tired. My stitches itch. None of this feels like mine anymore. It feels like someone else's wreck. Like some black, burned-out hulk you see on the side of the road and you think, Huh. I wonder what happened to *that* guy.

I get out of the car. I glance around at the other cars and think about the people they belonged to. (I know, I know: "It's about time you thought of other people, Eddy.") Were they hurt? Did they lose an eye or an ear or an arm? Can they walk? Are they dead? Are they around here somewhere, hiding behind the Toyota or the Buick, saying, Hey, guys, get a load of this one, coming back to the car graveyard to get all his crappy, broken stuff. What the hell does he think he's going to do with it? What the hell does he think it means?

I back away from the car that's not mine anymore. All the other cars are looking at me—I swear, they are looking at me—waiting to see what I'm going to do.

I drop the duffel bag. I turn and walk past the acres

of mangled metal back to the front office, where I buy a Nirvana cap, a toy truck, and a pair of earrings. $54.97 plus tax. I put on the cap. I sit out front to wait for the cab that Tony called for me. I sit and wait for the real story to begin.

Acknowledgments

One of the cool things about being a writer is that you can spend hours and hours watching movies and call it research. Thanks to the many filmmakers who work so hard to bring us their visions—whether they appear on YouTube or the big screen. Thanks also to Clarissa Hutton, Ellen Levine, Anne Ursu, Gretchen Moran Laskas, Carolyn Crimi, Esther Hershenhorn, Myra Sanderman, Esme Raji Codell, Franny Billingsly, Rosemary Graham, Audrey Glassman Vernick, Tanya Lee Stone, Tania Ortiz, and Mary Roach, for writing the Meatball's favorite book, *Stiff*. Thanks especially to JFMBH, who specifically requested a book about a player who gets his heart crushed/smashed/totally annihilated (maybe she was a little angry at the time). And, as always, thanks to Steve.

Acknowledgments

One of the good things about being a writer is that you [illegible]

Take a sneak peek
at Laura Ruby's new novel

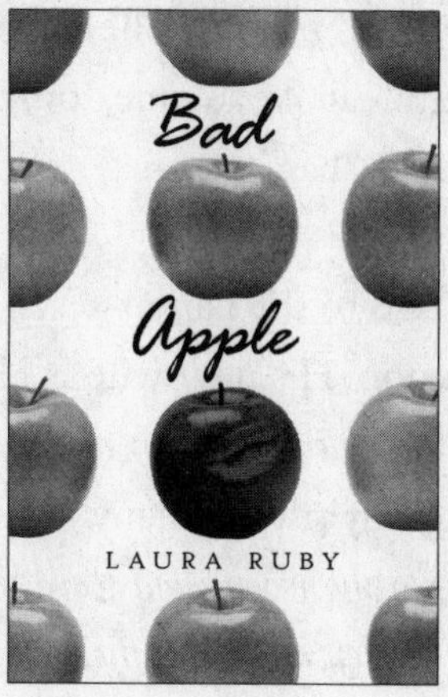

THE FUTURE IS GRIMM

Mr. Mymer, my art teacher, is tall and skinny with floppy hair the color of yams and a peculiar affection for "funny" T-shirts: CLUB SANDWICHES, NOT SEALS. YOGA IS FOR POSERS. FULL FRONTAL NERDITY. When my mother met him at parent-teacher conferences, she said he seemed like a very interesting person. She doesn't say that anymore. Now she says things like he's "evil," "a criminal," and "a predator."

After she says these things, she sometimes stares at me as if I'm a wounded bird flapping around her living room—

maybe something you want to help, maybe something you want to smack with a broom. She opens and closes her mouth as if she might call *me* a name, too, but she never does.

I think the name is "liar."

My father didn't go to the parent-teacher conferences. He was on his honeymoon. His new wife is Hannalore, which is German for *I keep poisoned apples in my purse.*

"No, stupid," says my sister, Tiffany. "It's German for *I haul spoiled stepchildren into the woods and leave them for the wolves. I gather the bones that are left and crush them to a powder. I drink the powder in my afternoon tea. It keeps my skin looking young.*"

Hannalore is six hundred feet tall and looks like one of those opera singers. You know the ones. They wear the metal breastplates and the big hats with the horns. They're always the last to sing.

Like Hannalore, the Brothers Grimm also came from Germany. We all know what kind of tales the brothers had to tell. Bad things have gone down in Germany.

"You're such an idiot, Tola," says my sister, her eyes narrow as punctures. "Ever hear of the Spanish Inquisition? The Salem witch trials? *Slavery?* Bad stuff goes down everywhere."

But my sister doesn't really care about the Brothers Grimm or anything else. After a few minutes of talking about it, she suddenly shrieks: "Shut up! Shut up about the Brothers Grimm! Why does everything you say have some sort of literary reference? Why do you carry around that stupid book? How pretentious are you?"

Someone who wears lavender contact lenses shouldn't talk about being pretentious. I refuse to call my sister Tiffany, so I call her Madge. Madge is eighteen going on Crypt Keeper and cries all the time. I often find her curled up on her bed, wailing like a lost kitten. When you ask her what's wrong, she can never explain. "Life," she says. Or, more specifically, "Everything." Sometimes she hyperventilates. She carries around a supply of brown lunch bags just in case she has to sit and breathe into one.

Only people named Madge breathe into brown lunch bags.

Madge has been to four doctors—one regular one and three therapists. She doesn't like therapists. She calls them voodoo headshrinker freaks. She says that all they want to do is blame our parents for her problems when it's the whole world that's in pain.

I myself have not been to any therapists, which is funny, considering that my sister is (was?) the golden girl and I'm the bad seed. Five years ago, at one of the parent-teacher conferences my mother enjoys so much, my sixth-grade math teacher told my mother that though I was doing better in class, I still stared out the window and appeared stupid. Those were her exact words, too. "She still stares out the window and appears stupid." This is not the sort of thing you say to my mother about one of her children. My mother used her coldest voice—the voice so arctic and furious that icicles spiked the air as she spoke—to tell off my teacher. It took a while. A half hour, maybe. (I'm not sure how long because I was staring out the window and appearing stupid.) My teacher got paler and paler as my mother told her how inappropriate and ridiculous and irresponsible this comment was and how rude and naive and inept the teacher was. My mother talked until the teacher blended in with the white board behind her. And then my mother grabbed my arm and yanked me from the room.

In the car on the way home, my mother used that same freezemonster voice to tell me that I'd better start paying attention in class and living up to my potential, or she would send me to a monastery in Nepal, where I'd spend my life combing fleas from the yaks.

I told my grandpa Joe what my mom said. He patted my hand and declared that he'd never met a yak he didn't like.

Me, Mom, Madge, and the yaks. Sounds bad, but it's not. It wasn't. Take the teachers. Most of them are nice. Sometimes I draw portraits of them and leave the pictures on their desks. That doesn't thrill some of the other kids, who think I'm a brownnoser. But that's not true, either. I like to draw, and the teachers are there just waiting to be drawn. Besides, the things

I draw aren't *always* the kinds of things that teachers find flattering. Like, say, putting Ms. Rothschild's head on a rabbit's body. Or drawing Mr. Anderson with a tail. Ms. Rothschild thought her portrait was hilarious; Mr. Anderson, not so much. Actually, that last drawing got me a trip to the principal's office.

The principal: "Is this supposed to be a joke?"

Me: "No, it's a present."

The principal: "A present?"

Me: "As in gift."

The principal (muttering): "You couldn't have given him an apple?"

Me: "You think he would have liked fruit better?"

The principal: "You're a smart girl, so I'm going to be blunt. I think you'd be a lot happier if you stopped acting so weird."

Me: "Who says I'm not happy?"

But maybe he was right, because nobody's happy now.

Before Mr. Mymer, these are the kinds of things that people said about me:

1. In third grade, Tola Riley ate nine funnel cakes at the school carnival and then puked them up on the Tilt-A-Whirl.
2. In fourth grade, Tola Riley stole Chelsea Patrick's American Girl doll—one of those creepy twin

dolls—and tried to flush it down the toilet, flooding the school bathroom and causing thousands of dollars' worth of damage.

3. In sixth grade, Tola Riley ran down Josh Beck, the fastest kid in the whole school, so she could rip out a lock of his hair to use in a spell.
4. In eighth grade, Tola Riley drew a picture of one of her teachers with a noose around his neck and was almost suspended.
5. In ninth grade, Tola Riley was caught making out with Michael Brandeis in the broom closet and was almost suspended.
6. In tenth, Tola Riley was caught making out with June Leon in the girls' room and was almost suspended.
7. In eleventh, Tola Riley was making out with John MacGuire at a party when, for no reason at all, she smashed him in the head with a fishbowl and swallowed the goldfish.
8. She has strange piercings in mysterious places.
9. She's descended from fairies, trolls, munchkins, and/or garden gnomes.
10. She has ADHD, bipolar disorder, Asperger's, and/or psychic powers.

I think this stuff is funny; at least, I used to. No one really believed any of the stories; they just needed something to talk about. Everyone loves a villain. Or maybe not a villain, exactly, but someone you can point out and say, "I might be weird, but I'm not weird like *her*." I was cool with that. I had my friends. I didn't need to be like the rest of the drooling high-school idiots—obsessed with sex, YouTube, MySpace, Facebook, texting, drinking, and UV rays (*Orange is the new tan!*). Let people think I was crazy; let them think I would say anything, draw anything, do anything—what did I care?

Now that I do care, now that I'm trying to tell my own story, no one is listening. Madge says I haven't helped my case by chopping off my hair and dyeing it a shiny emerald green (in addition to the nose ring my mother nearly had a stroke over).

I say, "About a hundred other juniors have dyed hair and pierced body parts. And that's just the guys."

"Congratulations," says Madge. "You're a teenage cliché." She goes back to applying her makeup, or reapplying what she's cried off. "Don't walk too close to me in the mall today, okay? I don't want anyone to know we're related."

"I never made out with Michael Brandeis, you know," I say. "He made that up."

Madge shellacs her bloodless lips with gloss. "Who?"

For the record:

1. I didn't throw up.
2. I buried it under the monkey bars.
3. Hell hath no fury like the boy beaten in the hundred-yard dash.

4. It wasn't a noose; it was a necklace of bones.
5. No.
6. It wasn't the bathroom; it was the art room.
7. The fish was saved.
8. The nose is strange and mysterious enough. Just try to draw one that doesn't come out looking like something that belongs on a grizzly bear.
9. Fairies, definitely.
10. I know what you're thinking right now.

You're thinking: *Is* she a liar? Or is she really crazy?

All I can tell you is that I read too many fairy tales about children left to be roasted by hags, vengeful stepsisters so desperate for love they'll cut off their own feet, and girls locked up in towers with only their hair for company.

I didn't know all the tales were true.

(*comments*)

A Willow Park High School art teacher, Albert Mymer, was suspended with pay pending an investigation into an alleged relationship with a sixteen-year-old student.

According to a witness, the teacher and student were observed lunching together at a New York City café. Sources within the school administration say that the witness, a fellow student of the alleged victim, described inappropriate personal contact. She also described an exchange of gifts, including a book. Other witnesses interviewed suggest that this is a pattern of behavior.

"I would like to say I'm shocked," said a coworker of Al Mymer, who wished not to be identified. "But I'm not."

Police and school officials are continuing their investigation.

—*Dana Hudson,* North Jersey Ledger

"Subject was interviewed at her house with mother present. She was cooperative but guarded during interview. Denied allegations of abuse but admitted that she wanted to protect her teacher from punishment."

—Detective J. Murray

"She sort of lost it when my—I mean our—dad left us, and my mom started treating us like we were in kindergarten. At least, that's what my therapist thinks. If you can trust the opinion of a therapist. Which, mostly, you can't. Therapists are crazy.

"Look, she's always been weird. She was born that way, so it's not like you can blame her—at least not totally. No one asks to be born."

—Tiffany Riley, sister

"It's true that I was focused on other things at the time. I admit that. I take full responsibility. Maybe if I'd been around a bit more, none of this would have happened."

—Richard Riley, father

"Do you really think that it was just that one time? Give me a break. That skanky little freak is getting exactly what she deserves. Sooner or later, everybody does."

—Chelsea Patrick, classmate

Laura Ruby lives in Chicago with her family. When she's not writing, she's watching tennis tournaments, Hitchcock films, *Forensic Files*, and *Law & Order* reruns. She is also the author of GOOD GIRLS, BAD APPLE, and several books for children and adults. You can visit her online at www.lauraruby.com.

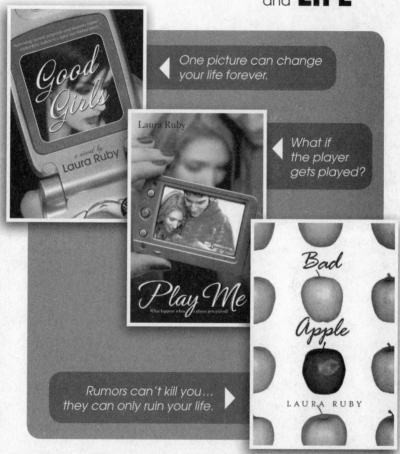